THE
LOST
QUEEN

THE
LOST
QUEEN

BOOK ONE

AIMEE PHAN

G. P. PUTNAM'S SONS

G. P. PUTNAM'S SONS
An imprint of Penguin Random House LLC
1745 Broadway, New York, New York 10019

First published in the United States of America by G. P. Putnam's Sons,
an imprint of Penguin Random House LLC, 2025

Visit us online at PenguinRandomHouse.com.

Library of Congress Cataloging-in-Publication Data is available.

ISBN 9780593697337

1 3 5 7 9 10 8 6 4 2

Printed in the United States of America

BVG

Design by Rebecca Aidlin
Text set in Ten Oldstyle

The authorized representative in the EU for product safety and compliance is
Penguin Random House Ireland, Morrison Chambers, 32 Nassau Street,
Dublin D02 YH68, Ireland, https://eu-contact.penguin.ie.

For ZZ,
my favorite dragon

THE
LOST
QUEEN

THE MYTH OF TWO SISTERS

There were two sisters. They were partners, queens, warriors who liberated Vietnam from the Han dynasty. They united coastal and mountain villages, appointed women to lead their army, and ruled their country for three years, until the ruthless Han invaders squashed their rebellion.

Refusing to surrender, the sisters jumped off a cliff and drowned in the Hàt Giang River.

But their legacy endured to inspire a nation.

That is what people like to believe.

Other versions say they were beheaded or slaughtered in battle, that they vanished from the sky or turned into stone statues. The same finale: they died, they died, they died.

This is what we used to believe.

There is so much more to this story.

Shall we begin?

1

THE POOL

We stared at the glossy turquoise water, some with suspicion, others with fear. The pool seemed to wink at us, the satiny aqua blue water neatly divided by green-and-yellow racing lanes. The backstroke flags whipped and snapped in the hot, dry breeze. We squinted in the September morning haze, shoulders curled and resentful, and sat on the sun-toasted bleachers, hugging our knees to our chests. Over the fence, the boys preened and stretched before their soccer unit, smirking in our direction.

Everyone dreaded the swim unit in gym. They found the chlorine water super harsh; it smeared their carefully crafted makeup, spoiled their straight-ironed hair, destroyed their mornings. How could they possibly return to class with a dripping ponytail and faded lipstick?

That was not my problem. My face was already makeup-free, my hair too short for a ponytail, too coarse for any product. I never liked the feeling of anything sticky on my face or in my hair. People who bothered looking my way were not counting the number of blackheads on my face (three) or wondering when I'd last washed my hair (last night . . . or maybe the night before). Unlike all the other unhappy reflections in the water, mine was smiling.

I couldn't help it. While the pool was their enemy, it was my friend. Underneath the water's gloss, I could paddle away from my classmates' scornful eye rolls. When gossip and rumors drifted near my ears, I could submerge under the surface and muffle their lies. I could float, somersault, and practice my handstands, and pretend those girls over there—my former friends—did not matter.

I always preferred water over land. Summers in San Jose without central air turned every kid into a fish.

While we sat and waited for Coach Turner to finish attendance, I glanced around, assessing the pool that should have been my second home. I still remembered the unanswered emails and voice messages from the coaches during preseason training, asking if I was sure I didn't want to try out. Promising that there was still a spot for me if I wanted it. I ignored them, and after a few weeks they stopped trying.

My eyes wandered to the gymnasium wall mural of the West San Jose Vaquero, the school's aggressively joyful cowboy mascot. Since the school's founding in 1980, Vaquero had appeared as a pale, red-mustachioed ginger, an obvious rip-off of that racist Looney Tunes character. But a recent student petition had rebranded the mascot into a cowboy of color; his mustache had darkened into a walnut brown, and his alabaster skin was painted over in a golden, racially-ambiguous-but-definitely-not-white glow.

For our swim test, Coach Turner hollered for the first group of students listed on her clipboard: "Hennessy, Marquez-Chen, Lyford, Pham, Patel, Rodriguez, Chang, Lam."

I rose from the bleachers, the backs of my thighs crimped and rosy from the metal grooves, and toed off my rubber flip-flops. We stepped over the pyramid of kickboards and fins, arms crossed over our torsos, dispersing to find an open lane.

My ex–best friend, Lana Marquez-Chen, pointedly skipped past me to stand next to Huong Pham, the pretty, popular junior who had moved here from Vietnam last year and now co-anchored *Vaquero Vision*, our high school's morning news show. She was the only junior in our class of sophomores, but I guessed she needed the gym credit. I tentatively approached Stacy Hennessy's lane and asked to join.

"As long as you go first," she said.

Aboard the starting block, I assumed the position, squatting neatly with my legs and feet tucked together, and watched as some of the others struggled to balance themselves. Lana and I peeked at each other. As former swim teammates, we knew we were each other's competition—that is if I cared, if I could gain even a sliver of satisfaction from beating her in an inconsequential heat in gym class.

I did care, I realized. After what she'd done to me, I would beat her.

"Fifty-meter freestyle," Coach Turner said, holding up the stopwatch app on her smartphone. "Focus on technique. I want to see elbows above water, arced arms, cupped hands, and tight scissor kicks. And, yes, your faces must go under the water."

A crisp whistle sliced the air. I leaped headfirst into the water.

Diving in felt so luxurious that I almost forgot to begin swimming. I pushed through the satin-smooth waves, absorbing the sensations.

After a few strokes, my hands felt something grimy. Without breaking stride, I instinctively rubbed my fingers together to determine the texture. Sand? Dirt? Our class was the first to enter the pool this morning, unless water polo had practice before school. That was possible, but not even a bunch of stinky boys could pollute the water this much. I glanced over at the other lanes but could barely make out my classmates' bodies through the murky water.

By the time I reached the other side, the water had cleared, the contamination evaporated. I frowned in confusion, passing Stacy Hennessy, who appeared to be clinging to the lane line mid-lap, already winded.

After my fingertips reached the wall, I popped up, breathing heavily, and glanced over to Lana's lane to make sure I won. She wasn't there. I looked back at the bleachers. They were empty, the rest of the class now standing near the edge of the pool. Tamara Lyford—bobbing in the next lane, mouth hanging open, chest heaving—began to scream.

My chest seized. I yanked my goggles up, my gaze whipping to the center of the pool, where Tamara was looking. Three lanes away, two bodies lay tangled together. Oh god. Lana. While I stared in shock, Coach Turner dove into the water, clothes, floppy sun hat, whistle, and all. After a second, I followed her.

Powered by adrenaline and terror, my feet pushed against the pool wall; my body wriggled beneath the water, slipping under the lane ropes until I reached the girls. Under the water, Lana and her lane-mate, Huong, glowed in a hazy mass of limbs, hair, and skin, but when I touched the closest arm, I knew it belonged to my former best friend. I wrapped my arms around Lana's waist, scooping her up and hoisting her against my side. Her body felt like an oversized sandbag. But she was alive. She had to be. I repeated this to myself over and over as I kicked my feet to regain balance.

To my amazement, the cloudiness returned, the water around us transforming from clear saline blue to a deep yellow haze. I blinked a few times in confusion, my eyes burning, trying to see through the foggy mess. Huong floated past us, her long black ponytail wrapping around her neck and face. I desperately stretched out my hand, grasping at her heel but unable to secure a proper grip. Her skin felt too slippery, disintegrating between my fingers and dissolving into the water, like it was no longer solid. A thin, mossy reed appeared out of nowhere, drifting between us. I swatted it aside in shock, reaching again for Huong while still struggling to hold Lana. The grainy golden water was so thick, Huong seemed to disappear within it. After blinking again, I couldn't see her at all.

What was happening? My body floundered as my heartbeat grew louder in my ears, the panic clutching my throat. Could it be happening again?

Maybe this was a dream. A nightmare. Please let it just be a nightmare.

An arm grazed my waist and I turned. Coach Turner bumped against me, taking Lana from my weakening grip. Two others surrounded Huong. Together, we pushed the unconscious girls up to the surface, gasping and spitting into the cool air.

On the deck, our dry classmates continued shrieking. *Omigod. Omigod. Omigod.* Someone pushed a lifesaver donut at me. I looped Lana's arm through so her head could stay above water, and we bobbed to the edge of the pool.

Hands reached for us, untangling us and pulling us out. Once Lana and Huong were safely on the deck, Coach Turner shouted for us to make room. I finally caught my breath, my nose and throat still burning, and looked back at the pool.

No kelp, no mud, no golden tint. Only clear water.

But the memory of my eyes stinging and salt lingering on my tongue haunted me. I shook my head, trying to dislodge excess water from my ears and the images seared into my brain.

The mud and plants in the pool—I'd seen them. I'd felt them. Swallowing back hot saliva, my throat sore and parched, I looked around nervously. Was I the only one?

They all remained focused on Lana and Huong. My classmates hovered around them, our wet hair and swimsuits enclosing them in a drippy circle of concern. Coach Turner pressed an ear to Lana's chest, then snapped around to look at us. "Who else knows CPR?"

"I do," I said, kneeling in front of Huong. Droplets from my hair sprinkled across her face as I tried recalling the Red Cross instructions.

"They knocked skulls," Madison Ha said behind us. "We could hear them from the bleachers. It was like . . . *crack!*"

Lana began coughing up water, moaning, and turned to her side, while Coach Turner covered her with a green-and-yellow-striped towel. Huong remained motionless, her wrist heavy in my shaky grasp. I concentrated on finding a pulse, but my fingers trembled. My eyes stayed fixed on her immobile nose and mouth still dotted with water. I pushed on Huong's chest with both hands, counting each compression aloud and pressing so hard that I imagined feeling a rib cracking. Huong was tall but thin, with hardly any boobs to cushion the chest pumps.

My classmates' commentary buzzed above us. I tried to ignore them, but Daphne Nguyen's voice pierced through my fog. My other former friend. She whispered with another classmate, Iris Thomas, pretending to look concerned.

"This is why we shouldn't, like, ever share lanes," Daphne said gravely.

"Who hit who?" Iris wondered.

"Well, Lana just flip-turned right into her. She wasn't even looking—"

"Huong shouldn't have been there. She wasn't supposed to take off yet, she was supposed to wait until Lana tapped the wall—"

While they gossiped, I continued to press on Huong's chest with my sweaty and slippery hands, trying not to panic as the seconds ticked by. Coach Turner stood behind me, prepared to take over when my hands got tired.

The others couldn't help but gawk. How often could they witness Huong Pham in such a vulnerable state? She was always composed and confident on *Vaquero Vision*—her glowing, dewy face streaming through the classroom monitors and the outdoor screen in the campus quad for ten minutes every morning, renewing collective envy from most of the girls at our school.

Even wet and unconscious, her face was impressively untouched, yearbook-picture worthy. Her skin, dotted with pool water, glistened in the sun.

As if to protest the gawking, Huong's body erupted. A few gurgles of water first as warning—her shoulders and chest spasming—and then, with a sudden lunge forward, she vomited onto the deck. A fountain of pool water, mingled with her morning blueberry smoothie, splattered Coach Turner, me, and a few others who had the misfortune to be kneeling over Huong.

Several girls screamed and gagged, hopping up and down in hysteria and disgust. I took a towel someone shoved in my face to wipe the purplish puke away. The vomit didn't actually smell that bad, more like sweet water than anything else. I gazed at the puke-stained towel in wonder, at how the violet chunks seemed to twinkle in the sunlight, and then threw it to the ground, hoping that no one else had noticed.

And they hadn't—everyone's attention was still on Huong. Once she stopped heaving and coughing, Coach Turner's arm around her shoulders, something resembling a sly smile flickered on Huong's face. It lasted only a second, but I glanced around quickly, wondering if anyone else caught it. They hadn't. Apparently no one had seen any of the weird shit I'd witnessed.

The school nurse and several aides arrived—someone must have alerted the health center—armed with towels, first aid kits, and the grim expressions usually reserved for earthquake or lockdown drills. They elbowed their way to the center of our group, where Huong and Lana lay on the deck.

Without the suspense of possible death, or at the very least an ambulance, our classmates drifted away. Daphne and Iris chatted with two boys through the fence, dramatically reenacting the accident, pushing up their chests and tilting their hips.

"Omigod." Iris sighed, resting a hand on her heart. "It was so, so scary."

"They. Could. Have. Died," Daphne said.

"Her vomit just flew in the air! It was like *The Exorcist*!" Iris said.

Of course, they were both dry as powder, their hair and makeup unaffected by the icky pool water and soaring body fluids. I turned around. "Could you guys keep it down? This is serious."

Daphne glared at me. "You don't have to tell me that. Lana is my best friend."

"Then maybe you should stop gossiping about her."

Daphne hadn't helped to save Lana, and probably resented that I had. I walked away before she could respond, feeling her eyes, thin and lethal, following me, her rage activating prickles along my back.

I frowned in irritation. My stupid hives. When they first started, I dismissed them as another side effect of my recently diagnosed anxiety, more evidence of my craziness. I tried hiding them with long-sleeved shirts and sweatshirts, but Bà Nội caught on and made an appointment with Dr. Bruckmann, who added another anti-anxiety pill to my meds list. The hives receded, my skin calming and returning to normal, but the burning sensation never fully went away. Sometimes I could feel the heat prickling underneath my skin, and it was almost always because someone was staring at me. Judging me.

Like now. Another reminder that I'd never feel normal again.

The school nurse checked Lana's vitals first. After the nurse moved on to Huong, Lana sat in a puddle wrapped in several layers of towels, staring at the pool with tired, bloodshot eyes like a little refugee, overwhelmed, confused, scared. Daphne was still too busy flirting with the soccer players to bother checking on her.

I walked over to her, summoning my courage. "Are you okay?" I asked.

"I guess," she murmured. "They think I might have a concussion."

"Well, yeah," I said.

"I don't know what happened." She shivered. "I didn't even see her."

"It was hard to see anything in that water."

Her forehead creased in confusion. "What do you mean?"

"Well, there was all that stuff in the water mucking it up."

"What stuff?"

"The mud and sand. It was like we summoned the ocean again."

Lana scowled, tightening the towels around her. "I don't know what you're talking about."

"Don't you remember?" Her face told me to stop talking, but I couldn't help myself. "Back in my grandparents' pool, when we were little?"

When we were seven, Lana and I spent most of our waking hours in my backyard pool. I lived in my neon-green polka-dotted swimsuit, indifferent to the penetrating rays of the brutal sun. My grandparents usually emerged at dusk, when the pink evenings exhaled a cool breeze across the South Bay. I couldn't bite into a watermelon slice or pop open a Sanpellegrino without remembering those lazy, perfect days when Lana and I were so close that I never thought things could be any different.

That was years ago, before the pool got cemented over. I'd get up early, float in the water before anyone else had awoken, stare up at the clear blue sky that hardly changed all year, even in winter. It had probably looked like that for millions of years before me and would look like that for millions of years after. That thought thrilled me when I was little, the largeness of the world, the smallness of me.

At breakfast, Bà Nội would secure my hair in two braids, but by the afternoon, I had undone them to enjoy the luxurious sensation of water flowing through my hair. For the rest of the evening, I would glide around the pool like a mermaid, scheming to return to the ocean, which I was fantasized was my true home. I loved living in the water, especially when my best friend was there with me.

"You have to remember," I said, trying to push past the awkwardness, hoping against hope she could. "We used to find plants and fish underwater and thought it was so weird that no one else could see them—"

"Stop," Lana warned, looking around to make sure no one could hear us. "Jesus, we were seven and playing make-believe."

"Oh," I said, trying to laugh it off, my face heating up. "Sorry. I just thought—"

"I don't want to hear any more of your lies," Lana said, her eyes rolling. "No one does. Haven't you figured that out yet?"

I turned away as Daphne and Iris swept in to talk to Lana, grateful that at least she'd kept her voice down. I practiced the 5-4-3-2-1 grounding technique to regain my breath, trying to keep the intrusive thoughts away. *This is why no one likes you. This is why you have no friends.* I focused on the sun on my skin, the warm wind rustling my hair, and breathing in and out until the sirens in my ears subsided.

One of the aides clapped his hands and ordered us back to the locker room. I waited until the rest of my classmates left so no one would see my face and ask what was wrong.

I passed Huong on the bleachers, a towel draped around her like a sari while one of the staff held her wrist to check her pulse. Her long legs stretched out in front of her like she was sunbathing instead of recovering. She waved at me.

"Thanks," she said.

I shrugged, walking past her, but I felt a strange sensation mid-stride, as if the cells in my body were stirring. It felt like the prickles I got with my hives, but more pleasant and warm. I gazed down at my arms. Instead of ugly red welts, my skin looked shiny and dewy, almost sparkling. I stopped and looked back at Huong, whose gaze hadn't left me. The others around us, however, remained still—too still. Like they were petrified in time. Huong blinked at me, smiling. Were we the only ones who could still move?

I felt a trembling, like a small earthquake, but within my body. I pressed my bare feet to the concrete, my hands gripping my towel, afraid my knees would buckle beneath me. I blinked and shook my head, waiting for the dizziness to go away.

This whole time, Huong just watched me, curiously, amusedly.

"See you soon," she said, and with a nod of her head, the world returned to motion.

I walked away, stumbling a few times over my own feet. What was that? The lack of oxygen had to be affecting my brain.

As I walked into the humid locker room, a burst of giddiness spread slowly, dreamily through my body. I couldn't remember the last time I'd felt this happy, especially for no good reason. Why? Because some popular girl I hardly knew spoke to me? Yet the inexplicable glee continued to flow through me as I showered and changed clothes, and I couldn't help but beam at everything.

I basked in the euphoria, an opalescent bubble carrying me through study period, where no one spoke to me, and into lunch, where I sat alone in the cafeteria at the same corner table with the other friendless freshmen and sophomores.

At first bite, my usual sandwich tasted different. I slowed my chewing in astonishment. I savored the salt in the pastrami, the creamy fat of the mayonnaise, the crunch of the butter lettuce and sourdough baguette. Had the cafeteria switched catering services for our lunches? Even the bottled water—the same brand the school had contracted for years—tasted cleaner, as if my tongue detected the mythical mountain spring advertised on its label. I chomped into my apple, a fresh Honeycrisp, detecting the rich, earthy soil, and inhaled the pungent evergreens from the Washington State farm where it had grown.

Not until I stood in front of the compost and recycling bins, separating my lunch remnants, did I realize what had been happening since Huong smiled at me. The discovery, so whole and abrupt, halted my steps in the crowded cafeteria doorway. The buzzing throughout my body swelled, warming me all over again.

A few kids hollered at me to move along or to get out of their way, roughly bumping my shoulder, but I barely noticed. At that moment, they didn't matter. None of it did.

Because, somehow, I was in the ocean, swimming down into the darkness until I found Huong sitting on the sand, waiting for me, her hair undulating above her. As soon as I reached her, Huong looked up and gave me that smile, a finger touching her lips. She shimmied along the ocean floor as I followed, until the water began to brighten, shifting in colors, like a rainbow had descended around us. Huong stopped, turning to me. Suddenly, we stood on a cliff overlooking a roaring ocean, the sun high and bright, the wind blowing through our hair, our hands clasping each other. She looked at me in gratitude.

I knew you'd save me, she said.

It wasn't a delusion. It wasn't a dream. I was having a vision.

Just like Ông Nội had told me, once you have one, once you experience that cosmic smack in the face, the electricity gliding through your bloodstream, you cannot ignore it. You cannot think about anything else. You wonder why or how you never felt it before, and how you could have ever existed without it.

THE PSYCHIC

Huong wasn't my first vision, but she was certainly the first good one. And way better than the last, which had essentially ruined my friendships, torched my reputation, and destroyed my life. Bad visions could do that, especially if you tried to ignore them. You pushed them deep inside your body and, inevitably, they erupted.

Just ask my psychic grandpa.

When people found out I was descended from a long line of psychics, they got excited, like I was related to a tech founder or a movie star. They asked a lot of questions.

Do they know where you are . . . like right now?

Can they see dead people?

Do they know when you're going to die?

Can they predict lottery numbers? The SuperLotto is up to 500 million right now!

Can they tell my future? I'd love to know if Fin likes me, if I'll get into Stanford, what questions Miss Haskins is going to use on our econ quiz, etc., etc., etc.

It was not nearly that fun. Which was why I hadn't seen my dad in over eight years. Why I sat alone at lunch every day at school. Why my former friends refused to speak to me. Once people got over the holy-shit spectacle of it all, the reality that my grandfather was a thầy bói, a fortune-teller, started to sound creepy. And when you factored in all the stereotypes, the idea of being psychic started to lose its charm.

Some of the biggest lies I'd heard about psychics:

1. They were all the same.

This couldn't be further from the truth. There were clairvoyants, spiritual diviners, sensitives, astrologers, precognitors, telepaths, feng shui experts, geomancers, lucid projectors, intuitives, and telekinesists among the many, many types of mediums in the world. Some abilities crossed over, but not always.

For readings, they could use tarot cards, rice grains, coins, tea leaves, and, yes, sometimes those sparkly crystal balls. Some had even updated their tools and used phone apps.

My ancestors never needed objects to perform readings. Ông Nội dismissed them as garbage. He wouldn't even hold your palm to pretend to read it. A good thầy bói knew what was going on when a person walked into the room and didn't need props.

2. They were fakes.

If this was what you really thought, then my ancestors' legacy as revered thầy bói in Vietnam would never sway you. You wouldn't believe that prominent village leaders and government officials visited our family home seeking advice on strategic planning, or that families from around the region would ask for the best wedding dates for their children or request horoscope charts for newly born grandsons. Granddaughters rarely warranted such trouble, unless they were rich.

You certainly wouldn't believe that my Ông Nội anticipated the end of the civil war. On the day Saigon fell, he warned our relatives and neighbors to not bother rushing the American embassy, because the handful of American helicopters on the roof were not nearly enough for the thousands already clamoring for refuge. He promised our family would escape. They'd just have to wait five years for the right boat. Ông Nội himself would navigate a grueling three-week odyssey through the South China Sea to eventually reach a refugee camp in Thailand that would grant them sanctuary.

You would not believe how Ông Nội called my dad one morning only weeks after my parents had eloped, when he and my mom were still living in a studio apartment in Venice Beach, and told them that they were pregnant with me. My mother was barely four weeks pregnant. "It's a girl, and you are moving home so we can help raise her," Ông Nội said, hanging up before they could protest or ask questions.

3. They were greedy, cheating swindlers. And they should be able to predict lottery numbers. If they said they couldn't, they were lying.

Okay. First of all, how could psychics predict lotto numbers and also be con artists whose sole intention was to take everyone's money? Since we live in Silicon Valley, the land of venture capitalists and startups, this greedy attitude is everywhere.

My family had never been rich. We lived in an affluent neighborhood in San Jose only because my grandparents bought their first home before the tech boom. Ông Nội used to take perverse pride in the dilapidated conditions of their house while increasingly being surrounded by snotty neighbors. *Let them look down on us,* he'd say, *they won't be here for long.* Whether he meant another tech bubble would be bursting or something worse, I didn't know and didn't want to ask.

4. They could foresee every disaster or tragedy, both small and large, including when you were going to die.

Come on. Psychics couldn't predict everything in the future and recall everything in the past. The world was too massive, chaotic, and messed up for any human being, medium or not, to possibly try to control. If the psychics in our family could predict everything, they would have avoided the war that resulted in the deaths of millions of civilians and soldiers and forced them out of their home country. They would have prevented my dad from leaving. They would have prevented my mom from dying.

She died in childbirth. Preeclampsia that the doctors hadn't detected in all those prenatal appointments. I never got a chance to meet her. We had very few photos of her in the house, but Bà Nội said she saw more of my mom in me every day, not only in my face and body, but in the way I crossed my arms when I was overthinking something, or biting my lip when I was mad.

Most of all, they would have foreseen Ông Nội's dementia—how it would slowly but surely steal everything imaginative, compassionate, and astounding about his powerful brain; how it would frighten away most of his clients. That was what dried up his business. Now, of course, he didn't say much of anything at all.

So even if psychics could make these epic forecasts and change history to improve their own lives, who would listen to them? Who would believe them?

They were frail, vulnerable, bewildered people just like the rest of us.

3

VISIONS

We lived on a cul-de-sac of ranch houses close to the freeway, bordered by a row of lush sequoia trees. At night, I could hear the hum of late commuters and the impatient whistles and grumblings of the overnight freight trains, the eucalyptus trees rustling in the wind. Even as I walked home that afternoon, the sidewalk vibrated underneath my steps, reminding me of the San Andreas Fault and the tectonic plates grinding deep below the soil, biding their time before some fantastic, destructive upheaval. I looked around uncertainly and checked my phone, which was set for alerts for earthquake activity. No notifications.

The house was quiet when I stepped inside. As I crossed to the kitchen, soft voices bubbled from the dining room. Stepping around the corner, I saw my grandparents hovering around the dining table with an unfamiliar older couple. Their heads converged over a pile of papers on the table. A tray of perspiring teacups and politely bitten dried salted plums sat forgotten on the sideboard. The smell of incense lingered in the air.

While I rooted around in the refrigerator for a snack, the voices in the dining room swelled. I didn't need to understand Vietnamese to know that Ông Nội was sitting with clients, and they were unhappy with his calculations. When I pushed open the swinging door between the kitchen and dining room to peer in, the older couple stood, shaking their heads in displeasure. The man jabbed his finger at one of the numbers on Ông Nội's charts, his face inches from my grandfather's.

I inhaled deeply and released a shaky breath, hoping, wishing for the clients' frowns to disappear, for them to even smile.

Ông Nội still had a few loyal clients who trickled in for the occasional horoscope chart, wedding date, or business reading. This couple had to be part of this minority of devoted holdouts. Bà Nội said the younger generations looked down on horoscopes as superstition. Americans didn't believe in psychics, only money.

As good business practice, psychics needed to strike a balance between what clients should and should not know. Ông Nội used to excel at this, carefully suppressing information he knew clients were not ready for, because above all else, they paid his fee. Who wants to buy bad news? He navigated this fine line with cryptic warnings and long-winded lectures.

Until about a year ago. At first we thought it was from boredom. Years of impatience built up from listening to self-serving, indulgent clients. Or his brain finally succumbing to all the destinies he had to carry. Whatever the reason, he started to tell the truth . . . about things his clients didn't ask for.

One can excuse the occasional rant from an eccentric psychic.

But then he began to deliver them more often, ignoring questions in order to obsess over an imagined apocalypse starting in San Jose. The gossip spread among his clients and their families, and, inevitably, to kids in school from our community.

His eventual diagnosis felt like both a relief and a death. Ông Nội was here and wasn't here at the same time. Despite Bà Nội's efforts, the house felt quiet, and the last thing I wanted to do was speak up and fill it with more sadness.

Bà Nội caught me spying from the kitchen. "Jolieeeee!" she called out, dragging out the last syllable into a wide smile. I dragged my feet across the carpet to stand in front of our unhappy guests. "This is our granddaughter. Jolie is a sophomore at West. Jolie, this is Mr. and Mrs. Phan."

I was being recruited as a distraction; the conversation had switched from Vietnamese to English so I could participate. And nothing brought Vietnamese people together like telling a kid what they should do with their life.

Mrs. Phan's frown melted away. "My children graduated from West."

"Oh yeah?" I asked.

"Jennifer loved being a Vaquero," Mrs. Phan cooed. "She was on student government, and the varsity tennis and volleyball teams. What about you, con?"

"Me?" I asked. "I do nothing."

"She is focusing on her studies right now," Bà Nội said, offering a tight laugh that sounded like a machine.

"STEM classes are very important," Mr. Phan said, snapping his chewing gum open-mouthed so that the little gray rubbery worm revealed itself on his tongue. "Who is that tutor we hired for Michael? Very smart boy with scholarship offers from Cal Tech and MIT. Have you already taken the PSAT?"

Mrs. Phan winked at me and my grandma. "Ah, don't ask her that! Jolie knows that school is much more than studies. You are a second year? You know Daphne Nguyen? Her mother and I see the same hairstylist. She's very good at coloring all my white hairs."

I smiled tightly. "Yes, I know her." Why was I surprised? Daphne's family knew all the Vietnamese families in San Jose.

"Jolie used to swim," Bà Nội said. "It gave her very broad shoulders. See? They are still so big."

My grandmother's diversion, while ill-chosen, worked. Mrs. Phan's eyes sparkled in understanding.

"Aah, my Jennifer's body was like that, too. She had to be careful not to get too fat."

I would have acted offended if any non-Asians were around to hear their criticisms.

"Jolie is fine," Ông Nội boomed, tapping his pencil on the table, his tic when he grew impatient.

"Of course she isn't fat," Bà Nội said soothingly. "This is a hormonal age."

"And her mother was white, so you never know how that affects the genes," Mrs. Phan said. "But she did give her pretty hair. Look at those golden streaks. And her skin." She looked me up and down like a potential purchase. "My goodness, she has beautiful skin. She looks like she's glowing. Did you go to one of those tanning salons?"

Bà Nội studied me, too. "She's right. Did you get a lot of sun today?"

I stepped back, suddenly self-conscious. It actually felt easier when they were criticizing me.

Ông Nội coughed loudly. "Are we done?"

"Not at all," Mr. Phan said, once again jabbing his finger on his expensive commissioned chart. "We still haven't settled on the date."

"We have," Ông Nội said. "You simply don't like the dates I've offered."

"But the reception deposit is not refundable," Mr. Phan said. "Perhaps you can look at the dates again. See if there is any flexibility about the fifteenth."

"No," he pronounced. "The fifteenth is the worst day of the month, even the next few months. The likelihood of an earthquake that week is also very high."

"Oh, we've been having earthquakes anyway."

"This will not be any ordinary tremor," Ông Nội said, wagging his finger. "Do you really want to be sitting in a crowded reception hall built alongside a crumbling cliff when it hits?"

They switched the argument over to Vietnamese, where their voices grew louder, pushier. My throat felt hot and prickly. I wandered back to the kitchen for a glass of water, gazing at the wild yellow flowers in our backyard.

My grandparents planted the yellow mustard flowers years ago, when they first moved in, a familiar and beloved blossom in Vietnam. They hadn't realized how quickly the plant would spread—like an invasive weed—and seedlings cropped up in the neighbors' otherwise pristine gardens. While our neighbors struggled to keep their grass green, ours always appeared embarrassingly overgrown and lush, which drew suspicion that we were violating our city's water usage restrictions. Like we were responsible for the droughts and wildfires that disturbed their summer vacations in Tahoe and Yosemite.

In our defense, we were the only house on the block without a pool. Bà Nội had ours paved over last year after I quit the swim team and she became worried that an increasingly forgetful Ông Nội might fall in and drown.

After the clients left, I walked back into the dining room. My grandmother was clearing the dining table, while my grandfather knelt on the floor to shove papers into a cardboard bankers box.

"The Phans have referred many families to you," Bà Nội reminded him. "We cannot afford to anger them."

"I calculated those numbers at least a dozen times," Ông Nội said from under the table. "If they don't like the results, that's their problem."

"They need your blessing," she said. "How can they move forward with a half million–dollar wedding when their fortune-teller says the day is unlucky?"

Ông Nội's head poked back up from under the table, his face red from either the exertion of crawling around the floor or anger. "Why are they so concerned with frivolous parties," he asked, "when they should be preparing to survive?"

"But how will I survive you?" Bà Nội asked, pulling him up to his feet. "You are tired and should rest."

While they went upstairs, I held up one of my grandfather's horoscope calculations. What should have had numbers and astrology figures instead had a pencil drawing of . . . a dragon. Another one. This one was hanging off a cliff by its front talons, its snout exhaling rings of smoke. With all the others he scribbled all day, we could assemble a coloring book.

My grandparents' voices vibrated through the popcorn ceiling. This wasn't new; they often carried on the most boring conversations at maximum volume, since neither of their hearing was prime anymore. But then I heard doors and drawers slamming, and thuds like they were throwing things against the walls and on the floor. I waited for it to settle down, as it usually did when Ông Nội gave up and lay down for his nap.

Yet the slams and crashes grew louder and bigger, the clangs sharpening and slicing through my ears. This was a full-on fight. Were they still throwing things? My hands crept over my ears, trying to block out the noise. Didn't they realize I could hear them?

The roar grew steadily louder, angrier, wrapping around and shuddering through my body. Then, as the ground underneath me began to tremble, something else occurred to me. Was this the big one? No. Earthquakes started from the ground, undulating in waves, the furniture rattling and bumping against the walls. But this had started upstairs. This was like a snow-globe shake. I looked down at my bare feet, trying to lift one foot, then the other, off the shaky floor, but they wouldn't budge. A thick, black mud surrounded my feet and was spreading across the tiles.

The pressure began crawling up my legs and then my arms, the pain so agonizing that I twisted to the floor, landing not on the twenty-year-old dusty Oriental rug that was supposed to be under the dining room table, but on a bed of rocks, lichen, and hardened mud. Panicking, I reached for a chair leg and found myself gripping something thicker and rougher. I frantically clawed at it again, feeling soft bark collect underneath my fingernails. It was a tree root.

Another vision, I thought grimly. This couldn't really be happening.

Beneath the kitchen doorway, a stream of water trickled in, slowly at first, but then growing, pushing the door open, rolling toward me. At the end of the dining room, a curling wave of foamy water hurtled down the staircase. The water rose fast, chilling my already shocked body, sloshing across my paralyzed legs.

I opened my mouth. Despite all the water around me, my throat still felt dry and scratchy. I inhaled, willing a hot breath to gather inside my lungs. With every ounce of power in my stomach and chest, I screamed.

"Jolie?" I turned around to see Bà Nội standing on the staircase, staring at me quizzically, a wrinkle between her eyebrows. She carried a thick book in her arms.

I no longer lay on the ground soaked in muddy water. Instead I stood on the familiar rug in the same dining room we'd eaten in for years. The walls of the room appeared dry and undamaged. I placed a shaky hand on the table to steady myself.

"Jolie," my grandmother said again. "Did you call me?"

"Did you feel that?" I asked. "Did you see the water?"

"What?" she asked me, her face calm and blank.

She hadn't seen or felt it. Only I had. It was a delusion. Another one. My face tilted up at her, and I struggled to blink my eyes.

"Nothing," I said, trying to control the trembling in my voice, though my heart continued to pound and my hands were damp from sweat. Only sweat.

She came down the stairs, set her book on the table, and stood in front of me. Now she was the one looking up at me, since I'd shot past her in height when I turned twelve.

"Mrs. Phan was right. Your skin is very bright. Are you swimming again?"

I looked down at my bare arms and hands, still very shiny, like after the vision this afternoon.

"We swam in gym today."

"Did those girls give you trouble again?" she asked, frowning.

"No," I said. "But something did happen in the pool." I told her about Lana and Huong's collision, and what I saw under the water. I wanted to tell her about what I had just experienced in the dining room, but something in her distressed face made me hesitate.

"You've always been very sensitive," Bà Nội said, smiling weakly. "You feel things too deeply."

The disappointment caught in my throat, my cheeks heating up in frustration. "You think I imagined this?"

Her smile faded and she stepped toward me. "The thầy bói gift doesn't pass down to women. You know that."

"I didn't say I was thầy bói."

"Be glad you are not," she said.

I shouldn't have said anything. Bà Nội already felt like she had to manage Ông Nội. I didn't want to be another burden. I turned away, the red leather book on the table catching my eye.

"What is that?" I asked.

"It's your Ông Nội's mythology book," Bà Nội said. "He's been sleeping with it under his pillow."

"Why?" I asked.

"I don't know." She looked tired and irritated. "He doesn't even read it."

"He probably has it memorized," I said, running my hand along the aged red leather spine. It had to be the oldest, rattiest book from his collection. He used to read these Vietnamese folktales to me when I was little. My favorite ones had been about the mythical, mischievous dragons that founded Vietnam. When Ông Nội's dementia began, he would talk for hours about the mythical creatures' return and revenge on this world, long after his clients—or we—cared to listen.

No wonder Bà Nội didn't want the book around.

"He keeps bumping his face into it, waking him up," Bà Nội said. "Then waking me up. When I try to put it back downstairs, he just finds it and sneaks it back under his pillow."

As if on cue, Ông Nội moaned from their bedroom, calling for Bà.

We both looked up at the ceiling. Bà Nội sighed. "Would you mind putting this back in his study?"

After watching her trudge up the stairs, I lifted the book with two fingers, once again surprised by its weight. How could old paper weigh this much? As I carried it to Ông Nội's study, a room he barely used anymore, the book seemed to grow heavier, enough so that I needed both arms. I dropped it on the desk with a thud. I walked out, pausing to close the door, when I heard a clatter from the desk. I froze and turned to look back in the study. The book seemed to have shifted, balancing halfway on the desk, threatening to fall on the floor. I walked back and pushed the book firmly onto the middle of the desk, checking again before closing the door that it was still there.

Back in my room, I closed my door and hurled my backpack toward the bed, where it bounced off the edge, landing on the carpet with a surprisingly wet squish. I stepped forward to look at the comforter where the backpack had landed, then pressed my hand on a darkened spot at the bottom. Bringing my hand to my nose, I smelled, then licked, two of my fingers. They felt damp and tasted of earth and salt.

THE MYTH OF THE DIVINE DRAGONS

In the beginning, there were four immortal guardian dragons. These gods were blessed with the prime elements of life and destined to rule and protect this world. Representing earth, water, fire, and air, these gods created the world as we know it today. They carved the land and sea into continents and islands, pushed up mountains, and sculpted rivers, oceans, forests, and deserts. The guardian dragons then populated the land and sea with creatures and plants of all sizes.

Their most beloved creations were their children: one hundred divine baby dragons. Each divine dragon inherited their own unique shade from the rainbow, from deep violet through blues, greens, and yellows, all the way to brilliant red. The guardian dragons endowed their children with the divine elements of earth, water, fire, and air. While not as supreme as the guardian dragons' prime elements, the divine dragons still carried immense power so they could continue their parents' legacy as caretakers of this young world.

But these new dragons, while strong and magnificent, were not as wise as their parents. Instead of sharing and nurturing the world, the children rebelled from their destiny. They bickered over the world's treasures, unable to appreciate their divine gifts. They squabbled over territory and power. They flew through the air and spun tornados, stampeded across the land and triggered earthquakes. They flooded valleys, breathed fire into volcanos, and howled inside the ocean waves to create tsunamis.

The guardian dragons tried to restore balance. They scattered their children to different parts of the world, so they'd have their own domains to rule. But the children always found each other, resulting in more chaos and destruction. They grew selfish and greedy for power. They resented their parents, realizing that the guardian dragons possessed more power than they ever would. A small but mighty faction of the children began to revolt, plotting to seize control of the world.

The guardian dragons realized that there would never be peace among their children. To save the world, they hid their prime elements so their children could never find and exploit them. Once they completed this sacrifice, the guardian dragons abandoned their thrones and vanished.

Left alone in this world, the divine dragons continued to search for their parents and battle for territory, provoking conflicts, wars, and devastation for centuries, their thirst for power never fading.

While we may no longer see them and many people no longer believe in them, they are still here. If catastrophe happens, always suspect the divine dragons.

And the prime elements? They are still lost. The divine dragons continue to hunt for them. There is a prophecy that these immortal elements will return. Whoever finds them will claim the guardian dragons' thrones and rule this world.

GIFT OR BURDEN

I read the myth of the divine dragons to my third-grade class. Our teacher, Ms. Adcock, had assigned us a history report about our ancestors' home country. Ông Nội' had helped me translate the story from his mythology book, and I was proud of how many details I recounted.

When I finished, my teacher gently suggested that I'd mistaken fantasy for nonfiction, which was a different writing genre. Zach Dillon accused me of lying to get attention and said that dragons weren't real. When we returned from lunch, someone left on my desk a picture of a dragon in green and red crayon with the words YOUR FAMILY. Even Lana was mad, saying I shouldn't bring up weird Asian superstitions that would make people laugh at us.

I crumpled my report and threw it away. When I returned home from school, I pulled Ông Nội's mythology book off the shelf in his study and found the pages that had humiliated me. I tried to tear them out, determined to destroy the lies. But the papers wouldn't budge in my grip, no matter how viciously my fingers scratched and tugged at them. The pencil-drawn dragons seemed to mock me as my hands shook and tore at their illustrations.

In my struggle I fell backward, bumping into Ông Nội, who had been standing behind me the whole time. I dropped the book, shame swiftly washing over me.

Instead of getting mad at me, he told me to ignore the disbelievers. Of course they would say that, he reasoned, because most people couldn't believe in dragons. They were too vain to consider that any creature could be smarter and stronger than themselves. And if a human ever did believe, they would try to control and destroy these magnificent dragons, as they did with everything else in the world. So for the sake of peace, the dragons made sure humans never remembered them.

"Then how can you remember them?" I asked.

"I am thầy bói," he said. "I share the elements with these dragons. We are connected."

"Can you tell Ms. Adcock?" I asked. "Because everyone in my class thinks I'm a liar."

"It is not necessary for them to believe. How would humans benefit from knowing that dragons are real and that they can come back to this world? Most humans are irresponsible, impulsive creatures. They are best left ignorant of truths they cannot control."

I wrung my hands in frustration, imagining dragons descending on us, on me. "I don't want them to come back, Ông Nội."

"They are not our enemies," Ông Nội said. "The guardian dragons created this world for us."

"But they're gone. And their children can hurt us."

"That is why the thầy bói are here. For now, the dragons only live in our dreams. It is not ideal, but it is better than them being here and causing trouble among us."

"How long can you keep them away? Don't you get tired?"

"It is my gift, Jolie," he said. "I have never seen it as a burden."

But maybe he'd think differently now.

After that day, I'd learned my lesson with my classmates. I avoided speaking of dragons again—not to kids and teachers at school, and especially not to my friends. When Ông Nội's gift turned into a curse, overwhelming his brain and destroying his reputation, Bà Nội and I were careful to always shush Ông Nội whenever he mentioned dragons. We hated hearing about them. We wished they'd leave him alone. But as Ông Nội always warned, you can only suppress destiny for so long.

While brushing my teeth before bed, I heard my grandparents arguing from their bedroom. Ông Nội was looking for his book, accusing Bà Nội of hiding it from him (true) and plotting against him (false). As he raged, I wondered if it was worth all this trouble. I could easily go downstairs and return the book to him, and we could all rest. Ông Nội had already lost so much. Why take a book away from him?

That night, I dreamed I was back in gym class, swimming after Lana and Huong, but this time I swam down into the pool, deeper and deeper, until the water turned red, then orange, then yellow. Farther I swam, toward a sliver of white-and-blue light that revealed a cave, and when I approached, I found myself enclosed in fire and smoke. When the bubbles around me cleared, there were giant white eggs nestled in a steaming pool of red lava. I didn't have to count the eggs to know there were one hundred of them.

As I swam above them, the eggs began to crack, baby dragons poking their heads from the broken shells, their eyes shut, their mouths open, their howls echoing through the cave. Their shrieks pierced my ears. Their screams grew louder and more terrifying.

I awoke with a start, my body shuddering and perspiring. Sitting up, I felt around me for my sheets, damp with sweat, my hair knotted and tangled from tossing and turning.

The thầy bói lineage could only pass through the males in our family. It's why my father left; he was trying to outrun his destiny. I was supposed to be safe.

Then what were these visions? Why was I dreaming my grandfather's dreams?

I pressed my fingers to my temples as hard I could, gritting my teeth against the pain, trying to squeeze out the throbbing inside my head. What was wrong with me?

WORLD HISTORY

I rarely paid attention to *Vaquero Vision* in homeroom, but when Huong's voice announced a call for volunteers for the school's annual beach cleanup, I looked up from my doodling and to the classroom's flat screen.

"This year's goal is five hundred volunteers, which our class president isn't sure we will reach," Huong said, lifting a perfectly threaded eyebrow. "Why don't we prove him wrong?"

As she gave further details, several classmates took pictures of the info or wrote it down in their planners. Huong Pham was the ultimate motivator. In a school already full of overachievers, she could easily recruit volunteers with a smile and a few words. Before Huong, hardly anyone paid attention to morning announcements. Then again, last year's *VV* anchors were two basketball players who spent most of their ten-minute airtime burping or mumbling inside jokes that only their friends understood.

My thoughts swirled back to Huong and Lana's crash and my delusion in the dining room. Those weren't the only times my mind had tricked me. I used to see my dad in different places—lingering behind the glass patio door of my grand-parents' house, bending over for a juice carton in a grocery store aisle, sitting in the driver's seat of our old Toyota in the driveway—even when I knew it wasn't possible. Who knew if he even looked the way I remembered him? And then there was the worst delusion, the one with Lana at the swim meet last spring, the incident people would come to remember whenever they thought of me. The one I tried every day to forget.

Contrary to school gossip, I could tell the difference between reality and fantasy. Most of the time, anyway. Since my return to the pool last week, it was getting harder. Maybe the lack of oxygen from being underwater so long had muddled my brain, allowing me to see things that didn't truly exist?

In World History, Mr. Sheridan introduced ancient China and the Han dynasty. Ever since we'd started the Asia unit last month, the class had turned on each other, dividing into ethnic factions, reigniting the resentments and grudges of our ancestors. The Koreans despised the Chinese. The Chinese loathed the Japanese. The Southeast Asians distrusted each other, but collectively agreed the East Asians were worse. Everyone ignored the South Asians.

All students outside of these groups, including mixed-race hapas like me, sat in the middle, like neutral Switzerland. Although Lana was half-Chinese, she used to sit with Daphne and the other Vietnamese kids, but Mr. Sheridan had separated them last week because they chatted too much during class. Lana made sure to never look in my direction, even though she was seated next to me.

This morning, Mr. Sheridan suggested we identify fact and fiction about the Han dynasty, so we could move to the next century the following week.

"Who can name a country that was once part of the Han dynasty?" Mr. Sheridan asked.

"There is only China," Milo Kim joked. "Because we're all Chinese."

"Shut up," Harsha Reddy said. He was a junior, but for some reason enrolled in our history class. He was also the first crush of most of the girls, and some boys, our year.

"Actually," Daphne said from her side of the room, "Vietnam was made up of a series of independent indigenous tribes and villages that united under the Trung sisters."

"For three years," Milo snickered. "That land was part of the Han dynasty for centuries."

"It was still enough time," Daphne said. "After the Trung rule, the Vietnamese continued to recognize themselves as their own people, separate from the Chinese. The country still has temples and parades to honor the Trung sisters. Their spirits supposedly cursed Ma Yuan, and his army soon succumbed to a plague."

"That's a lie!" Basil Liu yelled.

Daphne shrugged. "If you believe in superstition."

"Legends and traditions are important facets of history often used to inspire loyalty and patriotism within countries," Mr. Sheridan said, then turned on the projector to display several marble statues of Asian dragons. "Take dragons."

"My birth year sign!" Milo hooted.

"Most of your signs," Harsha reminded him. "Half this class was probably born in the year of the dragon."

"Many Asian countries worshipped dragons as their ancestors," Mr. Sheridan said. "Historical texts suggest that the dragons introduced warfare to humankind, and the current conflicts in Asia are extensions of ancient dragon battles."

"Ultimate sibling rivalry," Milo said. "They're why we fight."

"We're all enemies!" Basil yelled.

"But they're not real," Daphne said. "They're mythical. People who actually believe in them are crazy."

"So you're saying millions of people are crazy?" Harsha asked. "Most myths defy human logic. We don't have any issues with Buddhist or Hindu reincarnation."

I hesitantly raised my hand.

"Ms. Lam?" Mr. Sheridan said.

"My grandfather said that dragons have known for centuries how to live among humans without being detected."

"Maybe they're among us now!" Milo Kim cackled. "Can you see them, Loony Lam?"

The room exploded in laughter. Harsha grabbed Milo's beanie and threw it across the room, but the jerk continued to flap his arms, his mouth open and snarling. My eyes returned to the desk in front of me and the tiny, faint pencil and pen graffiti on the chair.

Stop talking. You need to stop talking.

I looked back at Lana, surprised she'd say that aloud. "Excuse me?"

Lana's eyes widened. "I didn't say anything."

"You did. You just told me to stop talking."

The dismissal bell rang. Lana slammed her book shut. "Why can't you just leave me alone?"

Daphne appeared next to us, pretending to look concerned. "What did she say?"

"Nothing important," Lana said, gathering her stuff and throwing it in her backpack.

"Quit talking about dragons," Daphne hissed at me. "You're going to make us all look crazy."

Like her crazy thầy bói and his stupid dragon tales.

"Don't call him crazy," I said sharply.

Daphne scowled. "What are you talking about?"

"Don't ever talk about my Ông Nội again."

"I didn't say anything about him."

"Yes, you did. Just now."

"Let's go, Daphne," Lana said, pushing at her shoulder. "There's no point in arguing with her. She'll never learn."

She's not worth it.

Around us, our classmates slid out of their chairs, packing up and moving on.

But even as they left, I could hear their thoughts echoing through my head, my heart tightening with fear.

Creepy. Creepy. Creepy.

6

LANA

Even as I rationalized that I could not have imagined Lana's and Daphne's words in my head, I knew the truth. I'd heard them. And they were right; I was creepy. Just like Ông Nội. My creepiness had torpedoed our friendship over a year ago and now it was making sure that my life would never feel normal again.

If they had ever stopped to really think about it, or answer any of my texts or calls—if they would have listened to anything I had to say, maybe things could have been different. Maybe I could have helped them understand. But listening never came easy, especially for Lana. The last thing she'd want to hear is that I'd been trying to save her.

It was the day of county semifinals. Lana, Daphne, and I were on the 400-meter freestyle relay, which should have been simple. Along with our teammate Stella Flores, we'd been shaving off seconds with each practice, and our coaches predicted an easy first place to advance us to regionals. They had arranged our lineup weeks ago: Lana, Stella, Daphne, and then me as the anchor leg. Lana tended to start strong and give us a sizable lead, Stella and Daphne maintained our momentum, and I didn't mind the pressure of making up time. I thrived on the challenge. During morning warm-ups, we felt optimistic about setting another team record, or even a county record.

The race began normally. At the starting horn, Lana dove in and finished her lap, then Stella, then Daphne, and finally me— a clean, smooth dive with a dolphin kick. Not only were we in the lead, but from my brief glance at the timer, I knew we were on the verge of breaking the relay record.

In the pool during a heat, my focus was usually on the water ahead of me, with each stroke, each kick, each inhale and exhale building speed and riding on this energy until my hand firmly slapped the pool's edge. That match, I don't know why my eyes drifted down. I saw Lana sprawled unnaturally still and calm at the bottom of the pool. My best friend, her skin swollen a purplish blue, her open eyes bulging, her body stiff and lifeless.

I swam toward her, tangling with lane ropes and other confused swimmers, trying to propel toward the bottom to reach her. But when you are alive, your body wants nothing more than to float up. The water rushed into my mouth and down my throat as I gagged and choked. When they dragged me out of the pool, I howled and kicked, my head smacking the wet concrete several times, the bright fluorescent lights clashing with the fireworks behind my eyes, the shadowy faces crowding around me like smoke.

"Lana!" I screamed, over and over. Someone had ripped off my goggles and swim cap. A voice instructed me to breathe, said that I was okay, that I was safe, that I needed to calm down, their hands around my shoulders, waist, arms, and legs growing tighter, pulling me down. "No! She's dead! Lana! Lana! We have to save her!"

Those were the words I remembered saying. They were seared in my mind and heart whenever I recalled that terrible day. On and on like this, for how long I wasn't sure. I think I passed out after hyperventilating and coughing up a bucket of warm pool water.

An hour later, I woke up in the emergency room. I looked past my red-eyed grandmother and the paramedics, searching for Lana. My heart rate and blood pressure had returned to normal. They thought I'd suffered a panic attack. They suggested I go to my family doctor to follow up.

"Your coaches pushed you too far," Bà Nội said on the drive home. "There is not enough oxygen entering your brain when you swim this much. What if you'd drowned?"

I ignored her, scrolling through my phone, trying to reach Lana. Though my messages showed they'd been read, neither Lana nor Daphne had responded. After making me rest for several hours, Bà Nội finally allowed me to walk over to Lana's house. The wind had picked up, howling through the sky, creating swirls of leaves across the sidewalk. I pushed the strands of hair away from my face and knocked on her front door. When she answered, I'd expected to see relief, maybe even a smile that I was okay.

Instead her face crumpled up, like she was going to cry.

"What?" The word sounded sharp and clipped, a tone she

usually saved for people she hated, not me. She was my best friend. My ride or die, from a promise we swore over bloody pinkies in third grade to always tell each other if we had food stuck in our teeth or period stains on our leggings.

"I'm so glad you're okay," I said. "I saw you—"

"I don't care what you saw," Lana interrupted.

"Oh." The wind picked up behind me, whipping my hair into my eyes. If only she let me describe it to her, the sickening sight of her lying there. Wouldn't she agree what a terrifying ordeal it was for both of us? Didn't she want to know how it happened? Together, we could figure it out.

"What is wrong with you?" Lana asked. "Why did you humiliate me?"

I stared at her, confused. "What are you talking about?"

"You acted like I was a monster! You said I was going to burn everyone!"

"No," I said, sputtering. "No, I didn't say that." The wind howled in my ears.

"You did, Jolie, we all heard you. Someone recorded it and now everyone's seen it."

To prove her point, she thrust her phone at me, her eyes shining with tears as we listened to the screaming on the video, confirming every terrible detail. On a grainy, wobbly video, several coaches held me down to prevent me from lunging at a weeping Lana. I watched in horror, a feeling that never left, even after hundreds of viewings. But I couldn't remember doing it. I couldn't believe it.

"You said 'it' was inside of me," Lana said, taking the phone back and turning from me. "What is the matter with you?"

"I'm so sorry," I said desperately. "I didn't mean it."

"What is *it*?"

"I have no idea. I just know I was trying to save you."

"From what?" Lana asked. "You ruined the meet, and you ruined my life. Just because you're some fortune-teller's granddaughter doesn't mean you can see things."

"I know," I repeated, feeling my body, my heart, recoiling.

"And fortune-tellers are scammers. They can't really predict the future. They just want to take people's money. My dad always said so, but I was too nice to say anything to you until now. They're liars. And you are, too."

She said some other things that I no longer recall. I may have responded, but it was useless, hysterical blubbering that would change nothing. What I could never forget was the feeling, the crack in my chest that made it almost impossible for me to breathe normally, deeply. Even now, eighteen months later, my rib cage rattled with grief. Her words continued to seep through my skin, moving through my veins like an efficient, enduring poison. She slammed the front door at some point, turning off the porch light so I stood there in the dark, sweating in my parka, fearing that my legs would give out right there on her porch.

I walked home, stepping over branches that had fallen from trees and assorted piles of leaves, allowing the warm, determined air to dry my face. I didn't stop after entering the house.

I walked straight through to the backyard. I shrugged off my parka, slipped out of my flip-flops, and staggered down the steps into the shimmering pool water, which slipped around my ankles, my thighs, my tightly coiled stomach. It felt warm and soothing.

When I finally emerged from underwater, Ông Nội was sitting at our patio table peering over me, a striped towel laying over his lap. I slung an elbow over the pool's edge and blinked at him in confusion.

"You had a vision," he pronounced.

I stretched back into the water, letting it slide through my hair. "Don't you mean a breakdown?"

"That's what regular people see."

"Girls can't be thầy bói," I reminded him.

"So far," he confirmed. "But nothing is permanent."

"Ông Nội, I can't," I said, staring up at the night sky.

I flipped in the water, swimming from one end to the other in one breath, waiting for my heartbeat to slow and calm. With each stroke, I watched the moonlight in the water sliding around me, allowing it to follow me, lighting my path. When I came back to the surface, Ông Nội was gone, and only the striped towel remained in the chair.

Alone again, I floated on my back, collapsing my shoulders and spine to allow the water to flow over my arms, chest, neck and face, so eventually only my nose remained above the surface.

Another benefit of water? You can't really cry beneath it.

SPEAK

I didn't hear anyone else's thoughts after hearing Lana's and Daphne's in World History. A week passed with only my lonely, paranoid voice inside my head. I even tried listening for stray opinions from my grandparents and quieting my mind to hear my classmates' thoughts at school, which was easy enough to do since barely anyone outside my house spoke to me. Maybe, I wondered with growing certainty, it had been my imagination.

The following week, during morning announcements on *Vaquero Vision*, Huong tilted her perfect face to the camera, as she usually did, to share the details of the upcoming football game.

This is all stupid and pointless, she said, but the words did not match what was coming from her mouth.

I paused, looking around, but no one else seemed alarmed or disturbed.

You know it, too, Jolie, don't you?

The pencil dropped from my hand. Huong smirked, seemingly right at me. I sank deeper into my hoodie, wanting to melt into my chair. My heart began to pound so loudly, I couldn't pay attention to anything else Huong or her co-anchor, KT, said, with or without their mouths. When I'd overheard Lana's and Daphne's thoughts, they didn't seem to know. But Huong seemed to be directing her thoughts at me. How was that?

In gym, I anxiously listened for Huong's voice, but she came to the pool late and slipped into the farthest lane from me. I felt relieved.

Eventually I put that task aside, allowing myself to enjoy the familiar silky glide of the water around my body. The calm eventually trickled up to my brain, until I forgot all about Huong.

After class, as I was leaving the locker room, I heard her deep voice calling out my name. It was out loud this time, echoing off the steamy tiles. My ears perked up, my spine straightened, as I waited for her voice to return inside my head.

Instead Huong jogged toward me, waving my phone. "You left this."

"Oh." I took it from her, a little confused since I usually kept it in the front pocket of my backpack during gym. "Thanks."

I shyly looked up at her face, wondering if I would hear her thoughts again. Did she know?

"You should really set a passcode," Huong said. "I turned it on to see whose it was, and I think someone changed your lockscreen."

My thumb tapped the screen on, my stomach already twisting, knowing. My usual screen background, which was a photo I had taken of a colorful tide pool in Monterey last summer, had been replaced with an image I'd been trying to forget. Me lying next to the pool, my body darkened from the shadows of my coach and teammates hovering above me. My hair wet, skin blotchy, eyes bloodshot, mouth twisted in fury and hysteria.

Scrawled across the photo: "Psycho in the water! None of us are safe!"

They'd used this photo so many times, changing the caption repeatedly to refresh the humiliation.

"Do you know who did this?" Huong asked.

"No," I said. Sadly, it could have been anyone at our school. I'd been an easy target for a long time.

I clicked open our Schoolbook's mobile app and went to my account profile. Nightmare confirmed: my profile picture was changed to display the prank there, too. The lockers around us swayed, the overhead lights somehow brightening. My fingers clumsily found the delete option on my phone. The Schoolbook app was our school's primary software that controlled our schedules, grades, attendance, emails, etc.

The posts started last year. At the end of our second week at West, I received an anonymous text linking to an encrypted video, and the texts kept coming until I finally clicked on it. A video opened on Schoolbook's forum page, proclaiming a top ten list of why Jolie Lam was San Jose's Psychic Psycho, followed by loops of me walking alone on campus, staring listlessly into my locker, tripping over doorframes, or dropping books in the hallway.

At first I suspected Lana and Daphne, but when I confronted them at school, they swore they hadn't done anything. It was one of the few times they actually spoke to me since we'd arrived at

West. After the county swim meet that summer, they'd stopped responding to my calls and texts, and sat as far away from me as they could, determined to shed me and my reputation so they could start fresh for high school. In our shared classes, they looked past my gaze, making it clear we were no longer friends. I kept hoping they'd get over it, especially Lana, or maybe even miss me and realize it was stupid to throw away eight years of friendship. But they didn't.

The videos had petered out this spring. I liked to think that I'd bored my classmates with a lack of material, learning to blend in and disappear. That maybe they'd forgotten me and I could reappear and resume a normal life. But I guessed not.

"It's easy to find out," Huong said as she watched me frantically jab at my phone. Her hand reached over my screen. I relinquished the phone and watched as Huong's index finger swiped, zigged, and zagged across the screen, her eyes crinkling slightly in concentration.

"Do you know anyone who lives on Hamilton Drive?"

I felt the blood drain from my face. "Are you sure?"

"That's where the IP address is. What's the person's name?"

"Lana Marquez-Chen."

"Oh, the girl who crashed into me in the pool." Her eyes carefully observed mine. "Friend of yours?"

"Not anymore," I said, struggling to compose myself. My body started to warm with anger. I tried to breathe slowly, like my therapist had taught me. Why did Lana need to dump on me? I knew I annoyed her at the pool, but I'd also saved her.

"Give me another minute," Huong said. "I think I can fix this."

Even while tapping on a phone, Huong looked poised, her posture as straight as a ballerina's, wearing a blue cotton dress and espadrilles. An amethyst necklace twinkled against her chest. She handed the phone back to me with a closed-lip smile.

I turned the screen in my palm. Huong had navigated to Lana's Schoolbook profile and switched her profile photo to a screenshot of her current grades. Yikes. They weren't good. My cheeks started to cool. I clicked over to my profile and saw my default student ID photo restored.

"It will take her a while to change it, until she can crack the new password."

"You're fast," I said, smiling gratefully. The school was overpopulated with aspiring coders and hackers who longed to drop out and work for a startup.

She reached behind her to squeeze out her wet hair, the droplets falling in a constellation on the hallway's tiled floor. "Why were you hanging out with that white girl anyway?"

I snorted a laugh and immediately felt self-conscious. "She's half-Asian," I said, "like me. But Chinese."

"Really?" she asked, tipping her head to one side, looking me up and down again, as if trying to detect it.

"There are a lot of mixed kids here," I said, though why I was defending Lana, I had no idea. "It's California."

"You only look Vietnamese to me." Her chin jutted out confidently, without any shame or sheepishness.

No one had ever said that to me before. People often looked surprised when first meeting my grandparents, sometimes even asking if I was adopted. Whatever was Vietnamese in me seemed stubbornly buried—sleepy, recessive genes yet to be activated. Bà Nội said I had my dad's dark hair and eyes, but everything else echoed my mom: freckles, pale complexion, and long arms and legs.

"What about that loud skinny girl she hangs out with?" Huong asked. "Delphine?"

"Daphne. Oh, both her parents are Vietnamese."

Huong frowned. "Yes, I remember seeing her at last year's student Tết festival. She's a downer. Speaks decent Vietnamese, though, unlike most of the Viet kids born here. How about you?" Huong asked. Her hands had risen up to her long damp hair, and she massaged her scalp with her fingers.

"Do I speak Vietnamese?" I asked. "No."

"Your mother didn't teach you?" She began dividing and twisting sections of her hair into a french braid.

I'd never been able to do one for myself, back when my hair skimmed past my waist. It always came out crooked or loose. Now my hair was too short. Bà Nội had chopped it off last year after discovering a bird's nest of knots on the underside. A bob required nothing from me. After watching the newspapers on the floor fill with soft piles of my neglected hair, I had stared fearfully at my new reflection—ugly, unlovable—and cried.

Eventually I got over it. Given enough time, people can get used to most anything.

"My mom is dead," I said. "She was white."

"Oh," Huong said, pausing her hair-braiding. "Sorry."

"It's okay. It happened when I was really young."

"You look like you can understand the language," she said.

"Well, I can't," I said, irritated, and then paused, rewinding her words in my brain. She hadn't said them in English, yet I'd swiftly understood and responded.

She grinned at me, revealing the top row of her teeth, so attractively even—exactly how I remembered her from the pool. She released her hair to stretch, like a cheerleader doing victory arms, then rested her hands on her hips. Her head tipped coyly to the side, her french braid trailing down her back. "Are you sure?"

"Huong!" From down the hall, Huong's best friend launched toward us, her purple empire-waist dress billowing with each stride in her tall black boots. Khanh-Thien Nguyen, also known as KT. Along with co-anchoring *Vaquero Vision*, KT was treasurer of the junior class, president of the school's National Honor Society chapter, head delegate of Youth & Government, and a member of countless other clubs. You could always spot her in a crowd with her shoulder-length, super-bleached platinum-blond hair.

On *Vaquero Vision*, KT often played the bad cop—rarely smiling, often barking her announcements—to Huong's good cop. While other students appeared pale or sweaty under the glaring studio lights, their breakouts in high definition, KT often radiated superiority, her flat-ironed hair never out of place. She signed off her morning announcements with the same threat: "The only acceptable place is first place, Vaqueros."

I didn't think I'd ever seen her without platform boots or wedges since she was barely five feet tall. Despite her height, she intimidated many, yelling at students in her gravelly voice to get out of her way.

"What are you doing with that freshman?" she hollered. "We're late!"

"She's not a freshman," Huong said. "Her name is Jolie and she's in my gym—"

"I don't care," KT said, pausing to look at me briefly before pivoting on her thick heel in the direction of their next class. "You are always disappearing at the most inconvenient times. Let's go!"

Huong turned to me. "Sorry, she's on her period. But KT's right, it's Mr. Savage's Econ, and he locks his door after the bell."

Her hand gently squeezed the curve of my shoulder before she left, but I was too absorbed in her previous words. I rewound the moment and realized again I'd understood her in Vietnamese. Alone in the hallway, I tried to repeat the words she'd just said but couldn't. They'd faded from my mind, and I couldn't grab them back. But their meaning, their feeling, remained, glowing inside of me.

See you later, Jolie, Huong's voice had whispered in my head. *I'm glad we could chat.*

I spun around the empty hallway, looking for her, finding no one.

Yet I didn't feel lonely. My face broke into a grin. Not anymore.

8

CURSE

While I grew up around my grandparents speaking Vietnamese, I never picked it up. Bà Nội enrolled me in language classes with Daphne at their family's Vietnamese Catholic church, but I barely lasted a month. The teachers claimed I had no ear to pick up the tones. Every time I tried to pronounce a word, it felt like I was hurting their ears. Daphne graduated as their best student and now volunteered on weekends with the younger kids' Vietnamese language and history classes at the church.

That evening, I sat across from my grandparents over steaming bowls of bún riêu. This was one of my favorite dinners, but I was too busy trying out my new gift to enjoy it. In addition to the recent vision, I could hear my ex-friends' and Huong's thoughts—and I could understand Vietnamese.

Of course it could have been my imagination, like Bà Nội said, but what if it wasn't? I needed more proof. I examined my grandparents, trying to clear my thoughts to make room for theirs. I could understand their murmurs in Vietnamese, which before had only sounded like a familiar melody. As for any internal conversation, I gathered nothing. Only silence. Unfortunately, I wasn't very discreet with my efforts.

"What are you doing in there?" Ông Nội asked suddenly.

I innocently focused on the rice noodles slipping off my chopsticks. "I'm just waiting for my soup to cool."

"Lies," he declared loudly. He'd caught me searching his thoughts and, strangely, didn't seem surprised by it. "If you want to know how our day was, just ask."

My eyes widened for a moment, but I recovered. "How was your day?"

"Not nearly as exciting as yours. Why don't you tell us what happened at school?"

Bà Nội took a sip of her soup and looked at me curiously.

I tried to laugh it off. "I don't know what you're talking about."

"Of course you do," Ông Nội said. "Your school is an inferno of traitors and spies!"

"Hush, old man, you are tired," Bà Nội said, taking the heat off me for a moment. She glanced back at me. "You are very quiet tonight."

It was worth a try. I took a breath and plunged in. "I was talking to this girl at school and she said something to me in Vietnamese, and I understood her," I said.

Bà Nội rested her hand on Ông Nội, who was staring at his bún riêu like a petulant child. She tilted her head. "Can you understand me?" she asked in Vietnamese.

I hesitated, counting three of my heartbeats before answering. "Yes."

Her face twisted in a mixture of emotions. Was she mad? Was she sad? I rested my chopsticks next to the bowl. I didn't know what else to do.

"Anything else?"

"What?"

"Can you hear anything else?"

Something in the way she said it warned me I'd revealed enough to her for now. "No," I lied.

She studied me, then wiped her eyes with the back of her palm. "I've heard of this before. You listen long enough and then suddenly, after many years, you can understand that language, especially if family—"

"That is not what is happening," Ông Nội interrupted.

"She is fine," Bà Nội said firmly. She looked over to me, shaking her head, as if trying to convince both of us.

"Of course she is. The gift is coming."

"She is a girl. It is not supposed to happen with girls."

"You think you know my ancestors' history better than me?"

"Ông Nội," I broke in, tired of them talking like I wasn't even there. "Do you remember your story about the first thầy bói? How the dragon taught him to understand all the languages? And read people's futures?"

He narrowed his glassy eyes at me. *You don't need me to tell you your future.*

I looked over at Bà Nội in alarm. "Did you hear that?"

She shot me a disapproving look. "Jolie."

"You didn't, did you? Only I could."

"Jolie, he is tired. I don't think tonight—"

"Why don't you want her to know the truth?" Ông Nội asked, his voice rising.

With one slap of his hand, the ceramic bowl of soup flipped in the air and landed back on the table. It shattered on impact, the broth, noodles, and crabmeat dispersing across my grandfather's lap, the table, and the floor.

I pushed out my chair and knelt, trying to sop up the red soup bleeding across the carpet.

Bà Nội rested a hand on my arm. "I'm going to help your grandfather change. Can you take care of this?"

I nodded miserably. They continued to argue as they left the room. The broken bowl couldn't be saved. He hadn't had an outburst like that in weeks. And I had to be the one who triggered it. We'd gone through these episodes before. Bà Nội would talk and soothe him through the episode until he finally fell asleep. Then she'd be too exhausted to come down and finish her dinner and would pass out next to him.

His tantrums were the first sign of his dementia. Before the rages, Ông Nội had been the calmest, coolest person I knew, hardly ever raising his voice. The first one happened in a department store when he couldn't find Bà Nội. Apparently he'd roamed the aisles screaming for her, afraid she'd been abducted by dragons.

We rarely went out with him, but for Tết, Bà Nội thought we should celebrate the Year of the Tiger with Dungeness crab and garlic noodles at their favorite restaurant. When the main course arrived, Ông Nội jumped up and ran through the dining room, circling tables of bewildered diners, yelling that we had to evacuate before the fires returned. It took three servers and the restaurant host to pull him down, and more than twenty minutes for the screaming to end. As we were leaving, I noticed Daphne and her family gawking at us from their corner table. My face burned in humiliation and anger. Our families had been part of the same community for years, and now they acted like they didn't even know us.

We hadn't eaten out since. Now, if Bà Nội was craving chả cá lã vọng or bánh cuốn, she made it herself or ordered in.

After clearing dinner and cleaning up, I walked into Ông Nội's study. I couldn't find the book at first. Bà Nội had hidden it on the highest shelf to prevent Ông Nội from finding it again. The red leather tome was heavy, and I nearly dropped it while pulling it down. It was nine by eleven inches in dimension, no larger than a notebook, so the heft of it always surprised me. There was no text on the cover or spine, similar to a blank journal. When I was little, Ông Nội said that it made the book more special: only those who knew could read and discover what lay in these pages.

One time in fifth grade when Daphne was over after swim team, I tried to show her the book. After turning a few pages, she said the stories sounded unbelievable, even for Vietnamese folktales. She preferred books from her Catholic church, which were newer and had prettier pictures. I never showed her the book again.

When I first opened the mythology book, it appeared blank. I frowned, turning the pages. Maybe I'd mistaken an unused journal for Ông Nội's book, but the cover was so familiar: the aged leather, the yellowing, jagged deckle-edged pages, the frayed black ribbon bookmark. I sat on the floor, letting the book rest in my lap. I pressed my hand to the center and the cover felt warm to my touch. I opened it again and found handwriting.

I inhaled sharply. Had I missed this the first time? The writing was in Vietnamese, but unlike previous times, when my eyes glazed over the artful symbols, I connected the consonants, vowels, and diacritical marks. Not only could I understand Vietnamese, I could read it.

The page was open to the fable of Lâm Xuân Hiển, our ancestor and the first thầy bói of Vietnam—my favorite story. Ông Nội told it to me so often, I wondered if I imagined my comprehension. Maybe these words were ingrained in my memory. I pressed my finger to each word, reading for the first time in Vietnamese.

THE MYTH OF THE THẦY BÓI
(PART ONE)

Over two thousand years ago, a young fisherman named Lâm Xuân Hiển had gone swimming in the ocean when he encountered a dragon under the water, napping in a cave of rocks. Most men would have panicked and tried to swim away. Instead our ancestor swam down to meet this magical creature.

Impressed with his courage and curiosity, the dragon spoke to him. She granted him ears that could understand her language, lungs that could breathe underwater, and eyes that allowed him to look into the past and the future. For hours they played, shared stories, and sang to each other.

She confided that she was protecting the most valuable treasure in the world, the prime elements, from her feuding siblings. He told her about his family of farmers and fishermen who had lived in the same valley between the ocean and mountains for centuries.

He did not want to leave her, but as a human, he needed to return to land. He'd already spent too much time away, and his family would be missing him.

But the dragon had grown attached. She still had so much more to share. So the dragon offered him a final present, one he could carry away from the ocean. She gave him a glittering yellow flower.

Once he consumed it, their spirits would remain connected, bonded for eternity. She would know what it was like to be a human. And he would know what it was like to be a dragon.

This gift, while generous and loving, changed their destinies forever. For this was not the dragon's gift to give, especially not to a human.

When Lâm Xuân Hiển emerged from the ocean, his feet could feel the change from silky water to pebbly sand. His hands and hair could sense the breeze from the air and warmth from the sun. But he could no longer see—not the beach or his dogs running toward him or his family members surrounding him, relieved that he was still alive.

According to his family, his eyes and hair had turned bright white, his skin had wrinkled and darkened. His night under the sea had aged him fifty years.

His family mourned his aging, blindness, and ridiculous chatter about the dragon he met under the ocean. They ignored his prophecies and warnings. They wished for their old father to return. He did not care. He was more interested in everything else he could now see.

9

THE CLIFF

I closed the book, which had grown warmer in my hands. I'd been so absorbed in my reading, I hadn't noticed the growing heat until it made my lap uncomfortably hot. Yet my grip didn't loosen, so the book's warmth traveled up my arms and into my chest. The increasing discomfort built to pain and finally release—like tiny heat blisters bursting throughout my body. My lips parted and a gust of air from deep inside my chest unfurled across the room. But unlike the heat in my body, the breath felt cool and clean, swirling through the air, gathering up the dust that had collected for months, creating an iridescent cyclone. It circled the ceiling, searching for a place to escape, spinning, spinning, spinning, until it disappeared through the walls.

Mouth open, I scrambled to my feet as the glowing book hit the floor. I paced the room, staring at the ceiling, waiting for the cloud to return, or maybe for my grandparents to wake up and rush down. Their bedroom was right above the study.

The room now smelled fresh and cool. I inhaled, tasting salty

air and rich earth on my tongue. The sensations felt both familiar and new, disturbing and calming, all at once.

Separately, I could explain away the visions, understanding
Vietnamese, the bizarre delusions. But denial just wasted time.
The signs kept coming, piling on top of each other. My inevitable
destiny. The curse my dad ran away from, the reason why I
hadn't seen him in years, the reason for all of my family's unhappiness over generations and generations.

I was becoming a thầy bói. I wanted to cry. I wanted to
scream. How could anyone want this? Want to never have
hope, because I'd always know the ending. I'd have no choices,
no possibilities, because there would only be one inevitable
outcome. Seeing the future was a gift I could never give back.
As a thầy bói, I'd carry this curse for life, and like Ông Nội, it
would ultimately drive me crazy.

Later that night, Bà Nội came by my room to check in on me.

"I'm calling his doctor in the morning," Bà Nội said.

"What if he's right?" I asked. "What if I am a thầy bói?"

"You know he says many things that do not make sense," she
said.

"That doesn't mean he's wrong."

She sighed, putting a hand over mine. "When I first came to
this country, I was afraid I was never going to learn English. I'd
listen to these very tall, very pale people shout and yell in my
face and they seemed like dogs to me, barking so much. Then
one day, the words made sense. And I realized they were not
angry. They were trying to help me. It happened like that.
Maybe that is what is happening with you. We have been speak-

ing Vietnamese around you for fifteen years. If anything, you are a slow learner."

I rolled my eyes, and she squeezed my arm playfully.

"Now we have to be careful what we say in front of you," Bà Nội said.

Bà Nội had married into a family of psychics, so she knew what she was getting into. Her father-in-law, my great-grandfather, had chosen Bà Nội out of all the eligible girls in their neighborhood to marry my grandfather, despite her family's lack of money and education, declaring they were destined to take care of each other.

The vision came true, like all of the thầy bói's predictions. The family's clairvoyance had protected the Lam lineage through Vietnam's many wars and foreign occupations and their eventual escape to America.

But that was a long time ago, when Ông Nội's reputation as the best fortune-teller in town brought our family financial support and respect from the community. Now we scraped by with my grandmother's pension and their social security deposits, but Bà Nội regularly fretted over their depleted savings.

After she left, I pulled out the mythology book I had swiped from Ông Nội's study and hid under my comforter. As I read, I imagined Ông Nội's voice reading the words to me. His voice was the soundtrack to my life, especially after Dad left. He worked as a geologist and was always away on field expeditions. On his last trip, he never returned, and only occasionally sent postcards from whatever remote location he was stationed. Even when Dad was around, it was Ông Nội who read to me, corrected my homework, and answered all the questions parents usually did for their kids.

I remember once, after listening to another bedtime story, asking Ông Nội if he ever disliked being a thầy bói. At the time, it seemed like a superpower: to always know more than everybody else. He said there were good and bad things about it, but that he couldn't ever renounce it.

"That is like regretting living at all," Ông Nội said.

That night, the first thầy bói came to me in a dream. He looked just like my grandfather but younger, with thick black hair, dressed in all white. We stood on a grassy cliff, the sky streaked with white smoke. The ocean waves below crashed against the rocks. The ground shuddered with tremors.

The thầy bói pointed at the creatures perched on the rocks over the cliff's edge. There were dozens of dragons, in all different colors of the rainbow and beyond. They wailed up to the clouds, crying out for their departed parents.

The sun rose and fell many times. Eventually the baby dragons began to take flight. First, the black and red dragons took off. Then the green, blue, orange, indigo, violet, and every shade in between. Finally only two dragons, one lavender and one yellow, remained. The yellow dragon looked especially small and helpless, but the lavender dragon wrapped her body around hers. They stayed on those rocks for a long time, weeping into each other's necks.

Why don't you fly away? I finally asked them.

The dragons looked over at me with shining white eyes.

We can't, they said. *We gave them all to him.*

I followed their gaze to the first thầy bói, whose eyes shone white, like the dragons'. Before I could ask what they gave him, the thầy bói raised his hands, levitating from the cliff. We watched him soar higher and higher, through the white smoke, until we could no longer see him.

10

THE RESCUE

The next morning, I woke up exhausted. Fuzzy head, achy muscles. It could have been from gym. Or maybe I was sick. Viruses were always floating around this time of year.

I checked my phone, the memory of Lana and Daphne's prank descending. No surprise texts or emails, but there was an update on a postponed football game because of an earthquake damaging the fields in San Leandro. My guidance counselor had sent me details of a new math tutor assignment. With everything that had happened, I had almost forgotten that I was failing algebra.

Lana and Daphne lurked around my locker after school, slouched in various poses of fake chill. Daphne's head dipped as she whispered to Lana, their hair blending in a conspiratorial curtain of golden brown and blue black.

Daphne reluctantly slid over to allow me access to my locker. Their eyes traveled from my uncombed hair and gray crocheted sweater down to my baggy jeans and Reef sandals. I ignored their judgmental expressions as my fingers fumbled to find my locker combination. It wasn't like they looked so much better, Lana in warm-up sweats and Daphne in a Vaquero hoodie and ripped denim short shorts.

They peered over my shoulder as I opened my locker. Their bland, identical thoughts filtered through my brain, noting the lack of photo collages, cards from friends, and practice schedules. I had only a small oval mirror magnet, where their reflections surrounded me.

"You changed my password," Lana said. "I need it."

Oh, right. The Schoolbook profile. "I didn't touch your account," I said.

"My mom goes into my Schoolbook to check on my attendance," Lana said. "Please give me the password."

I focused on changing out my textbooks for tonight's homework. "It would be a lot faster calling the help desk or resetting it yourself," I suggested.

"That doesn't explain why you were in my account," Lana said.

"Why were you in mine?"

They both feigned ignorance, exchanging meaningful glances with each other. What Lana and I used to do together. A slow, resentful heat simmered underneath my skin. I'd been the one to introduce them to each other when Daphne first moved here. I'd been the glue of our trio. Not anymore.

"You changed my profile photo," I said, grabbing my phone to show them the screenshot of their prank.

They both stared at it for a few moments, like they hadn't seen the viral photo before.

"That is sick," Lana finally said.

"Do you mean me, or what you did?" I asked.

"That wasn't us," Daphne claimed.

"Stop lying," I said. "I don't know why you chose a photo that has already been used over and over again. Not very original."

"Why would I want to be reminded of that day?" Lana snapped.

"Fine," I said, slamming my locker shut, turning to face them. "None of us will admit anything then."

"Can you try to be mature?" Lana asked. "I want to resolve this so we can leave each other alone."

"We can do that without speaking to each other. You came here. I didn't want to talk to you."

But they didn't leave me alone. They surrounded me, suffocating me with their thoughts.

I'm so tired of her bullshit.

I can't believe we were ever friends.

This is how I knew I had not imagined their words, because these thoughts were much worse than anything I could come up with. My neck and arms seethed with heat. I was not going to back down.

I felt my lips parting, the smoke rising inside of me.

"Jolie," another voice said, and I looked up. Huong and KT walked toward us. "Is everything okay?"

Time stilled, the squeaks and slams of lockers fading, the conversations around us quieting. A gray cloud over the hallway's skylight drifted past us, allowing the afternoon sun to pierce through the glass windows. A cool breeze swept through, a waft of fragrant flowers enveloping us, quenching the smoke inside of me.

To my wonderment, I exhaled a sweet glittery mist, and watched the sparkles rise through the air around us.

"Everything's fine," Lana said, her voice soft and breathy. "Just chatting."

No one else seemed to see the mist but me. Lana and Daphne stepped back as Huong and KT reached us, their shoulders drooping, their gazes suddenly transfixed on the diamond-patterned tile floor. Their fear whirled incoherently through my head. This was probably the first time a junior had bothered noticing them. And if they wanted one to notice them, they wouldn't want it to be KT.

Huong and KT were only a year ahead of us, yet they looked much older and more sophisticated. Huong wore a loose yellow blouse, dark jeans, and chocolate-brown flats, while KT had on a Peter Pan–collared white blouse, a gray jumper, and her thigh-high black boots.

Only their facial expressions matched, which I didn't think happened often. KT wore a permanent stink eye, while Huong typically exuded kindness, from her warm eyes to her easy, bright smile. Except this afternoon. Cast frostily at Lana, Huong's gaze was as intimidating as her scary friend's.

"Then why does Jolie look upset?" Huong asked, tilting her head. "Why are you in her personal space?"

"And who's wearing the pissy perfume?" KT barked, her nose sniffing the air. "It's making my eyes water."

"We're not!" Lana said sharply, then her face puckered in regret. "We're having a private discussion."

"Jolie broke into Lana's Schoolbook account," Daphne said. "We just want to know why."

"Oh, that wasn't Jolie," Huong said, a sweet smile breaking out on her face. "That was me."

The girls stared in stunned silence, while KT popped a bubble in her gum.

"Didn't you break into hers first?" Huong continued. "We needed to make sure you hadn't taken anything from her, like swapping assignments."

"We've heard it happens," KT said. "Cheaters are the lowest form of scum."

"Why would I want her assignments?" Lana sputtered.

"Most of us have seen your fall progress report," Huong said, shaking her head sadly.

"How?" Lana asked, her face blushing with rage.

KT held up her phone, revealing a picture of Lana's transcript alongside her profile photo. "It's right here. Someone just forwarded it. Both of yours."

Daphne, who always prided herself on her GPA, looked like she'd been slapped.

"Yeah, you, too, dummy. It looks like the whole school received your progress reports."

The girls scrambled for their phones to check, their faces reflecting the horror they found in their messages. My own phone buzzed in my pocket, but I ignored it, too fascinated by the unfolding real-time reactions.

"Well, of course," Huong said calmly. "Who would click on their Schoolbook profile photos? Better to send to everyone to make sure we all know who they are and what they're worth."

Daphne and Lana continued to gaze at their phones. Lana's eyes had teared up.

Huong rested her shoulder against me, immediately calming me. "Do you feel violated? Helpless?" she asked my former friends, her eyebrows rising. "I want you to remember this feeling whenever you feel the itch to bother Jolie again."

They departed quickly, Lana dragging a catatonic Daphne away, not looking back as they hustled down the hallway.

Huong turned to me, beaming. "I'm your math tutor. I couldn't wait until four o'clock, so I thought I'd find you now. I'm glad we did."

"First-years can be so mouthy," KT said.

"She's a sophomore," Huong corrected.

"Whatever! They haven't grown tits or accomplished anything yet. What is there to be so proud of?"

"Jolie isn't," Huong said, patting my arm. "Mouthy, I mean. And she has boobs; nice, cute ones."

"Being mute is only marginally better," KT said, turning to cast a crippling glance at me as I crossed my arms. "Do you speak at all?"

"Stop," Huong said before I could open my mouth. "Jolie knows there is more wisdom in listening than speaking."

"She'll have to speak up someday," KT said. "Don't expect us to always rescue you, Julie."

"It's Jolie," I corrected her, to which she shrugged.

Huong turned to me. "You want to come over to my house? The library's air conditioning gets too cold for me."

"I guess I should find my dummy," KT said, pulling out her phone.

We listened to the echo of her boots stomp down the hallway.

"Why is she even a tutor?" I asked after I felt sure she'd left the building.

"KT?" Huong asked. "Oh, she's the president of the tutoring alliance. She's all bark. She convinced me to do it. And now I'm so happy she did!" She linked her arm around mine, her skin silky and smooth, the smell of jasmine rising between us. "Because I'm taking you home."

11

PRIME NUMBERS

More eyes followed me on that walk to Huong's car than ever before. How weird to be inside her spotlight, even if it was more like her shadow. I pulled at my hair, hoping they wouldn't notice me and frown, or even worse, say or think something nasty I could overhear.

Huong barely noticed, brushing past classmates who tried stopping her, some of them calling for her to text them later. Her strides appeared graceful and fluid, like she was gliding, even if only to a parking garage. She'd only moved to San Jose last year yet had made a deeper impression than I had in fifteen years.

"I don't even know that girl," Huong muttered after waving at a cheerleader who hopped on top of one of the stone vaquero statues to blow a kiss at her.

We stopped in front of a metallic blue Tesla. The car interior smelled like cotton candy. A plastic pink cat bobbed on the dashboard.

"Do you know how to drive?" Huong asked.

"I'm fifteen," I said.

"So?" She smiled. "I could teach you."

Bà Nội had been wanting to teach me too, so I could help with more chores. But I'd been afraid to learn, since I already got nervous riding on freeways or going over bridges too fast.

Once off campus, I turned to her. "Thanks for defending me, but you didn't have to."

"Why not?" she asked.

"You barely know me."

"But I really like what I do know."

We drove through West San Jose, where almond and cherry orchards used to surround the area. Some of the trees remained, their brown spindly branches casting sprawling, intricate silhouettes across the roads and fields. I spotted a rainbow stretching over the horizon. I hadn't noticed any rain that day, but I marveled at the vivid colors arching through the clear, brilliant sky.

Huong turned into a gated community of identical sprawling mansions. She pressed a button on her visor for the garage door. Her front yard had several cherry trees with gorgeous purple blossoms.

"Your trees bloom in the fall?" I asked as we pulled into garage.

"Weird, right?" Huong agreed. "Probably climate change."

We could smell the blossom fragrance when we opened the car doors. I inhaled deeply, the sweetness overwhelming my nostrils. Huong's car was the only vehicle in the pristine four-car garage, which also didn't have any boxes, laundry machines, bicycles, or other spillover junk you'd expect. Once inside her house, we slipped off our shoes on the bamboo doormat.

"Are your parents home?" I asked after hearing someone in the kitchen.

"No, that's our housekeeper, Phung," Huong said.

Phung looked barely older than us, dressed in a white polo shirt and jeans, her long hair pulled back in a low ponytail. When Huong introduced us, Phung smiled joyfully and called me em—Vietnamese for "sister"—even though we'd just met.

Huong carried a plate of mango wedges with us upstairs. Except for a few sweaters and a nightgown on the floor, several sticky notes on the mirror, and cosmetics scattered on a rustic white vanity table, the room looked immaculate, with decor and furniture transported directly from a Pottery Barn catalog. Wall-to-wall gray carpet. A violet duvet with an array of decorative bolster and lacy pillows and a matching crocheted blanket neatly folded at the end. A desk sat under a window, which looked out on a panoramic view of the caramel-colored San Jose hills.

There were no posters, just a clock shaped like the country of Vietnam.

The afternoon sun was melting, a pink haze rising behind the hills. When I was little, the hillsides reminded me of giant camel humps hiding on the horizon, holding up the sky. The branches and petals from the cherry blossom trees scraped against the window, casting soft, bubbly shadows across the carpet.

On her desk was a photo collage of KT and Huong in various

cut-out selfies: preening, pursing their lips in front of the camera at sleepovers, sunbathing on the beach, snowboarding, sailing on the bay with the Marin Headlands and the Golden Gate Bridge glowing behind their sun-bronzed faces.

"Most of our stuff is back at our house in Hanoi," Huong said. "All this furniture came with the house."

"This is a rental?" I asked, taking a seat on the carpet. Huong also knelt on the floor, stretching her legs.

"No. My parents bought it in case I attend university here," she said. "I told them there was no chance I was sticking around."

"They were okay with that?"

"Why should they dictate my life?" There was no spite or anger in her voice. She sounded downright cheerful. "You shouldn't let yours either."

"Luckily, they're not around anymore," I said, then instantly regretted it. I sounded stupid and careless.

She rolled over on her stomach to look at me. "What happened?"

"My mom died in childbirth," I said. That was the easy part of the story. "And my dad left when I was seven."

"Why?" If anyone else had asked that, I would have been offended, but Huong sounded sincere.

I explained that he was a geologist doing field work abroad, and hadn't been home to see our family in years. "He always seemed too busy for me," I said. "My grandparents raised me."

Huong reached over, placing a hand on mine.

"My parents feel like ghosts, too," she said. "They spend most of their time in their apartment in San Francisco. But I have to stay here because it has a better school. Sometimes I think we should just agree to live separately."

It was a strange thing to hear, but it made me feel better.

Huong's eyes drifted over to my backpack, which I'd opened to find my algebra textbook. "What's that?" she asked, nodding at the thick red book nestled inside.

I'd forgotten I'd brought the mythology book along. I'd impulsively thrown it in that morning, in case I had extra time to reread the thầy bói section and see if it matched up with my dream.

"It's a Vietnamese mythology book."

Her eyes sparkled with curiosity. "Can I look at it?"

I placed the book between us, flattered that she was interested. Huong leaned forward to turn the page to an illustration of four dragons, the story of the world's first gods. I didn't remember this from last night. In fact, I didn't recall ever seeing this illustration before.

The next illustration spanned two pages to display the hundred children of the guardian dragons. They indeed represented all shades of the color spectrum. Some of them looked fierce and large, and others small and fragile. Their common trait was their white eyes, which allowed them to see every color and element in the world, in both darkness and light.

Huong turned to the chapter about the divine dragons in Asia, where a trio of dragon brothers ruled ancient China. Two dragon sisters preferred the coastal land that would become Vietnam. For centuries, the dragon gods left each other alone, until the brothers began coveting their sisters' land, which was full of lush fruit and wildlife.

Eventually the dragons' spirits manifested into human warriors. The brothers became generals of the Han dynasty in China, while the sisters transformed into the Trung sisters, the queens of Vietnam. In their human incarnations, they led their countries against each other in further wars. After the Trung goddesses died by suicide, the Han gods also disappeared.

"That part of the story always bugged me," I said. "What happened to the Trung sisters' bodies? The Han really couldn't find them? You'd think it would be important to locate them and ensure they're really dead."

"Books can only tell you so much." Huong smiled mysteriously. "Only the sisters know what happened."

"Maybe," I said, closing the book. "But I can't keep avoiding my algebra homework."

"Oh, we'll finish that quickly. I have all the tricks to show you."

"I feel lucky we got matched."

"I was just kidding about that. When I saw your name on the list, I made sure to grab it," Huong said. "How could I not help my hero?"

My face flushed, the warmth spreading through my body, down to my fingers and toes. "I'm not a hero."

She cocked her head, strands of hair falling over a cheek. "You were the first one to swim down to save us. Why?"

"I don't know—" I said, but then stopped. I needed to stop lying. But she didn't know my history, hadn't yet dismissed me as a freak. "I . . . knew I was supposed to. I knew what was going to happen."

I told her the story. My family history, my breakdown at the swim meet and friends ditching me—the condensed version. She didn't recoil. Her face didn't sour in disgust. Instead she was resting her head on my shoulder by the time I finished.

"Wow," she marveled. "So you and your Ông Nội are thầy bói?"

I tried not to tense. "Well, he used to be." I exhaled a shaky breath. "Still not sure about me. I hope not me."

"Why not?"

"I don't want to know the future," I admitted. "I already feel powerless enough. I want to believe I have some control over what's going to happen."

Huong lifted her head to gaze at me. "You don't yet believe in destiny," she observed. "I think yours may be greater than you think."

I looked away, my cheeks reddening. Huong did not sound like any of the kids at our school—no *likes* or *ums* from her. Every word felt deliberate and meaningful. I thought about our conversation last week in gym but felt too shy to ask her to switch over to Vietnamese.

We spread out across the carpeted floor, sharing the textbook and graph paper in front of us. I sat hunched over, cross-legged, while she lay on her side, a velour pillow between her head and the floor, walking me through differentials, which hadn't made any sense when Ms. Jennings started the unit last week.

We were stuck on prime numbers. I tried to focus on Huong's words until I could follow her thought process and understand the equation. I even tried to see if I could listen to her thoughts, hoping that could unlock the obstacle. But when I did, she seemed to bristle, looking up at me.

"I'm just not sure why I need to understand that prime numbers are important," I admitted. "Can't we just say they are, and move on?"

"Because they're the building blocks to whole numbers," Huong said. "No math, no computers, no progress would be possible without them. Prime is everything."

Huong knew when to slow down and when to repeat, never rushing through the steps, like she could intuit the looping, confusing logic trail inside my brain to guide me back on course. There was something inside her voice, inside the words she chose. Like I could understand what she was saying before she even finished a sentence.

"You're yawning," Huong observed, resting her pencil on my textbook, where it rolled softly to the floor.

"I have to get home," I said, rubbing an eye. "I have other homework to do, and you probably do, too."

"You need a nap," she said. She walked over to her bed, shook out the folded throw blanket, and looked over at me expectantly.

"I don't know," I said uncertainly.

"We still have a lot of work to cover," Huong said. "A power nap will help you, promise. I'll set an alarm."

After we agreed to twenty minutes, I crawled onto the bed.

My head settled on a fluffy pillow. My eyes glided along the stained grooves and gnarled knots in the wooden beams across the smooth white ceiling. The air conditioner had clicked on, and a gust of cool air drifted by, raising goose bumps along my skin. Hong slipped the blanket over me, and I pulled it up under my chin.

The bed felt soft underneath me, like I was floating, and my body was neither too hot nor too cold. The air conditioning had warmed, so it felt like a balmy wind floating across my skin. Between my toes, I felt the tickle of dewy blades of grass and damp soil. Strange. My head lolled to the side and my eyes opened.

Huong was asleep beside me, her hair neatly tucked behind her against the pillow, face warmed and tinted by the sun.

The sun. My eyes narrowed in confusion. I turned my head to the ceiling, but there was no ceiling. Instead it had burst open to reveal a mango-colored sky. Huong's bed, her room, had disappeared. I blinked a few times, my lashes feeling heavy and thick, and turned my head to find Huong awake, smiling at me. That smile. Her face glowed the color of trust, her eyes sparkled with ideas. Tiny flies buzzed above us and swirled around our ankles, but they didn't feel bothersome. The grass had grown tall enough that we hid among it, a billowy cover from the sun. Huong pushed on the grass between us and squinted, like she was still trying to see me, like maybe it hurt to look.

"Can you hear me?" Huong murmured.

To my surprise I could. I nodded eagerly. Her question was both ridiculous and reasonable, impossible yet accurate. Like everything else happening around us, it made perfect sense.

Somehow her fingers had laced into mine, and we took turns squeezing each other's hands. We sat there enjoying the tickle of grass, the warm breeze, the bright light nourishing our skin, fortifying our hair, invigorating the tips of our fingers and toes. We were surrounded by purple and yellow blossoms, the fragrance filling my nose, their soft petals cushioning my head, back, and limbs. Above us, an intensely vivid rainbow arched over the bright sky.

It felt like we'd stepped inside the pages of Ông Nội's mythology book, the illustrations of ancient Vietnam brought to life.

"We need to stay here," she said softly, pulling a piece of dried grass from my cheek, "until I say we can move."

"Okay," I answered.

Huong looked pained, her mouth slightly open, the words hanging on her lips.

"What's the matter?" I asked, my head lifting slightly in concern.

She didn't answer, her face darkened by the clouds above us. I followed her gaze, my head settling back in the soft soil. The rainbow had vanished. The sky, which had looked so lovely and dramatic just a moment ago, had deepened into a clash of red and silver. Shadows that looked like birds circled in the air above us. They weren't birds. My chest filled with dread.

Ashen clouds of smoke billowed across the sky, flowing into our lungs, making us cough. I put my hands to my mouth, and when I pulled them back, I realized that they were stenciled with dirt and dried blood. My head turned back to

Huong, whose face was streaked with ash. Her eyes brimmed with tears.

"Don't move," she whispered. "They're coming."

I turned back to the gray sky. Han warriors stood over our bodies, holding their swords to our bloodied necks. We were surrounded by flames that were creeping closer to us. I was wearing armor, and the hot material seared my skin. The soldiers laughed, enjoying our torture.

My eyes closed. When I opened them again, there was no sky. The air felt cool and fresh. But the dark, blurry figures still loomed over us.

"Who are you?" I demanded.

The figures drew in closer, and my lips parted to scream. An arm reached forward, and the room exploded with orange light. I could now make out the ceiling behind the face in front of mine. The face retreated a few inches, fingers moving away from the bedside lamp—the source of the orange glow.

I recognized the face from World History, and that sigh. Harsha Reddy. Varsity soccer player. Prom prince. Huong's boyfriend. I'd seen them walking together in the hallways. Harsha and I used to swim together on the city swim team back in middle school. He held the record in the 200-meter backstroke. Behind his shoulder, another figure poked her head up: KT, her glossy lips puckered, eyes narrowed, hands on her hips. Next to her was a taller, lankier boy: Quentin Hua, her boyfriend, a creepy grin on his braces-wired teeth.

Everyone at our school knew about KT and Quentin. One of

the most PDA-afflicted couples at our school, they liked to make up and break up in public. People steered clear of them in the hallways whenever they started hollering, and KT would stomp away, while a towering Quentin reluctantly followed behind her.

"This is the puppy you rescued this afternoon?" Quentin asked.

"Can't you tell by the sad eyes and trembling?" KT responded.

"Shut up," Huong said. Her words vibrated through our shared pillow, tickling inside my skull. During our nap, our heads had somehow nestled ear to ear, like a pair of conjoined twins. I struggled to sit up, the dream floating around my head like a nimbus.

"Didn't you get my text?" KT asked. "There was an earthquake in San Mateo half an hour ago."

"Really?" Huong asked, sitting up. "We must have slept through it."

"How is that possible?" KT said, shuddering.

"They must have been really tired," Quentin said, his repulsive smile spreading wider.

"Q, stop scaring the virgin," KT said as she moved toward the bed. It was strange to see her bare legs outside of her boots. She jumped atop the bed on her hands and knees, bouncing a few times, the bedrails creaking.

"I've been texting you, too," Harsha said. He wore a muddy soccer jersey, flip-flops on his feet.

"Sorry." Huong yawned. "I didn't hear it."

"Right," KT said, crawling in and settling between us in the middle of the bed. Her elbow poked my side, her heel digging into my calf, pushing me away. "Is she any good, Julie? Or did she just say everything is easy?"

"Yeah, is she?" Quentin asked, leering.

I scooted back on the bed, uncomfortable with their appraising gazes. While I struggled to come up with a smart comeback, Huong glared coolly at Quentin.

"No, we're both difficult," Huong said. "And her name is Jolie." She gestured to the boys. "This is Harsha, and idiot Quentin—"

"I know who you are," Harsha interrupted. "You're in my history class."

"What are you doing in a sophomore history class anyway, Harsha?" KT asked, a mean smile lighting up her face. "Who fails World History?"

"I'm sorry not all of us can be smarties like you," Harsha said.

Huong sat up. "You can't trust history anyway. It all depends on who's writing it."

"I heard you helped Huong after she knocked into that girl in the pool," Harsha said. "Thank you."

"Oh, sure, no problem," I said, my cheeks growing flushed. I kicked a leg out and stepped onto the carpet, looking outside where the sky glimmered a dark, deep blue. I reached inside my jacket to find my phone and checked the time: 7:30. We'd been asleep for two hours, yet it had felt like two minutes. I had several texts and missed calls from Bà Nội.

"I thought you set an alarm," I said to Huong.

"Sorry," she said guiltily. "Want me to talk to your grandmother? I'm really good with adults. They believe me."

"It's true," Harsha said. "She can convince anyone to do anything." His delivery was so deadpan I wasn't sure if he was kidding or not.

"It's okay, I just need to go," I said, texting a quick message to Bà Nội. "It's late."

"It sure is!" KT said sarcastically. "It's probably your bedtime, isn't it, Julie?"

"We can take you home," Huong offered.

"You don't have to," I said, zipping up my backpack. "I can call someone."

"It's okay," Huong said. "I want to pick up some boba, and it's on the way."

"You don't know where I live," I said.

"There's good boba everywhere in San Jose," Huong said.

I watched nervously as they all got up to leave. "You really don't need to drive me," I said.

"I want to make sure you get home," Huong said. "I was the one who brought you out here, wasn't I? I'm responsible for you now."

12

THE DRIVE

Quentin drove a forest-green RAV4 that looked harmless until you opened the passenger door, where several layers of soda cups, Red Bull cans, and crumpled up fast food bags greeted you. The odor of sweat, rotting sports drinks, and french fries wafted around us.

"This is disgusting," Huong declared.

"It's either this or your Tesla, Princess. And I know you don't want to drive," Quentin said.

KT took shotgun, while Harsha, Huong, and I squeezed into the back seat. I scooped away the freshest layer of fast-food remnants from the seat. My feet kicked several stinky sweatshirts and socks aside, while my backpack balanced on my lap. Huong sat in the middle, Harsha on her other side. A thumping bass growled through the speakers when Quentin started the engine, and he leaned over to punch it down a few decibels.

Quentin did not use turn signals or check his blind side when changing lanes, probably because he and KT started arguing over the quickest streets to take as soon as he left the driveway.

A few blocks later, Harsha leaned forward to look at me. "You used to swim, right? On City?"

I nodded.

"You used to win in your age group all the time. Why'd you quit?"

"I thought she looked familiar," Quentin added from the driver's seat. "You and your relay partners drew bubbles on your backs before meets."

"Why were you looking at their backs, you pervert?" KT asked.

"Wait, shut up, I'm remembering something," Quentin said, turning back to look at me when he should have had his eyes on the road. "Didn't you, like, freak out at one of our meets? The county qualifiers last year?"

My hateful glare remained hidden in the shadows of the car.

"What?" Harsha asked.

"Quentin," Huong said in a warning voice.

The jerk smacked his hand on the steering wheel like a conga drum. "Dude, how could you forget? It was at Cupertino." He turned back to me, a stupid, delighted sneer on his face. "Didn't they have to call an ambulance? What happened, Bubbles? Did you really swallow your tongue?"

I said nothing, struggling to ignore the growing smile of satisfaction on his face.

"No shit, really?" Harsha turned to stare at me. "That was you?"

"You need to shut up," Huong said, her glare so dark that Harsha quickly sat back and fell silent.

But Quentin kept laughing, even after KT pushed him roughly on the shoulder, making the car swerve, jolting all of us inside.

I should have said something sarcastic, withering. But my lungs had already constricted, muffling any words that could have fought off his insult. The words were never available anyway, not when I needed them most. I hated how weak I appeared. Why couldn't I defend myself?

Harsha and Quentin were part of that sweaty, smug mass of boys swaggering through the hallways in their practice uniforms or warm-up sweats as if they had no time for normal clothes. While Lana and Daphne thought these older boys were cute, I only remembered how they'd splash and taunt the younger swimmers. I couldn't understand what Huong saw in Harsha, how KT could even tolerate Quentin, how any girl could have a crush on these losers, let alone date them.

The heat continued to crowd inside my throat, so I coughed, hoping to relieve the irritation . . . and a puff of yellow smoke appeared in front of me. My eyes widened, watching it dissipate, and, jaw dropped, I unleashed another curl of smoke into the car. I exhaled again, this time seeing flames flicker out of my mouth. My head snapped back in surprise. How was this possible? I breathed harder, harder, harder, until I felt Huong's hand slip into mine.

Her hand felt cool and soothing, and a fizzy sensation blossomed in my chest, immediately calming me. My heartbeat slowed to normal, my breaths returning through my nostrils. The smoke was gone. I looked over at Huong, and we both smiled.

"If we are digging up childhood humiliations, Q has lots of stories to share," KT said.

"So does Harsha," Huong added. "Why are you retaking World History, again?"

"All right," Harsha grumbled. "We get it."

"What *are* you doing in a sophomore class?" KT wondered aloud.

"I disagreed with Ms. Ongerth on a few of her thoughts on the British Empire. Anyway, I don't mind a redux. Sheridan is a much cooler teacher."

"You didn't quit, that's the important thing," Quentin said. The jerk smirked at me from his rearview mirror. "You could learn from that, Bubbles. Is that little meltdown what's keeping you from swimming? It happened a long time ago. If that's the reason you quit, that's weak."

"That's not the reason," I said, confused as to how I had become the target of attention in this car.

"Are you sure?" KT asked, looking back at me. "One of those girls was wearing a swim team hoodie. Ex-friends always make the worst enemies."

"There are much scarier things than fifteen-year-old girls," Quentin sneered. "If you don't learn to stand up to them, how you going to survive, Bubbles?"

"You don't even know me," I said.

"I know enough," Quentin said. "Why are you hiding? What are you afraid of?"

"You don't think I've tried?" I asked, starting to feel warm again.

"You need to show people you're not scared," Quentin declared, "starting now."

"Why now?" I asked.

He nodded in the direction of his window, and I turned to look. It was Daphne. In her pink MINI Cooper, the car she'd been putting on her Christmas wish list for years and finally received on her sixteenth birthday. When we were younger, she promised she'd drive us all around the city to go to the mall and swim practices. But she and Lana stopped talking to me before that could happen.

Daphne stared at us with terrified eyes.

"That's her, isn't it? She's been staring at you like she wants to kill you."

Daphne turned back to the light, hands gripping the steering wheel.

"It *is* her!" KT squealed, jumping in her seat. "That no-tits perfume sample."

Their heads turned while I sat back in my seat, allowing Harsha and Huong to get a better view from my window.

"I remember her," Harsha said. "Daphne, the know-it-all in our World History class."

"Seriously." Quentin snorted. "You're shaking over this little insect? What's so special about her?"

When Daphne transferred to our school in fourth grade, I wondered that, too. She barely said a word that year. She sat with me and Lana at first because Daphne's parents had introduced themselves to my grandparents at the Asian supermarket, and Bà Nội promised I would be her friend. One afternoon at her house, she showed us her K-pop playlist, and we all bonded over our shared crushes. She taught us the dance sequences so patiently, especially with me. She used to never dance in front of anyone but us. It took months to convince her to post herself online. Now, she and Lana posted dance videos on their @LanaAndDaphne account without me.

The stoplight turned green and the MINI Cooper sped off. But Quentin also slammed on the gas, the acceleration pushing me back into my seat.

"What the hell, Quentin!" Harsha yelled.

"This is for you, Bubbles," he said as he continued to weave through traffic after Daphne's pink Cooper, ignoring the beeps from frustrated commuters.

Daphne was trying to lose us, but Quentin was relentless, tailing her car so closely that I was sure we'd crash into her. My heart began racing. I was lightheaded, a buzzing growing between my ears.

"Okay, she's scared now, we can stop," I said breathlessly after he followed her through a red light.

His eyes met mine in the rearview mirror. His face appeared distorted and shadowy from the car and streetlights. "I know when to stop," he said.

My eyes grew foggy, my head filling with air. It felt like we were underwater, like I could float out of this car. I held on to Huong's arm for a moment to stabilize myself, and she squeezed my knee.

"Q, it's a cop," Harsha said.

We turned to look out the rear window. Several cars behind us, a police car with its flashing lights wove through the lanes in our direction. Instead of braking, Quentin slammed his foot on the gas. Our bodies snapped back.

The next few seconds did not speed up. Instead, strangely, they slowed. I watched as we slowly hurtled toward Daphne's car. We were on the brink of crashing when I felt the air from inside my body rush out of me. Yellow smoke gushed from my mouth, rippled out of the car windows, and created a barricade between our car and Daphne's, pulling us back to a stop. Quentin stared down at his feet in confusion, his foot still on the gas.

We still made contact. It was the smallest bump, but KT screamed and Harsha cursed. Huong buried her face against my neck, and I turned my own into her hair.

After a few seconds, I looked up. Daphne's car sped down the street. Quentin pulled off on a side street and paused in the driveway of a gated community. He put the car in neutral and turned to give us a satisfied smile.

That must have been another delusion. It had to be. Quentin must have stopped at the last second. But I could still see the yellow smoke around us, which no one else seemed to notice. How could they not see it? It was floating through our hair, fogging up the windows. The yellow haze felt bright, almost glaring, as I squinted through it. My heart continued to race, my eyes following the smoke as it finally began to disperse, the buzzing draining from my body.

"What the fuck, Quentin?" KT seethed as the police car screamed past us on the main street.

"What?" he asked, looking genuinely surprised.

Huong put her hand over my fidgeting fingers. "Are you okay?"

I nodded, struggling to find my breath again, trying not to freak out, not wanting a sequel of the pool meltdown. Huong and her friends probably already thought I was weird. They didn't need to know how much so.

"You're all such pussies," Quentin declared. "Don't you know you're safe with me?"

When we returned to the road, Quentin turned right, unbelievably, in the direction of Daphne and the police car. We passed Daphne's Cooper, my heart pounding loudly in my ears. The cop had pulled Daphne over, the blue and red lights still flickering. Traffic had congested from the lookie-loos, and Quentin deliberately slowed the car so we could see her sitting in the driver's seat, waiting for the officer to finish writing up her citation.

"Wow," Harsha marveled once we'd safely passed them and gone several blocks. "You are certifiable, Q."

"Daphne could have crashed her car," I finally said, not caring how mad I sounded. "She could have been hurt. We all could have been."

"Oh, she has a name now?" Quentin asked. "Why are you acting so ungrateful, Bubbles? If that girl is any smart, she'll leave you alone now."

I turned to look behind us, Daphne's car and the flashing blue and red lights growing smaller and fainter. The yellow smoke had disappeared, and when I turned back in my seat, Huong's head returned to my shoulder. I closed my eyes to rest, counting each heartbeat until they slowed.

LOSER LAM

I didn't say anything to Bà Nội, who had waited up for me with my reheated dinner. She'd prepared thịt kho—braised pork belly and hard-boiled eggs in a caramel sauce over steamed rice—with a side of garlic mustard greens.

She didn't need any more stress. Ông Nội had had another bad day. He was cranky and hostile, complaining again about dragons during lunch, so she'd given him a sedative and sent him to bed early. The earthquake had also made her nervous, especially since I hadn't arrived home or answered any of her texts.

"Did you think the earth swallowed me up?" I teased.

"You shouldn't joke about the big one," she said.

"But it wasn't," I said. "And look, we're all okay."

After helping with the dishes, I left Bà Nội to her favorite Vietnamese variety show and went upstairs. Alone in my room, I pulled off my jeans and sweater, opened my closet to find a nightshirt, and pulled out one of my dad's old T-shirts from Cal. They'd begun to thin and shrink from being washed so often, but the bottom hem still fell to my knees.

This had been the longest day ever. I felt dizzy remembering it all, much less trying to make sense of it. And I had no one to talk to about it. I fell forward on my bed and groaned when my toes began to buzz, the prickles soon traveling up my legs and down my arms, like I was rolling around a bed of broken glass.

So gross. What was wrong with my body? It was like I'd swallowed an alarm clock I couldn't turn off. I reached for the mythology book. I flipped through the blank pages until the text appeared again and found the chapter I'd read with Huong that afternoon. Then I reread it, because I must have misremembered. With Huong, it described all the dragons in Asia, yet this time, the passage only talked about the Trung sisters.

The illustration showed two women perched on elephants, wearing royal turbans on their heads, carrying bows and arrows slung behind their shoulders and massive swords alongside their bodies. My index finger brushed along one of the largest illustrations of the two women. Their faces looked nearly identical: proud, upturned noses, fierce eyes, defiant chins.

As the founding queens of Vietnam, they led an army of women against the Han overlords. One of their generals gave birth on the battlefield and then tied the wailing newborn to her back so she could continue fighting. Of course, this fierce female army couldn't last long against the Chinese, barely surviving three years. There were several theories about their demise: they were decapitated by the Han general Ma Yuan, they perished in battle after their army deserted them, or they drowned in the Hát Giang River. One legend suggested they'd vanished into the sky.

The final battle illustration was especially graphic: the Han warriors standing over the bloodied, injured Trung sisters. The warriors' faces looked demonic, like they were going to devour the women. Even looking at it hurt my eyes, the colors and details growing in intensity the longer I stared. The queens' swords seemed to glint off the page. I pushed the book up to the corner of my desk, where their faces somberly stared out at me. Like they were waiting for something. Someone.

The last few weeks, I'd been suppressing and wishing away these visions, but they kept coming, infringing upon my reality. Because they were becoming my reality. What if I stopped fighting them? What if I tried accepting them?

I looked up at my bedroom ceiling and opened my mouth, exhaling as hard as I could across the room, and inspected the air.

Nothing. No yellow smoke or mist. Nothing but my typical invisible breath. I exhaled again, shaky, shallow breaths. Whatever it was, I couldn't control it at will.

I decided to finish my homework, because at least math, especially how Huong explained it to me, made more sense than whatever was going on with me. My phone buzzed behind me on my pillow while I submitted my worksheets online.

"How are you?" Huong asked.

"Fine," I said, smiling. "Why are you calling?"

"You don't want to talk to me?"

"Why don't you just text?"

"I like hearing your voice. It feels good."

I understood what she meant. Huong sounded warm and comforting inside my ear, much better than an abbreviated text.

"I'm sorry Quentin was such an idiot," she continued. "He's usually not that awful, but I think he wanted to show off."

"To who?"

"Oh, he doesn't care. I doubt he thinks too hard about anything he does. But I'm proud of you. You stood up to him."

"Hardly," I said. "I doubt he heard anything I said."

"That's his problem. You can be book smart, but stupid in all the other ways." She let out a little sigh on the other line. "Enough about him. What are you doing now?"

"Submitting my math homework, thanks to my excellent tutor."

After clicking submit, the screen redirected me to my school email. My eyes scrolled down through the usual school announcements and reminders, until they fixated on a familiar email subject line, one I hadn't seen in months but had learned to recognize and dread: "Loser Lam: The Origin Story."

"What is it?" Huong asked, after hearing my gasp. "What's wrong?"

My index finger slowly lifted and came down to click on the link. A garish color palette lit up the computer screen like a bright orange stain, casting a hideous glow over my bedroom walls.

How did Loser Lam inherit her curse?

The words bled into a super-pixelated video at a restaurant. The camera panned around to show red tablecloths, servers in white blouses and black pants, banquet tables, and a floor-to-ceiling aquarium. My heart sank as I recognized the silver-haired man throwing a tantrum in the center of the video. The yelling, gasps of horror, squeaking chairs, and the manager's barking. How the camera shook and vibrated trying to follow him up and down the aisles. How the servers tackled him just before he was going to crash into the aquarium.

I closed out of the video. My head was draining. My right hand pushed the mouse away, but my fingers refused to straighten. My other hand reached over to try to relax the fingers, but my left hand had curled in as well, like paralyzed talons.

Huong called out my name, but her voice sounded very far away. The sender's email address was of course anonymized: a bunch of numbers and symbols.

"Who did this?" I whispered.

"I see it," Huong said. "They emailed the link to the entire school. Give me a sec and I'll find out the sender's IP address."

Before, I was the only target. Kids mocked my face, my body. They'd thrown plenty of insults about my grandfather, my absent dad, even my dead mother, but they'd never done anything like this.

"I found it," Huong said, her voice low. "Do you want to take a guess?"

"I already know," I said, trying to breathe. "Daphne's family was at the restaurant that night, too."

Her face from that evening flashed in my mind: so furious and humiliated. Sitting in her car, watching us sail by while she was pulled over by the cops. She and Lana both despised me, but after the car chase, Daphne probably hated me. I recalled that night as we hurried out of the restaurant with my ranting grandfather, thinking I'd caught a look of sympathy on my former friend's face. But the next day at school, she walked right past me, smiling and gushing with Lana, continuing to pretend she never knew me, had never gone over to my house hundreds of times, had never called me sobbing the day her cat, Zinfandel, died.

The room suddenly felt stifling and bright, yet I couldn't look away from the screen. This was the man who used to drive us to swim practices and meets. Who used to get us boba after school. He never talked much to my friends, but they knew him. They knew he was the closest thing I had to a dad in my life. And now they'd reduced him to a viral video loop that they could laugh at forever.

They didn't have to send it to everyone.

"I'm so sorry," Huong said. "I should have helped you sooner."

"How could you have known?" I asked. "I'm texting them."

"Jolie," Huong said. "Do you think that's a good idea?"

Too late. I'd already resurrected our old group chat, which had been dead for the last year; the most recent messages were of me pathetically trying to get them to talk to me again.

Me: Take down that link now

Ellipses as they read, as they frantically determined how to respond. Eternally long seconds passed.

Lana: ????

Me: I see the video, Lana, take it down now. Daphne, I know it's yours

Daphne: That is NOT mine

They were probably together, sitting right next to each other, tag-teaming their toxic texts.

Me: You are such a liar

Daphne: When would I have TIME? My parents have been screaming at me all night after you and those juniors CHASED ME DOWN

Lana: Ya, Jolie, that is so MESSED UP

Daphne: You think it was funny to scare me that way? It's HARASSMENT. You're lucky I don't tell my parents

Me: Like I care. Take down the video now

Daphne: I don't even know HOW. It's not mine

Me: I can't believe I ever thought you were my friends. Don't ever talk to me again

Daphne: THEN STOP TEXTING US

Lana: (liked) "THEN STOP TEXTING US"

I took a screenshot, closed out of the chat, blocked both of their numbers, and shared with Huong the screenshot of the conversation.

"Don't worry," Huong said. "I'll handle it."

"How?"

"You take care of me, I take care of you. I'm hanging up now. Go to sleep, okay? The video will be gone in the morning."

"But—"

"Trust me. Sleep. Goodbye."

With a click, she was gone. I held the phone to my ear a few seconds longer, wondering if she'd return. I could fake a fever and stay home tomorrow. The thought of returning to school, of being surrounded by all those gloating, insufferable faces and their whispering, made my skin crawl. The heat steamed in my throat again. My heart pounding, I reached over for my water bottle and drained it. When my mouth opened, a breath of pale-yellow steam released.

I stared grimly as the cloudy mist swirled across my ceiling. It didn't feel as cathartic as it had before. Maybe I was a freak, just like the kids at school said.

I pulled back the covers and crawled into bed, remembering how just a few hours ago, I was sleeping like this alongside Huong. Her sheets had felt softer, cleaner, safer. I hardly knew Huong, but she already made me feel less lonely than I had in months. I tried to hold on to those feelings, remembering her kind smile, her reassuring words. I wasn't crazy. I wasn't alone. I looked over at the mythology book on the desk. I leaned forward and impulsively pulled it toward me. I opened it to an illustration of two large eggs washed up on a beach. I inhaled deeply, my eyes feeling heavy, and allowed the words to lull me to sleep.

THE MYTH OF THE EGG

When the elders recounted the story of the ancient egg washing ashore in their small village, the color was never the same. Some said it was violet, others orange, and a few said it changed color throughout the day. What they could agree upon was that no one dared to come near it. Five times the size of any chicken or duck egg, it was larger than the biggest durian. Many people in the village speculated that the bulbous sphere harbored evil spirits, and they warned of getting too close, especially when the fissures started appearing, spindling along its glowing shell.

Once an egg begins to crack, it is only a matter of time before the creature emerges. But that didn't happen. Days, then weeks, passed. The curiosity grew into alarm, until a village meeting commanded the egg's exile back into the ocean.

It took several villagers to drag the egg across the sand toward the water. With every roll, some of the men claimed to feel the egg growing heavier, denser. During the struggle, the sky darkened and it began to rain, which seemed to help the men, as the egg began to slip toward the water. When the sand-speckled egg finally touched the lapping waves, a cloud of steam exploded from the largest crack, filling the beach with fog. The villagers who'd been watching farther up the beach strained to see past the mist but heard a piercing scream.

The cry came from one of the men running toward them, pointing back to a large black talon curling over the top of the jagged eggshell.

It was hatching.

The men had pushed the egg as far as they could and retreated to watch from the shoreline with the rest of the villagers. Yet the egg remained inexplicably buoyant, its heaviness defying gravity, as its cracked shell bobbed and danced along the waves. Several more black talons poked through the shell, a scaly lavender tentacle emerging on top, as if waving to them. The villagers watched, breathless, unable to move or look at anything else.

But the creature, whatever it was, did not break through. Instead, amid the lapping waves and fizzy sea spray, a buzz grew, quiet at first, then steadily building in volume.

The creature was crying, howling.

Finally one person emerged from the still crowd, a young woman, the new wife of one of the wealthiest farmers in the village. She strode through the sand, wading through the waves, until she dove under the water toward the egg, which had begun to finally sink.

Several tense minutes passed. Some of the villagers wondered loudly if she'd drowned. A few of them privately hoped this was true. A small sacrifice for the good of the village. At least it wasn't them.

When the young woman reemerged on the shore, to the insincere cheers and shouts from the village, she was not alone. In each arm, she carried a tiny, howling human baby. Both had soggy tufts of black hair pasted along their foreheads, scrunched-up red faces, little hands balled in tulip-shaped fists, their feet knotted around the farmer's wife's arms. What everyone remarked upon later was how their skin glowed, twinkling in the sunlight. Some of them swore that when the babies' eyes opened, there were no visible pupils: their eyes shined white like the moon.

They were also undeniably human. No large black talons. No scaly tentacles or monstrous sea creatures. Just two crying babies. Yet no one stepped forward to help her.

This is how the Trung sisters first came to the Vietnamese people. Later, their human mother would tell them that she heard them calling for her, that she could see them struggling in the water. All her life, she could see and hear things that others could not, just like her grandfather; she was the first and last female thầy bói in her lineage. These were the queens the divine dragon under the sea had promised would come. All her life, her ancestors had been waiting for them to arrive, and they did not disappoint.

14

DANGEROUS

That night, I dreamed I was enveloped in darkness, folded up in the fetal position. I blinked a few times, waiting for my vision to return, but I only detected layers of night, with the occasional sparkle of light on the periphery. My skin felt damp, my arms and legs sticky with goo. When I struggled to stand, my head smacked something hard. My arms stretched out to feel the walls around me. It felt like I was encased in box or a shell.

Then I heard murmurs and my ears perked up. I realized they weren't words, but laughter—hysterical, high-pitched squeals. I recognized the chorus of gigglers.

"Stop it," I said, but the laughter continued.

I said it again, pushing my arms against the slimy barrier above me. My hands traveled across the surface, my fingers digging deeper into the goo. It initially felt dense but softened and cracked as I continued to push against it. My hands curled into fists and I punched again and again, the laughter from the outside growing, Lana's and Daphne's voices filling my ears.

When is she going to get the hint?

We don't know what it is. It could be dangerous.

No one likes her.

Send it back to where it came from.

We never wanted her. She should just leave.

"Stop," I shouted, feeling the rage inside my throat creating steam around my face, the power growing in my fists. "Stop, stop, stop!"

With that last word, my fist punched through the shell, the air from the outside gushing through the fissure. With that crack, it was easy to pull apart the top of the shell until I could reach up, peek outside, and finally confront my enemy.

On a beach in ancient Vietnam, my former friends surrounded me, dressed in their pajamas. It was the middle of the night, the moon bright and swollen white.

Daphne popped a pink gum bubble and held up her smartphone, her screen displaying the spectacle of Ông Nội. She turned it toward Lana, shaking from laughter.

"I told you to stop," I warned, puffs of yellow smoke erupting between my quivering lips. But she didn't lower her arm. Her dumb, smug, superior smile grew wider.

I waited one second, two seconds, hoping she'd come to her senses, waiting for her face to change.

On the third, I opened my mouth and unleashed the fire.

15

DUMB LUCK

The next morning, my hands were roasting under the blankets. I groggily turned on my back. Seven hours of sleep, and I still felt exhausted. Holding my hands up, I blinked. They looked like puffy, bloated red boxing gloves. My heart tumbled inside my chest. I stepped out of bed and stumbled toward the bathroom.

My palms looked ruddy and blistered, and the backs of my hands were covered in bumpy, dry scales. Confused and alarmed, I soaked them under cold water, then slathered them with aloe vera. I tried taking a calming breath, but my throat and chest burned with irritation.

Back in my room, I spotted the mythology book on the floor. There was a small dent on the cover, which I didn't remember from last night.

I picked up the book, opening to a random page. My gaze fell on an illustration of the Trung sisters. I stared at their fierce, unblinking eyes. These women faced down a Han battalion. And I was scared of mean girls. My dream of being trapped in the egg, my rage against the girls, especially Daphne, had felt so real.

I set the book aside and swiveled the chair to my open laptop, my index finger gingerly tapping the mouse. True to Huong's promise, the video link had vanished. I searched my email, texts, and even my browser's history and cached files. Tension seeped out of my limbs. Huong had scrubbed the internet clean of my nightmare. Well, one of my nightmares.

After my hands shrank back to a somewhat normal size, I headed downstairs. I noticed that the books from the living room shelf were scattered on the floor, and the paintings on the walls were lopsided.

"Another earthquake?" I called out to Bà Nội in the kitchen. "Didn't we just have one?"

"A 5.4 in Berkeley," Bà Nội affirmed. "It woke me up, but when I went to check on you, you were still sleeping."

"Seriously?" I asked. Since I was little, I'd wake up from any earthquake, no matter how small or far away the epicenter. The fear of being buried under the big one gave me nightmares. Now I'd slept through two of them in the last twenty-four hours.

"Earthquakes so close together are unusual," Bà Nội said, concern in her voice.

"Maybe it's relieving the pressure."

"Or leading up to the big one."

I sat at the counter for breakfast. Bà Nội watched me struggle to hold my cereal spoon, left the kitchen, and returned holding a glass vial of sparkling emerald liquid.

"I have to go to school," I moaned as she unscrewed the

116

tiny red cap. The pungent menthol immediately filled the air around us.

"The smell lets you know it's working," she said, dabbing out a few drops and rubbing her hands together before reaching for mine. "Oh, Jolie." The pads of her fingers caressed the bumps along my hands. "You can barely bend your fingers."

I watched as her liver-spotted hands kneaded mine. My eyes closed at the gentle pressure. "They feel different," she remarked, holding my hands up closer to her suspicious eyes. Then her gaze caught something, and she reached behind my ear, brushing her fingers against my hair. She peeled something off me, tearing out a few hair strands, which made me wince. She then held it up between us: a yellowed leaf, stained with mud and what appeared to be dried blood.

"What is this?" She looked at me suspiciously.

I stared at it with equal wonder. "I don't know."

Bà Nội studied my face for a moment before dropping the leaf on the counter. It lay on the marble, curled next to my cereal bowl. I held the leaf under my nose, inhaling. Aside from the stinking menthol smeared on my palms, I smelled timber, smoke, and minerals. The leaf felt plump, not brittle, which meant it had been freshly plucked from whatever tree it came from.

"What did you dream about?" she asked me in Vietnamese. It was a question Ông Nội used to ask me every morning before his dementia, and now Bà Nội had taken it over. I thought it was just an affectionate habit, but this morning, it felt more pointed.

If I was honest with her, she'd want to call Dr. Bruckmann. "We know they're not just dreams, Bà," I said in Vietnamese.

Regular people had dreams. Not thầy bói. We had visions.

She half smiled, like it was painful. "Well, we always hoped you'd speak Vietnamese one day."

"I didn't think it would be like this," I admitted.

"How does it feel?" she asked.

"It feels right," I said honestly. "It feels like I've known how my entire life."

"What else do you know?"

I shared with her the most recent visions and dreams. From the flood in our dining room and the dragon dreams to the strange yellow smoke in Quentin's car and last night's dream about the eggs. There were others, I was sure—too many. It felt exhausting to retell them, and they were only a fraction of my dreams. It was why I felt so exhausted in the mornings, like I was living many lifetimes while I slept. When I finished, she placed her hand in mine.

"Those kids didn't see anything when they were with you?" Bà Nội asked.

"No," I said.

"Is there anything else?" she asked, staring pointedly. *Be honest with me, Jolie.*

Oh god.

I nodded guiltily, and her frown deepened in disapproval.

"How did you know?"

"I can feel you. I learned to recognize it with your grandfather and your dad. People can sense it if they're perceptive enough. It's like a quiet fly humming inside your ears."

"This happened with Dad?"

She nodded. "He didn't know how to turn it off. He'd have nightmares. It started around your age, too. But I thought you'd be protected from this."

"I was going to tell you," I said. "There's just a lot that's happened."

She looked at me with such sad, defeated eyes. I was afraid she'd react this way. I wandered through her mind, her fear and dread, already imagining me following the same journey as Ông Nội.

She put her hand on mine. "Please do not read my thoughts. You can ask me, Jolie, and I will be honest with you."

"I'm sorry," I said, immediately ashamed. "I don't know how to control it. I can't seem to control anything right now. And since I can't talk to Ông Nội, I've been reading the mythology book."

"You took the book from his study?"

"Yes," I said sheepishly. "I was hoping it could help."

"That's not just a mythology book," Bà Nội said. "It's a guide for the thầy bói. It contains all Ông Nội's premonitions. It was passed down through his family, and it's the only possession he brought over from Vietnam. He was saving it for your dad."

All the strange occurrences while I was reading it now made sense. "Maybe it's now meant for me."

"Where is it?" Bà Nội asked.

I ran upstairs to my room to retrieve the book and brought it to the kitchen. The binding of the book felt tight, the pages stuck together as I struggled to open it, finally wrenching it apart. Bà Nội leafed through the pages while I ate my breakfast.

She looked up at me. "I can only see the pictures," she said.

I leaned forward to the page in front of her: a map of Vietnam. I turned the page, and another: intricate drawings that detailed the tropical landscape and topography of the country. Sketches of peasants, scholars, mythical dragons, fairies, and animals. The last pages illustrated the Trung sisters and their army, their weapons—bows and arrows, and many swords. But no words.

"I swear I read a story from this book last night," I said, frantically flipping through the pages. "I don't understand. Could the pages have fallen out?"

I held the book upside down, re-examining its binding, but all the pages seemed to be intact, no evidence of ripped or missing pages. And I remembered from that one time when I was younger trying to tear the pages out that it had been near impossible.

"Let's ask your grandfather," Bà Nội said.

We went upstairs, where Ông Nội was dozing in their bed. The room smelled of menthol and jasmine, two scents I'd always associated with my grandparents. Bà Nội knelt at his side, gently pushing at his shoulder until his eyes blinked open.

"Jolie is having visions, Chồng," she whispered in his ear. "Just like Xuân did when he was her age. Just like you. We thought your book could help us, but we don't see anything. Do you? Can you help us, Chồng?"

His yellowed eyes briefly studied the open book, and for a few moments, I believed he was actually examining the pictures. But then his eyes glazed over, as they often did, and he turned over on his side to sleep again.

"I can try again later," Bà Nội said. "It's getting late. You need to get to school."

"School? Isn't that the least important thing right now?"

"This doesn't have to change your life," Bà Nội said. "This is only part of it. As you grow and mature, you will learn to control these gifts. Just like your Ông Nội."

"Until I can't," I said. "Look what these gifts did to Ông. And my dad! What do these premonitions mean? Am I supposed to do something?"

"Yes," Bà Nội said, closing the mythology book. "You are still Jolie. A sophomore who shouldn't be failing algebra. Go and focus on school."

"What if we're wrong, and I'm not a thầy bói?" I asked as she continued to push me toward the front door. "What if this is all just dumb luck?"

"Dumb luck is American tradition," she reminded me. "Understanding your destiny, both good and bad, is ours."

GONE

Arriving at school, I braced myself for heckling and stares because of Ông Nội's video. But no one said anything or even looked at me. I couldn't detect a malicious thought, or even sympathetic thought, directed at me.

During homeroom, I watched Huong and KT on *Vaquero Vision* benignly reading off the day's announcements. They reported on the Berkeley earthquake, which had apparently caused a lot of structural damage to downtown and the UC Berkeley campus.

My mind couldn't help overhearing the wild daydreams around me. People's inner thoughts were infinitely more interesting than the things they said aloud—Walter Panebianco freaking out over his SAT scores, Kai Herron practicing his NASA science internship interview answers over and over, Mason Chun wondering if his girlfriend, Audrey Frederick, was cheating on him, Audrey Frederick confirming Mason's suspicions.

I tried not to smile or react in any way as I spied on their thoughts. The more I practiced, the easier it became to control, to slide into minds carefully and quietly. None of them seemed to notice my presence in their heads like Bà had that morning.

It wasn't their secrets that delighted me. Instead I was more relieved that no one was thinking about my grandfather's video. Had none of them seen it? How could Huong remove every trace of it?

In World History, Lana arrived late and without Daphne, and chose a desk two rows away from me, which was better anyway. I ignored her, too, and despite my poor sleep, I retained all of the lesson. In Algebra, I worked through the problems on our latest quiz and they didn't look like random doodle marks anymore. My mind quickly calculated the steps faster than I could write them down. My lab partner, Yookyung, and I flew through our experiments in Chemistry. When we handed in our lab report early, first in the class, I caught Lana in the back corner sullenly glaring at me. For the first time in months, I felt brave enough to smile at her. I no longer felt afraid.

In gym, I spotted Huong at the edge of the pool and hugged my towel in happiness at the sight of her. My mind calmed, hummed, as she came closer to me.

"I can't believe it," I whispered. "The video is just gone."

"Of course," she said as we found an empty lane to share. "I always mean what I say."

Once submerged in the pool, my body melted into each stroke as I swam through the clear blue water. Every time Huong passed me, I could see her smile and wave, deliberately brushing me as she passed. I luxuriated in the sensation of the water gliding over me, relaxing every muscle, softening my spine, arms, and legs. The water transformed from blue to yellow to green, warming me. These changes in my vision no longer frightened me. The colors swirling around me felt like home.

During Coach Turner's nutrition lecture, I realized that the irritation on my hands had calmed. No more puffiness or angry blisters. The lifelines on my palms looked clear, my finger pads slightly crinkled from the water.

Huong rested her head on my shoulder. I smiled, allowing myself to enjoy this feeling. The air around me seemed to cool, a breeze trickling along my damp arms and through my wet hair.

On the other end of the bleachers, Lana sat by herself, her towel over her shoulders. I avoided looking in her direction, annoyed at her pitiful thoughts, all because Daphne was absent and their childish prank failed. I still couldn't shake the image of Daphne laughing and holding up her phone, me exhaling fire on her—I felt a cold chill slide through my body. But it had been a dream. She probably had called in sick, sulking over her speeding ticket. She did not deserve pity.

After school, Huong and Harsha stopped by my locker.

"You're coming over today, right?" she asked.

"Is tutoring every day?" I asked.

"You need consistent practice," she said. "I can't let you go away from me for a few days and regress."

Harsha nodded at me. "How's it going, Bubbles?"

I shook my head. "No."

"I'm kidding. I thought those bubbles on you were cool."

"I bet I could still beat you."

"I bet you could."

His face looked sincere, and I begrudgingly realized he was different from Quentin and his other obnoxious friends. I could maybe see why Huong liked him.

"My car wouldn't start this morning," Huong said. "Can I borrow yours?"

Before taking off, Harsha kissed Huong for way too long. I pretended to scroll through my phone. He massaged the back of her neck with one hand while her fingers smoothed out the wrinkles in his soccer jersey. When he finally left, Huong's smile faded.

We watched him walk down the hallway, stopping to chat to a group of freshman boys. Huong gazed at him like she couldn't bear to look away.

I felt like I'd tripped into a K-drama.

"Are you sure you two don't want to hang out?" I asked.

"Sorry," Huong smiled sheepishly. "Being with him makes me feel like time doesn't matter. Then when he leaves, the rest of the world comes rushing back."

I nodded in fake understanding. "Sure."

She saw through me and blushed self-consciously. "I sound sappy."

"I've never had a boyfriend," I said.

"Neither have I," Huong said. She gave me the side-eye. "That surprises you. I was never really interested before I met him. Harsha wasn't in my plans."

"Plans?"

"You know, the future. I was raised to think of myself first. But I can't seem to help it. Now I'm finding it's nice to think of other people. Like him. And you."

"It's hard growing up as an only child."

"No kidding," she said. "I didn't realize how lonely I was before this year." She frowned at me. "What's wrong?"

"I don't know," I said honestly. "It's been a weirdly good day. That doesn't happen very often."

"Then you should enjoy it." Huong took the books out of my arms and shut my locker door, studying my face. "Why are you crying?"

I wiped the wetness off my cheeks and took a deep breath. Another. "This last year," I finally said, my voice shaking, "it's just been pretty unbearable."

Her face softened and she reached over to rest her hand on my arm.

"You didn't deserve any of it," she said.

She sounded so confident. I almost believed her.

"What if I did?" I asked. "Maybe I did bring this on myself. Why do you even care?"

"I care about you," Huong said, and the way she said it didn't sound corny or cheesy or weird at all. "You're worth caring about, Jolie."

I laughed, feeling myself blush. "You barely know me."

"I disagree. From the moment we met, I felt like I understood you completely."

She hooked her free arm around mine, pulling us hip to hip, as if her relaxed, calm body could melt my awkwardness. Huong liked touching—hugging, kissing, holding hands with everyone she was close to—her boyfriend, friends, and now me. We weren't strangers anymore, but what did she know about me besides that I was deficient at math and my former friends hated me? Yet she still wanted to be around me.

"If you can understand me, then I'm sorry about that," I said.

"Stop that. Why do you always blame yourself? It's them, Jolie. Those silly fake friends are the worthless ones."

"Daphne didn't come to school today," I said.

"Oh." She looked confused. "And?"

"Maybe she got in trouble."

"You're too nice," Huong said. "She's a nasty, despicable peasant who doesn't deserve another breath between us. Why were you even friends with her? Or Lana?"

"I don't know," I said. "We grew up together. We probably liked the same colors in the crayon bin."

"But you're not five anymore," she said. "I know why I want to be your friend."

I exhaled. "Why?"

"Because you're a warrior," Huong said. "You are fierce and brave and willing to risk your life for others. You saved my life."

I laughed. "I did not."

"Yes, you did. Under the water, I saw your face and I knew I was going to be okay. You were always meant to save me."

She didn't understand. And I didn't see any point in hiding it from her, because she'd eventually figure it out, too.

"I'm a freak," I said, taking a deep breath, looking around to make sure no one was close by. "You might as well know. My old friends realized I was becoming a thầy bói, like my Ông Nội. That's why they call me crazy. That's why they went after him last night."

Huong cocked her head at me. "So you think you're a thầy bói?"

"I know I am."

She smiled. "No, you're not."

I stared at her, confused. "How do you know?"

These things you can do, she said in my head, *you think you're the only one?*

Huong observed me for a moment, waiting for me to catch up.

You can hear me? I asked.

She nodded. *But only what you want me to hear. And same for me to you.*

So that morning when I thought I heard her speaking to me through *Vaquero Vision* wasn't another hallucination. My mind whirled, absorbing this revelation.

How long have you been doing this?

She shrugged. *Time doesn't really matter so much to either of us.*

What does that mean?

"Sh," Huong said, pressing an index finger to her shiny lips, her eyes flickering at the throng of people trickling around us. They were moving strangely, walking slowly, silently, as if the world was stretching around us while Huong and I remained normal.

My eyes widened; my mouth dropped open. "Huong—"

She winked at me, and with a nod of her head, the kids

around us accelerated and the noise of the locker room returned.

I couldn't believe it. It reminded me of when we met, after
rescuing Huong from the pool. The euphoric floating. The feeling of time stretching around us.

Time.

I turned back to Huong. *You can stop time?*

"Kind of," she said out loud. "I can slow it down, really, really
slow it down, and only when I'm with you. But it's not because
we're thầy bói. What we are is much better than that."

My eyes closed briefly, my head spun. "What is happening to
me?"

"Don't look so ill," she said cheerfully. "Let's get out of here.
We're taking a field trip."

17

REMEMBER

We could smell the smoke before we even entered the parking garage. Quentin lay slumped in the open trunk of his RAV4, smoking with his friends Milo and Basil, the jerks from my World History class.

"Here comes Huong's newest pet," Basil sneered when he saw me.

"Where you going?" Quentin called out as we passed them. "Can we come?"

Huong didn't even pause, holding up a manicured middle finger behind us.

"Aw, you girls. Always leaving us out."

"I don't know why Harsha likes those losers," Huong muttered to me. When we were almost at the car, I turned to look again. Quentin was still watching us, a haze of smoke around him.

We headed west toward the ocean. Huong preferred driving with the windows rolled down, even on the freeway. She cranked up the music as loud as she could, and the concrete sidewalks and office buildings outside my window transformed into green grasslands, Monterey pine and cypress trees, and the twinkling bay.

Questions swirled in my head during our silence. Maybe I was still stunned, or afraid I was experiencing another delusion, and if I spoke, it would wake me from this fantasy. But when I looked over at Huong, so calm and reassuring, my body relaxed.

We parked in front of a beach house that she said belonged to Harsha's family. Instead of going inside, Huong walked around it, leading me to a trailhead at the wildlife preserve.

"I didn't bring hiking shoes," I warned, although my Converse appeared sturdier than her wedge sandals. Yet she marched up the rocky trail, skipping over a tangle of coastal scrub without even a stumble as I tried to keep up with her. The sun shone directly overhead, right into our eyes, so we both wore our sunglasses. We hadn't brought water bottles, and after the first mile, my forehead brimmed with sweat and my throat itched for moisture.

When we reached the summit, my thighs and calves straining from the two miles of steep switchbacks, Huong pulled me next to her so our feet toed dangerously close to the edge of the cliff. I hung back, my heart in my throat.

"It's okay," she assured me, the wind whipping her hair across her face. I looked around us at all the open air and water, listening to the roar of the tide. We could fall. We could die.

I turned back to Huong's face. She'd hardly broken a sweat,

her makeup still perfect. My arms pulled away from her, but her grip softly tightened on me, steadying us.

"How do you know?" I asked, trying not to think of the strong waves and sharp rocks below us, trying not to imagine my head splitting open on a boulder, the ocean devouring my body.

"Take my hand," she instructed, and then pulled me forward with a strength that surprised me. She sensed my reluctance, my desire to retreat. "Don't be scared."

"Move back, then," I suggested, twisting to look at the trail, which appeared solid and safe in comparison to the rocky, crumbling cliff in front of us.

Huong pushed her sunglasses up on her head so that her determined eyes squinted, then connected with mine. "We're not going to fall. Not unless we want to," she said.

I couldn't decide if confidence or madness lay behind her eyes. What did she mean? She pulled harder on my hands and walked off the cliff.

My mouth opened to scream, but nothing came out. We hadn't fallen. We weren't in the water. Instead we were suspended on a cloud of what looked like lavender smoke. The sturdy mass of purplish wind hummed steadily under my shoes.

Below us, time had stilled again. The green waves seemed frozen, waiting to crash against the rocky cliffside. The cliff grew farther away as we floated higher above the ocean. Yet I felt balanced, the wind supporting me under my feet, Huong's hands holding on to mine.

"Do you understand now? Fall, don't fall, it doesn't matter. This realm cannot hurt us."

"How can you do this?" I asked, my breath shaky and gasping.

"We've always done this," she said.

We?

Always?

"Yes," she answered aloud. "You have only forgotten."

She wasn't making sense. And her delusion was infecting me. Maybe we had fallen, our bodies tumbling in the rough waves of the icy ocean or sprawled broken across the jagged rocks, and these were our final thoughts. Maybe we were already dead. Around us, I detected a familiar floral scent.

Huong tilted her head, lips pursed impatiently. "Tell me," she said. "What do you dream about?"

Flashes of being trapped in the egg, breaking out on the beach, the girls laughing, the flame inside my throat. I remembered not only last night's dream, but the others before it. The dreams stretched back to days, weeks, years ago, unfurling a ribbon of images and sounds, until we were in an ancient land that felt both familiar and new.

Vietnam. An orange sky shrouded by mountains and trees. A farmhouse by a lake, a mother kneeling in the garden, a father riding a horse with two little girls. These same sisters play sword-fighting by an evening fire.

Those girls. I knew them. In every moment, Huong was there, right next to me.

"I dream about us," I said in Vietnamese. The words didn't feel silly or trip awkwardly from my mouth. They felt like the truth. The familiar heat returned, the buzz traveling up my spine, my mind and body fizzy with happiness.

Her face broke out in a smile. "Finally," she said, also in Vietnamese. "I was wondering when you'd see."

She blinked at me several times as her dark brown eyes slowly transformed to a sparkling white. I recognized these eyes. While I couldn't see my face, the heat prickling behind my own eyes told me mine had turned white, too. Our original, divine eyes. She delicately lifted away my sunglasses and tilted my head back so we both gazed directly into the sun.

It didn't blind us. It didn't hurt. In fact, the sun glittered with golden and silver dust. I didn't want to look away. It was hypnotic; the sun's center glowed and undulated with every blink, offering a multitude of swirling colors. The colors spun and stretched, eventually forming into the silhouettes of what looked like dragons.

Not just any dragons. I recognized them. I recognized us.

Huong's hands cupped my cheeks, turning my gaze back to her.

We laughed, clutching each other by the elbows, our foreheads pressed together. As we exhaled, curls of glittery smoke spiraled between us. She could do it, too. We both could. The sight of her blurred as my eyes filled with tears, my laughter growing, a cloud of joy around my lungs and heart, so every inhalation felt sweet.

The epiphany seeped into my skin, memories of our childhood and our reign together. What I'd read and what I'd dreamed, had been dreaming, for months. I could then recall the grass, the flash floods in our home village, the willow trees, the impossibly beautiful sunset, and that terrible fire. Our father. Our mother.

The things we could do. The powers inside of us. Visions returned of the two of us slowing time with a wave of our hands, rising in the air, flying through the sky above armies of soldiers watching us from the ground.

Ông Nội's stories, the tales in the mythology book—they were our stories, our lives. Emotions hurtled through me, warming me, despite the ocean wind whipping around us. Huong was my sister. I knew this. I'd always known.

"I knew you'd find me," Huong said. "I've missed you."

And without even thinking about it, I said my truest words: "Me too."

18

SISTER, MY SISTER

"You must have questions," Huong said.

"I have ALL the questions."

"Soon," she promised. "But first, we must go back."

"Where?" I asked, still trying to catch my breath after our laughing fit of insanity.

"Home," she said. "Our true home. Vietnam. We'll go back together, while you're awake this time."

"You mean the dreams—"

"Are not dreams," Huong interrupted. "They're memories of our past life there."

With her finger pointed up to the air, she drew a flaming purple circle. She reached inside the circle with both hands and stretched it open, tearing a large hole in the sky. Flashing me a confident smile, she stepped into the burning portal, her body disappearing into the void. She turned to wave and disappeared.

Are you coming?

Before I could answer, my body hurtled through the portal

after hers. When I tried to look back through the void, the Northern California sky and ocean darkened for a moment, then lit up so bright, all I could see was white. My eyes blinked against the surrounding glare.

The light eventually dimmed. We were traveling across a valley. Soldiers, mostly women, surrounded us. Our iron armor and helmets, and lavender and gold garments, were heavy on our limbs. I carried a thin sword, a bronze bow, and a case of arrows, while Huong carried her sword and shield. We rode atop a massive elephant in a parade of horses, chariots, and elephants.

We were in ancient Vietnam.

We were queens.

The Trung sisters.

The truth washed through me, along with every other feeling: awe, giddiness, terror, confusion, all while trying to balance on this massive creature bobbing along a dirt road. It was crazy and true, it made no sense, yet I believed all of it completely.

I struggled to maintain composure, though my hands could not stop shaking. Swirls of sherbet colors stretched above us, the poppy-yellow sun melting into the pink sky. Huong rode behind me, her chest against my back. Her arms felt tight but steady, digging the armor into my skin.

"They're coming," my sister whispered in my ear. "Can you hear them?"

Even before she finished her question, the first flaming arrows struck the grass. Our soldiers immediately turned, pointing their arrows to the sky.

"Toward the mountains!" a voice bellowed in the seat behind me. Though the voice sounded deeper and hoarser than the one I was familiar with, I recognized it as Huong's. No, Trac's. Her first human name. She pushed off my back, standing on the elephant and raising a heavy sword. "Warriors. Prepare for battle!"

With those words, her sword glowed bright white. I remembered these weapons: ancestral swords forged from the same steel, one engraved with a fairy, the other with a dragon. After our father died, I inherited the fairy, and my sister the dragon. The dragon was a heavy and thick double-edged blade, while the fairy was long, thin, and sharp like a needle.

We looked east at the smoke cascading down the mountains. Soldiers in red and black emerged from the smoke, line after line, spreading through the valley. The Han.

The ground shuddered as a boom reverberated through our bodies. *Boom. Boom.* A familiar dread trickled down my back. A bronze drum pounded as our soldiers positioned themselves for battle. Rows of archers and warriors surrounded us. Everywhere I looked, more soldiers appeared, populating the valley in their violet and yellow armor like colorful wildflowers.

I climbed to my feet, realizing I could also balance atop the massive elephant. I reached behind my shoulder for my bow and arrow and pointed to the sky.

Trac nodded at me in admiration. "You remember," she said.

"This was our final battle," I said. In our minds I added, *This was when we died.*

No, she replied. *This is our rebirth.*

We heard the galloping before we could see the horses, the first line of red, orange, and black chariots pouring in from the forests. The Han army wore a dark armor made of steel that reflected the light of the sun, designed to blind and disorient their enemies. It was why Trac positioned our army to the west, so we could see them clearly.

As the drumbeats escalated, I loaded and pulled back my first arrow—bronze-tipped and forged in our allied villages— and shot it into the sky. It soared toward the clouds and exploded in a yellow cloud of dust, my elements creating a temporary veil of protection. Our soldiers quickly followed, their flaming arrows joining mine. My arm muscles thrummed with energy as I aimed and released more arrows. They looked like golden, lethal birds soaring through the air, striking down multiple Han soldiers.

The Han responded with their own arrows. I watched in horror as soldiers around us crumpled after being hit. Some of them were screaming. The smell of burning flesh was awful and undeniable. The fires from the flaming arrows spread quickly through the tall grasses around us. The galloping of the Han's approaching horses grew louder, until it became a roar in my ears.

We'd soon be overwhelmed, the last of our soldiers meeting their deaths.

Trac placed her hand in mine. *Let's go.*

I shook my head. *We can't abandon them.*

But this was the plan. They were sacrificing themselves for our escape.

This is our destiny.

Two of our generals appeared at our side as our elephant knelt down for us to jump off. The generals helped us mount a waiting chestnut-colored horse. They placed Trac behind me, and she slumped against my back. The heat from the surrounding flames grew, making it difficult to breathe. A wetness soaked into my hip where the armor separated, and I realized it wasn't my blood. My sister was injured.

"Go," one general pleaded. "We will hold them back!"

We galloped through the carnage, and although my focus was on racing away from the battlefield, my eyes lingered on the bloodied bodies in the mud, the arrows poking from limbs, necks, and heads, my ears absorbing the moans and screams of our dying soldiers, the hollers and chants from the Han soldiers. Behind us, we left a trail of purple and yellow smoke that rose to the sky, creating a barrier between us and the battle.

Look to the river, my sister urged me.

When we saw the waves of blue water, I recognized the spot. This uphill climb toward the cliff, the strain in my thigh muscles, the arms around my waist. As the Trung sisters, we were riding toward our demise, the choice that would seal our fates in history books. Our final act of solidarity: choosing death over conceding defeat. We would never surrender to the Han.

When the horse abruptly halted at the edge of the cliff, Huong slipped off the side to stand on the grass and gaze out at the water. The Hát Giang River wound and looped to the sea below us. I dismounted from the horse, my feet landing softly on the grass.

Up close, Trac looked different from Huong: thicker eyebrows, a pointier nose, sharper cheekbones, her long black hair coiled atop her head in an intricate crown. Her frame was smaller and thinner underneath her lavender and gold garments.

"Why are we here?" I asked.

"This is our original realm, the first time we lived together in human bodies. It was also the last time we were together, until now."

"We can travel through time?"

"Yes. I created a temporary portal with our elements to travel here. But it will not last long."

"Why not?"

"We haven't fully reincarnated. We are still waiting for the rest of our elements to return."

I looked down at the water, the white waves crashing onto the rocks, and then back at her.

"We can go back to the battle," I said, thinking of our army. "We don't have to jump this time. We can help our soldiers."

"We cannot change the past here," Huong said. "This was the moment when everything changed. We only had a few minutes before they would catch us, and this was our only escape."

"How could we kill ourselves," I asked, "if we're immortal?"

"Our spirits are immortal, not our vessels. To escape the Han, we had to abandon our human bodies. Our army fought them off to give us time."

I turned, my eyes trying to absorb everything around us, and looked east toward the mountains. Black, orange, and red smoke ascended from the valley. The remains of our troops lay on the ground. The Han soldiers in their chariots surrounded them like vultures, picking off their weapons and armor.

"We planned this," I said.

Huong looked at me solemnly. "We knew our brothers didn't just want the land. They wanted our parents' prime elements; they wanted power. The only way to make sure they wouldn't chase us to the ends of the earth and sea was to—"

"Disappear," I finished, realizing. "Destroy ourselves."

"Like the guardian dragons did before us. It was our parents' prophecy, as it became ours. We needed the world to believe we were gone in order to save it later. Without our human vessels, our spirits scattered. We spread our powers, both prime and divine elements, across the world, exploding them into fragments as tiny as sand and casting them wide and far enough that our brothers could never find them.

"Our elements are supposed to reunite. We just didn't know when. For a long time, I was afraid your elements hadn't."

I turned to stare at her in amazement. "You found me."

Huong smiled. "We found each other, like we promised. Our brothers have been ravaging and exploiting this world for centuries, and now, Nhi, we are here together to stop them."

Nhi—my origin name. I looked down into the valley. We could feel the vibrations of the Han troops' approach traveling through the soles of our feet, up our bodies. Above us, large dark shadows circled the sky, at times eclipsing the sun.

"Do you feel it?" Huong asked, tears mangling her last words. We held hands at the edge of the cliff, and when I turned my head, I saw my sister's face struggling to stay calm. Her grip on my hand had loosened, our hands looking transparent and weak.

"Let's go," she said, her shoulders facing east, searching for the threatening invasion. I could see through her translucent body, to the valley and the approaching black, orange, and red smoke. "Jump, now."

"I need more time," I said. There was too much to take in and remember.

"We'll be back," she said, taking my hand and pulling me toward the edge of the cliff so I could see the rocks and dirt spilling over into the water.

The gallop of the horses and the battle cries of the Han soldiers grew louder, filling our ears, thumping in our hearts. The sky darkened to ash, the birds or vultures or whatever flying above us growing closer.

"Our portal is weakening. We have to return now. Are you ready?"

My answer came in our jump together, my heart traveling up my body, into my throat as we fell, faster, faster, until we should have touched water.

Instead our feet landed back on the cliff in Santa Cruz, not a scratch on us, the strong breeze cooling our reddened cheeks and rustling our hair so the strands reached out and touched each other's.

19

DESTINY

We got stuck in rush hour traffic on the car ride back to San Jose, staring at a sea of red brake lights amid the gray concrete road and cotton candy–pink sky. It seemed silly that we could travel through realms within seconds but still get snarled in Bay Area traffic.

While the cars around us sat idle in a bored standstill, chaotic thoughts, both good and bad, swirled in my brain. What had just happened? I'd never felt so exhilarated and afraid in my life. I thought of what we'd just done in ancient Vietnam, what I was apparently capable of doing now. I looked over at my sister. *My sister.*

"Sorry," Huong said sheepishly as she cut off an Audi. "I used most of my elements for the portal, or else we'd already be home. Our spirits need time to recover."

"You're out of elements?" I asked.

"Just low," she said. "They replenish after we use them. They're our energy source."

I smiled at the thought. "So it's like . . . food for our souls?"

"Geez, Jolie," she said, half wincing, half smiling.

"How can we tell which ones are mine and which ones are yours?"

"Our elements can only return to their origins. Every god is distinguished by a unique color. It's how our parents could tell us apart. Mine are violet and yours—"

"Are yellow," I said, looking down at the sleeves of my lemon-printed hoodie, realizing how I always gravitated to this color.

Her white eyes glanced again at me. "What are you reading?"

During the drive, I'd pulled the mythology book from my backpack, curious to see how our experience matched up with the stories.

"Our history," I said.

"You're fact-checking me?" she asked, her eyes returning to brown.

"I'm supplementing. These stories are about us."

"Yeah, told by men who weren't there. I know you love your grandfather, but I think our memories are probably more reliable than a mortal's."

"Until mine return, I want to fill in the gaps."

"Or you could ask me. I'm right here."

"Okay," I said, closing the book and turning toward her. "When did you first know?"

Memories of our past life started returning to Huong in dreams. Last year, while on a rock-climbing trip in Vietnam, she fell and landed against a boulder. When she gripped the rock to climb back to her feet, an electric charge surged through her body, reawakening a memory of Trac. She began encountering more elements and memories of our lives as the Trung sisters in Vietnam.

Her dreams urged her to come to California. When her father was transferred to Silicon Valley for work, Huong understood this was destiny. But when she arrived, she found nothing. No new elements or memories. Bored, she settled back into her life as Huong, wondering if those memories were only dreams. For months she believed she was alone, until that day in the pool during gym class, when our elements reconnected.

"Ever since you saved me, I've been growing stronger and regaining elements every day. And so are you. Every dream you have, every time you feel that jolt in your body, it means more are returning."

I thought about the bad dreams, the swollen hands, the buzzing I felt in my body. I wasn't a freak. I was a powerful god.

Huong braked suddenly, cursing at the Kia who cut in front of her without using their turn signal. Someone had just cut off a god. I smiled.

"When will we know that we're fully reincarnated?" I asked.

"Once we can control the four elements," Huong said, still frowning at the Kia.

"Like, tell them what to do?"

"Sure. The elements will obey our wishes. You'll be able to harness wind to make tornados, burn down a rainforest with lightning, or wash away a city. The little things we can do now—blowing smoke from our lips, starting a spring shower inside a classroom, or stopping a car crash with our breath—will seem like nothing in comparison."

I blushed suddenly. The ride in Quentin's car. "You saw that?"

Huong nodded. "Of course. That was incredible. Well, except when you wanted to attack Quentin."

"You should have let me."

"He's irrelevant." She frowned at the traffic. "We can't waste our power on insignificant people. Once we reincarnate, we won't need these worthless mortal vessels to keep us together."

"You don't like our current bodies?" I asked. While I could see mine using an upgrade, Huong's body looked fit and strong and perfect.

"I mean, they're fine. They just have an expiration date. We've done better."

"As dragons," I said. Even saying the word aloud felt ridiculous.

"Now, that was ideal—much more powerful than these bodies." The way she said it sounded like she was comparing outfits. Her eyes turned a bright shining white.

I inhaled in surprise. "How do you do that?" I asked.

"You don't have to do anything, Jolie. It's like breathing."

She looked amazing, intimidating. I sat back in my seat, feeling suddenly tired.

"Can you change them back?" I asked. "They're creeping me out."

She did, dramatically rolling her brown eyes. "You're going to have to get used to them. And much more, sister."

"It's just a lot," I said. "You've had more time than me."

I closed my eyes, feeling dizzy. The joy and exhilaration of our trip back to ancient Vietnam was wearing off, and the anxiety and fear of all I didn't understand crept in.

"Well, I'm older," Huong said. "I'll catch you up. We'll need to before the Han find us."

It sounded ominous and exciting. We were queens. I was a queen. Not just a queen, a goddess. One with power that others wanted for themselves. I gazed at Huong, trying to sense these elements she kept talking about. The streetlamps beamed into Huong's car after we exited the freeway. I examined my inadequate shoes and sloppy clothes between the flickering shadows. I did not feel like a warrior queen. I couldn't manifest it yet in my blood or bones as I thought I should.

"Is that part of the prophecy?" I asked.

"Ever since we disappeared, this world has been in chaos because of our brothers. We came back here to fight them again. This time, we will win and restore peace."

She seemed so happy and excited, yet a sliver of dread uncurled in my body. History recorded in detail how relentlessly the Han hunted down the Trung sisters to end their rebellion.

"So where are they?" I asked.

"I haven't sensed them yet. They could be anywhere. It's probably good they don't know we've begun our reincarnation. We need more time."

"What if they find us before that?"

"We'll figure it out. Our only chance of defeating them is if we do this together."

Her words sounded so vague, yet that didn't bother me. Despite my fears, I felt so happy. We didn't need to figure everything out now. I could just enjoy this. I could get to know my sister. My sister.

"Do your parents know?" I asked.

"No," Huong said. "Why would I tell them? There's nothing they could do." She raised an eyebrow. "Are you telling your grandparents?"

"I don't know," I said. I *thought* I was going to.

"We should wait until all of our memories return," she said. "Saying something now would only upset them."

Huong had a point. Bà Nội already didn't seem to know what to do with the idea that I could be a thầy bói. This would be exponentially more distressing.

Huong reached out to pull me into another hug.

"You may only feel like Jolie," she said, her voice muffled into my shoulder, "but you're not. You are so much more."

At home, my grandparents didn't seem to notice anything different about me. They had the same mundane conversations and bickered at dinner, oblivious to my secret smiles and cheerful nature.

Later that night, I pulled the mythology book from my backpack. The leather-covered book felt even heavier than it had this afternoon. It hummed in my hands like it was happy to be near me again.

My fingers traced the newest words on the page. They felt firm and permanent, like they'd always been there even though they only just appeared today.

Trac stood in the center of the page in her armor and dark violet turban, while Nhi stood slightly behind her wearing a bright yellow turban. Their gazes appeared identical: serious and proud. They each held a sword in one hand, the others wrapped around each other.

I looked down at my muffin top tummy bulging over my pajama pants, my plump legs. How my body had softened since I'd quit competitive swimming. Would Nhi recognize herself in this body? Would she be happy with this reincarnated life? How would these two lives intersect? Or would Nhi swallow up Jolie?

Perhaps that would be better. What did I have here in this life that was so special?

If I forgot about Jolie, I could forget about the last year—the last couple of years, really—and everything before that. The tears, the panic attacks, the hives would disappear as if this pathetic life had never happened. I could leave behind these bad memories forever.

My phone buzzed. A message from Huong: **Look outside**.

I walked to the window and gazed up toward the sky. It was several hours after sunset, and the sky should have been dark. But tonight, the sky lit up in a golden yellow with deep violet clouds, the same two colors we'd worn as Trac and Nhi in ancient Vietnam. Our origin colors. They took my breath away.

I was about to text back, but then tried something more direct. *It's beautiful*, I told her through our thoughts.

I'll show you how to do it, too, Huong responded. *Trust me. I'll show you everything.*

20

DREAM

When I fell asleep the dream began immediately, the world brightening from black to orange, returning me to our old realm.

I was dressed in a white hemp blouse and pants and stood next to a young girl in the same clothes. They felt rough and thick against my skin. She smiled at me, and I recognized Huong in Trac's young body. I looked over the tall, sharp reeds in front of me and into the pond to see my own reflection: my chubby cheeks, my hair in pigtails.

"This is where our unconsciouses can meet," Huong said, her reflection appearing next to mine, "and we can revisit some of our memories."

"You've done this before," I said.

Huong nodded. "So have you. You just don't remember yet."

"So is this like what we did earlier on the cliff?"

"That was a portal jump into our original realm," Huong explained. "This is a dream. Our bodies are still asleep in San Jose. Like yesterday in my room."

My fingers brushed over the spiky grass, marveling at how I could feel both the cool, tickling leaves and the warmth of my bedsheets back in San Jose. To feel cold and hot, young and old, all at the same time. It felt confusing and intoxicating.

"Why are we here?"

"Do you remember this river?"

I looked around, recognizing the main house and the circle of huts, the surrounding gardens and fruit trees from previous dreams. In front, I spotted the purple cherry blossom trees from Huong's house, surrounded by the yellow mustard flowers from my grandparents' home.

"This is where we grew up," I said. "I read about this in the mythology book."

"You'll learn it's better to reexperience these memories than read about them," she said.

"Trac!" A man came out of the house carrying two swords, the dragon and the fairy.

"That's our father," I said, recognizing, remembering. "Our human father."

"Yes," Huong confirmed. "If it wasn't for him, we never would have overthrown the Han. He taught us how to fight and ride horses and command an army."

He approached us, his face golden and warm, his smile spreading wide across his face. "Are you ready, my fierce queens?"

"Don't you remember?" our mother called out. "Nhi is staying with me this morning. The seedlings have to be planted today."

"Oh, fine," he said in mock defeat. "Trac, it's you and me today. But soon, Nhi, you and I will dance with the dragon and the fairy."

While Trac and our father raced across the meadow, jumping over streams to try to beat each other, I approached the garden, where our mother squatted in the herbs, aerating the soil with her hands. I stared at my chubby fingers combing through the rich dirt, the exquisite relief of the crumbly, muddy soil cooling my sweaty palms. I bit my lip in concentration, feeling truly content. I'd never felt more at peace than in the garden with our mother, standing close to her, learning and doing what she loved.

This was something my siblings and I never thought to do. While we treated this world like our personal playground, taking, always taking, humans approached it differently. They recognized their mortal limitations and experienced the dangers. They learned to grow and cultivate the earth in order to nourish themselves and build a community. They labored and practiced patience through the seasons, appreciating every fruit and vegetable they harvested from their efforts.

In the absence of inherited powers, these humans cared for each other. They created their own powers.

Our mother reached over to help filter some soil into my patch. "Father allowed you to stay with me today," our mother said. "But you should study with him tomorrow."

But instead of agreeing, my answer surprised me.

"I don't want to learn to fight," I said, my voice so high and sweet my heart ached. I hadn't known anything back then. I hadn't understood what would happen.

"You cannot expect your sister to always protect you," our mother said. "You need to fight for yourself."

"Will she also learn to farm?" I asked.

"No," she said. "She has always been a warrior. She is not like you."

I frowned. How would Huong feel if she heard this?

Our mother suddenly looked up, her head turning back and forth, her eyes searching past me. I froze, afraid that she could sense something different about me. That she could sense Jolie. Her shoulders stilled, her face full of concern.

"What's wrong?" I asked.

"Do you see this?" she asked, pointing to a bright yellow mustard blossom in the soil. "Do you think it's pretty?"

"Yes," I replied cautiously.

"It looks like a mustard flower, but don't let it fool you. See how it sparkles in the light? That is how you can tell the difference. People who find it and do not know any better will try to eat it. They cannot resist its beauty, its fragrant smell. But it tastes bitter to humans, the worst taste that will burn in your mouth for days. But not you, my child. Only you can eat it."

With that, our mother grabbed it at the base of the stalk, curling her fist around it, and yanked it from the dirt. The root that emerged was twice as large as the diminutive flower, already showing evidence of its lethal spread. Our mother held it to my disgusted, startled face.

I held my breath as her eyes seemingly locked on to mine.

"Try it, Nhi," she said. "Trust me."

I dutifully opened my mouth, and she fed it to me: the petals, the stem, and even the roots.

The taste was bitter and my tongue recoiled. But as I chewed, my face began to warm, the energy pouring down my body until my eyes flashed white, my skin and hair glittering with sparkles, the golden dust surrounding the two of us.

She didn't look surprised or startled. "Do not tell anyone," she said quietly. "Not even your sister. These flowers are only for you."

I closed my eyes, searching for my sister in the dream. I found her in the meadow wielding swords with our father. He let her use the dragon, a sword as tall as she was. Huong appeared deep in concentration, listening to our father's instructions, as if sword-fighting wasn't already ingrained in her. The clashing swords generated brilliant white sparks that danced in the air around them.

The sun began to dim. When we looked up, smoke had filled the sky, our dream fading.

When I blinked again, I was back in my bed, alone in the dark.

I sat up and checked the clock: 2:30. I leaped out of my bed, rushed down the stairs, and stepped out into the backyard.

It was silent in the middle of the night, only crickets and the occasional rustle from the squirrels. The soil and dried grass prickled under my bare feet. In Bà Nội's garden beds, I knelt in the dirt and began to dig out the vegetables with my hands, initially careful and hesitant, then growing faster, until I was yanking out more vegetables, hungry to find what I needed.

Buried several feet deep, I discovered the twinkling yellow flower from the dream. I wasn't sure why I knew it had been buried right here. Something inside me just knew. I crammed it into my mouth, feeling it melt down my throat.

It started as a hum, vibrating with energy, until the divine elements traveled through my hands, then arms, an electric, not entirely unpleasant feeling. My hands began to glow red, emitting orange and pink sparks, singeing my fingers. The heat crept up, until the burn crawled through my limbs, scratching and prickling my skin. I took several calming breaths, but my veins began to bubble, the boiling in my bloodstream growing intolerable. Even in the pale moonlight, I could see the ugly red welts spreading along my arms, radiating in the darkness. I fell onto my back, my head spinning, and turned to curl in the fetal position, my bare feet pushing against the garden bed planks.

My body began to smoke, a golden cloud swirling around me, the same glittery fog I'd seen when Huong created the time portal. These were my immortal, divine elements: the yellow sparks seared my body, embedding in my veins, so my skin began to illuminate. My glowing hands clawed at my head, pulling at my hair. My scalp burned with pain. I struggled to breathe as the heat enveloped my body, overtaking my eyes, until all I could see was a bright white light.

Images then surrounded me: our mother and father, Trac and me racing through the fields—first as children trying to play together, and then fully grown, leading our soldiers through jungles and valleys, hiding in a swamp while Han soldiers galloped by us on the hills—lying in the grass next to my sister, exhausted, injured, bleeding. I was crying, but also raging. Screaming Trac's name.

The memories continued to shuffle through my brain, lodging themselves inside my head, and with each subsequent memory, I could feel my body calming, cooling off again. A steam rose around me, a silvery swirling fog comforting my exhausted body.

I wasn't sure how long it lasted, but when I awoke, I was still lying in the garden, my hands clenching fistfuls of mustard blossoms. There was soil everywhere, chunks of upturned vegetables cast about in piles. Was that what reuniting with my spirit felt like? It was nothing like the joy I felt with Huong at the pool or on the cliff. Maybe it would be different every time. Maybe this was a bigger piece of my elements. Whatever it was, my heart still hammered through my body. I didn't want to go through that pain again.

ÔNG NỘI

In the morning, I woke up with a burning sensation in my nose and sinuses, the taste of salt water lingering on my tongue. Curling veins of dried blood spread across my pillowcase. I gagged and ran to the bathroom. Blood had also dried in intricate lines along my nose, mouth, and chin. In the shower, the warm water stung my body, the droplets hissing off my skin. I made the water colder and colder, hoping to quench the percolating heat. The bathroom filled with a thick steam. I watched as layers of blood and dirt flowed off my disgusting body. Had I rolled in that much mud last night? Afterward, I wiped the steam off the mirror to see my reflection: a little better. Still haggard and exhausted looking, but with clean hair and skin.

Bà Nội was sitting on my bed when I returned from the bathroom, the mythology book next to her.

"I have my acupuncture appointment this morning in San Francisco, so I need you to stay home with Ông Nội."

It was Saturday. With no school, Huong and I had planned to meet up and search around town for more of our elements.

"Okay," I said, swallowing my disappointment.

"I'll be back by this evening. You just need to make sure the doors are locked and he doesn't wander out again."

I nodded, trying not to stare at the book, which was humming and glowing next to her. Bà Nội didn't seem to notice it at all.

"Are you all right?" Her face looked concerned.

I managed a weak smile. Since I'd come home last night, Bà Nội still hadn't asked about me being a thầy bói, nor about my being gone for so many hours with Huong. It was like she'd forgotten our conversation yesterday.

Maybe that was for the best. The prospect of telling her everything that had happened yesterday felt exhausting. I couldn't imagine having to adjust from accepting me as a thầy bói to me as a reincarnated goddess. Huong was right. There was nothing my grandmother could do anyway but worry.

I texted Huong that I was stuck at home. In the kitchen, I prepared Ông's breakfast of cut-up fruit and a bowl of nuts while I reread the updates from the mythology book. It was like a more-rewarding version of a Kindle.

The Trung sisters chapter had altered again and was now twice its initial length, including more of the memories I'd experienced in last night's dream. The only thing missing, I noticed, was my mother's lesson about the flower.

I found a longer account of the sisters' rebellion against the Han. How they rose to protect their village from an attack after their mortal father's murder. How women followed them to form an army, including their mother, who joined as the medical chief, using her expertise of herbs and flowers to help heal wounded soldiers. How the sisters created monsoons and tsunamis to fight against their brothers, but the Han, led by Ma Yuan, also attacked with their own catastrophic forces—earthquakes, lightning, and wildfires. Ma Yuan, along with his brother generals Geng Shu and Liang Song, relentlessly pursued the Trung sisters to their final battle.

I was so absorbed in reading that I didn't see Ông Nội in the kitchen until he sat across from me at the counter, a cup of steaming tea between us.

Sometimes he did this on his better days, slipping back into his morning routine like nothing was amiss. He still wore his pajamas, even though it was noon, and his shock of white hair stood taller and wilder than usual.

"Good morning, Ông," I said, closing the book.

"You found it in the garden, didn't you?" Ông asked, taking a sip from his teacup.

I inhaled sharply. "What?"

"I can feel it in you. Welcome back, Nhi."

He then leaned over and, with his right hand, dropped a tiny mound of pastel-blue pills and red-and-white capsules on the table. His medication, his sedatives. Several days' worth.

My heart began to quicken, not in fear but with impending discovery, like when Huong helped me understand a math equation—two disparate links fusing together for the answer. "How do you know that name?"

"We've met in another lifetime," he said, "when you chose my

160

ancestor as the first thầy bói. My ancestors and I have been protecting you for thousands of years."

"Me?" I asked, stunned.

"Of course," he said. "Do you think our true purpose was to select people's wedding dates and create horoscope charts? You were our first calling."

He blinked at me, his eyes glowing white for a moment before returning to their natural color. My eyes flashed white in response, detecting elements shimmering in his face and hands. They were not as bright as mine or Huong's, but like the subtle glints of light you find in the sand at the beach.

"Do you know why our eyes turn white?" I asked.

"These are divine eyes," he said, "so you can see all the elements and colors in this world."

Over the next hour, Ông Nội talked and I listened. He'd sensed my immortal spirit before I was even born, and he called my parents to tell them they were expecting. He knew from his ancestors that the elements would remain dormant in their children's vessels, and the thầy bói's responsibility was to protect and nurture them to survive another generation.

"You are meant to restore order and balance," he said. "All these natural catastrophes in this world? Especially here in California, with the earthquakes and wildfires? They're because the elements are in chaos."

"My brothers," I said.

"They've only gotten worse in these past years. But when I woke up this morning," Ông said, looking at me with awe, "I could feel your spirit in this house. Protecting us. I never realized I'd be able to witness the great reincarnation in this lifetime. You are destined to bring peace."

I leaned back in my chair, taking it all in. "So yesterday, when Bà Nội asked you about this, you were just pretending to be asleep?"

"She cannot know. Her ignorance protects her, as it once protected you."

"But she told me about the mythology book. She already knows."

"Not since this morning," he said.

I recalled her behavior this morning, how casual and oblivious she seemed. "How did she forget?" I asked.

"Again, Nhi, you are underestimating the thầy bói's power. Remember that humans are made up of the mortal elements of this earth. This includes their minds, their memories."

I watched him as he took another long sip of tea, finally understanding. "You can erase memories?"

Then I heard him, inside my own head. *You are the one who taught me.*

My heart leaped with joy. I felt the urge to run upstairs to find my phone so I could text Huong, or better yet break the news in our heads, but Ông raised a hand as if in warning. "You cannot tell her yet."

"Why not?"

"We are not strong enough. She is more powerful than you right now."

"She's been helping me."

"She thinks I'm just another fortune-teller who gives out

horoscopes. She doesn't realize the full power of the original thầy bói. No one else knows about me but you."

"Why?" I asked. "Can't she sense you?"

"I am connected to you—not your sister. She thinks she knows more than you. For now, she is stronger and remembers more, but you must catch up. You have to, before the dragons arrive."

My heart sank. Was this another one of his delusions? I searched his eyes for the cloudy confusion, bracing myself for his ranting again.

Instead they looked clear and calm. His hand reached over to cover mine. His touch felt frail, cold, but then I felt our eyes flashing white, our skins glittering in recognition. As his memories flowed into my mind, I could see dragons—black and red in the gray sky, the same ones from last night's dream. As they circled closer, I recognized them.

"My brothers," I said. "They're coming for me."

"And you'll be prepared to face them. The immortal guardians chose you out of all their children to fulfill their prophecy. Didn't you read your book?"

"You mean your book?" I looked at the book and back at Ông Nội, finally understanding.

"This book has always been for you. Over thousands of years, the thầy bói have been recording our history so that this information could help you."

I opened the book, my fingertips prickling with energy as they traced the words and illustrations. This had been for me, all along.

"Is that why the text keeps changing?"

"It is connected to your spirit. You are coming together, these memories returning. The book fills as you come closer to reincarnation."

"Can you at least tell me where the rest of the elements could be? You knew about the one in the garden."

"Elements find you when you are ready. They will arrive slowly—earth, fire, water, and air—because each power comes with responsibility. This world can change on a god's whim, and has."

I absorbed his words. My body already felt overwhelmed with the elements I'd regained. I couldn't imagine how it would feel when I was fully reincarnated.

He held up the mythology book. "Keep this safe and always in your possession, so when the words return, you are the first to read them."

This was the longest conversation we'd had in over a year.

"Are you back, Ông?"

He furrowed his eyebrows at me in confusion.

"This past year, you haven't been yourself."

"Neither have you."

Ouch. Harsh, but true. My breakdown at the pool, my confusion, my misplaced memories. He wasn't the only one who looked crazy.

"We're not going to dwell on that," he said, putting a hand over mine to calm me. "That will only waste time, which we don't have. We still have much to prepare."

22

OBLIGATIONS

After traveling back and forth over thousands of years and discovering I was the incarnation of a Vietnamese warrior goddess with a sister I never knew, going back to school on Monday felt like a significant letdown. But Huong said we had to. We hadn't seen each other all weekend because of human obligations: me watching Ông Nội, and she with Harsha and KT. We needed to get back to work.

When I opened the door to Huong's car, her eyes flashed white at the sight of me.

"You found more elements," she said, almost accusingly. "Why didn't you tell me?"

I climbed into the car and fastened my seat belt. Her eyes returned to their human color and scanned me suspiciously from the top of my head to my Adidas Sambas.

"It was the middle of the night," I said.

I could feel her thoughts mingling with mine, reading me.

"You knew the whole weekend," she said, her glossy mouth

pouting. "Was this after the dream we shared together? You should have called. How did it feel?"

"It . . . hurt."

She nodded knowingly. "Sometimes that happens. They're not all orgasms."

"Huong!"

"What do you want me to say? You find a better word to describe the feeling."

I could feel my body blush.

"What, you've never had one before?" Huong asked. "Do you want to? I could ask Harsha."

"Huong!"

"Don't be such a prude. I've seen the way you look at him."

This heat in my body was all human, I realized, nothing like the burn of our elements. Yet it consumed me all the same. I buried my face in my hands, twisting my shoulders toward my window. "Please shut up."

"Jolie, we're a part of each other. What's mine is yours!"

"I thought you cared about him."

"I do, that's why I'm offering him to you."

"Thank you," I said. "It's a sweet and bizarre offer, but unnecessary."

"If you ever change your mind . . . Now, I want you to talk. Tell me about the element fragment. Where did you find it? What did you see?"

"It was in my garden."

"Seriously?" She looked surprised, her brain absorbing the

information slowly. "Huh. I wouldn't have guessed there. And you're sure they're divine elements?"

The mythology book had described the two types of immortal elements: the guardian dragons' prime elements and their children's divine elements. While both could create—and destroy—the prime ones by far surpassed the divine's powers. After we'd given up the prime elements to become human in our first lives in ancient Vietnam, we hadn't felt their presence again.

"I assume so. We can't carry prime elements as humans, right?

"Right. But do you feel anything else?"

"Should I?"

"Usually, a memory reattaches itself when you reunite."

I didn't know why I couldn't tell her. The warnings from our mother in Vietnam and Ông Nội were confusing, but I wasn't ready to share. Not yet. "Maybe it was just a small piece."

"I don't know," she said, her eyes traveling over me intently. "You look different . . . can you . . . do anything?"

I looked at her pointedly. "What do you mean?"

She leaned over and pulled up the sleeves of my shirt to reveal the hives and burn marks.

"I used to get them too," she said, "until I stopped trying to suppress my true powers."

"I wasn't hiding them," I said.

"I know," she said. "But you're changing. It's happening quickly. I'm not letting you out of my sight."

I looked behind us as we sailed through another intersection.

We were almost at school already, in half the usual time. "We haven't hit any red lights on this drive," I said, looking back at Huong.

"We can do many things, Jolie," she said, passing through another freshly turned green light. "You haven't been paying attention."

At school, people appeared noticeably distressed, whispering to each other and wearing those freaked-out expressions usually reserved for midterms or finals weeks. In the sophomore hallway, a small crowd assembled in a corner. They surrounded Daphne's locker, which had been decorated with flowers, glittery cards, and sticky notes saying "ILYSM" and "MISS U" and "COME BACK SOON!"

"Humans," Huong whispered. "They're acting like she was kidnapped when she probably ran away for attention."

"What is this?" I asked.

"Daphne's parents reported her missing," Huong said, not even slowing past the shrine while I tried to crane my neck for another look. "There's an Amber Alert."

My heartbeat quickened. "Why didn't you tell me?"

"I thought you saw the Schoolbook alerts. They sent a bajillion of them."

The dream of Lana, Daphne, and the giant egg returned to me. The night of the car chase and Ông Nội's video. The dream had been more like a nightmare. All I could see, feel, and hear was Daphne sneering, laughing in my face, and how I stopped her.

How I burned her.

My dreams were not just dreams.

Huong realized I had stopped and turned back to me. "What is it?"

"It was me," I said, swaying slightly at my abrupt stop. Students glided past me through the hallway, faster and faster. "Oh god, it was me."

Huong stepped forward, putting her hands on my shoulders to steady them.

The details of my dream, when I broke through the eggshell to find my friends on the beach in Vietnam, poured into her mind. Huong patiently absorbed this, the concern spreading on her face.

I killed her, I wailed into her head. If she hadn't been supporting my shoulders, my legs would have buckled and sent me to the floor. *I'm a murderer.*

We don't know that, Huong said, pulling me to the side of the hallway to avoid the flow of student traffic. *Not yet.*

Even as she said that, our minds veered toward another memory from our previous life: one of our first battles against our brothers, facing down a Han army of over a thousand soldiers. We were easily outnumbered. As Trac plotted an escape route for our soldiers, the panic inside me grew hot and uncomfortable. We were attempting to cross a river to find safety in the jungle when the Han surrounded us. As our soldiers started to flee across the stream, I turned to the Han, opened my mouth, and released a sheet of fire. While our soldiers successfully escaped, I burned half of the Han army. My fire killed them—the same fire I used on Daphne.

The shame washed over me, chilling my bones. I was a murderer.

When our minds returned to California and the locker area, I was shaking. Huong stood next to me so I could lean on her.

She spotted something behind me and wordlessly turned me around.

Vice Principal Agrawal walked down the hallway with two police officers and a couple. My eyes flashed white to see them better: Daphne's parents. I stepped back and felt Huong's hands supporting me behind my backpack. They stopped at the locker shrine, their faces streaked with grief as students flowed around them, whispering, grabbing not-so-discreet selfies as they passed by.

I have to tell them, I said.

What are you going to say? That you burned their daughter in a dream? They're not going to believe you. I'm not even sure I believe you.

She pulled me down the hall and turned into the girls' restroom. After checking to make sure the stalls were empty, she overturned the trash can by the door and pushed it under the restroom window, which overlooked the hall. She climbed onto the trash can, gently nudged open the window, and motioned for me to hop up. I wiped my eyes on my sweatshirt sleeve, took several deep breaths, and followed her.

Huong had calculated correctly: the window looked right over Daphne's locker. From this perch, we had a full view of Agrawal, the officers, and Daphne's parents. Unless they turned around and looked up, they wouldn't see us.

Daphne's mom glanced around the hallway for a moment, her face pink and splotchy from crying. Daphne's dad, who I remembered only in suits for most of my life, wore a T-shirt and track pants.

"Daphne rarely uses her email," her dad said. "Why wouldn't she just text?"

An email! That had to mean she was alive. Huong realized the same thing because her hand squeezed mine.

"She could have logged on to a computer," the police officer said. "Her phone location hasn't been active since the night she disappeared."

"It's not her," her mom said. "She'd never say those words."

So either she ran away, or someone hacked into her account. My throat felt painfully parched, the regret and guilt twisting through my abdomen. My eyes closed for a moment, and when they reopened, I noticed someone had joined the adults, hovering behind them. Before I could wonder who it was, the person turned to face me, looking up, her eyes meeting mine.

Daphne.

"Oh my god," I whispered.

"What is it?" Huong asked.

I glanced quickly between Huong and Daphne. They couldn't see each other—their gazes were fixed only on me. I inspected Daphne more closely. Her straight black hair was rustling, falling across her face like there was a breeze around her.

Daphne lifted her chin, and as I blinked, her face began to fade, along with her chest, her wavering arms and legs. Her body transformed into a silhouette of glittery golden dust.

Huong persisted. "What do you see? Tell me."

Something inside of me resisted telling Huong. No one could know. Not yet.

Daphne's mouth opened and closed as if she was speaking. I knew that she wasn't a ghost or a hallucination. Daphne was dream traveling; her spirit was here, but not her body.

I suddenly felt cold, and the hallway flooded with a gust of frosty mist. I exhaled, watching my cold breath appear, but no one else noticed. A darkness was approaching us, a curl of black smoke slithering through the fog.

It was hunting her.

You need to go, my mind told Daphne. *It's not safe here.*

Her lips continued moving frantically, but I couldn't make out her words. The hallway had filled with a howling wind that seemed to affect only Daphne, whipping her hair around her face and rustling her clothes as the vice principal and adults continued, undisturbed, in their conversation. I tried to listen for Daphne's thoughts, but all I heard was the roar of rushing air. Daphne's hair lifted around her, her body rising up to the ceiling.

Huong's hand dropped from mine, her eyes focused on where Daphne hovered. She could sense her now, too. Huong stepped off the trash can, brushed off her hands, and pushed open the restroom door.

I jumped off the trash can to follow her.

Go now, I thought more urgently at Daphne, but when I turned the corner of the restroom to look down the hallway, she remained frozen, terrified, as Huong walked toward her. At the other end of the hallway, the smoke was slithering closer. Huong hadn't noticed it, her focus on Daphne's spirit. The adults were still absorbed in their own conversation, oblivious to us.

My body acted before my mind. My elements stormed across the hallway toward Daphne, surging past my sister, so when the smoke reached Daphne, she had already vanished.

Huong arrived in time to watch her disappear inches from her face. The smoke retreated, rushing back into the fog. My sister turned around to face me, but Vice Principal Agrawal had already stepped between us.

"Is there a problem, Ms. Pham? Why are you not in class?"

I retreated into the restroom, trying to catch my breath, my spine aligning against the restroom door. Even if Huong was pissed—and I suspected she was—I'd done the right thing. Daphne, wherever she was, felt safe for now.

I heard footsteps, first going one way and then the other. When a shadow bobbed along the floor, I looked through the small rectangular window in the door. I spotted her caramel-colored ponytail. And then her alert hazel eyes. Searching, then focusing. Lana.

23

DAPHNE

At lunch, I sat down in my old loner corner in the cafeteria. After Daphne's visit and disappearance, Huong was mad, refusing to connect with me for the rest of the morning even though I tried several times to speak through our thoughts.

Classes blurred by. I could barely hear or understand anything my teachers and classmates said. I wasn't sure how to face Lana. Had she seen only me or Huong, too? Maybe she thought we were just being nosy snoops. I remembered Ông Nội's gift to erase memories, and I wondered briefly if I should do that to Lana. Maybe he could teach me, and I could delete that morning from Lana's memory just to eliminate any suspicions.

The shame washed over me at even the thought. What was wrong with me? Burning old friends, erasing people's memories? I felt like a monster.

At my table, Huong took a seat next to me like nothing was wrong. She opened her bento lunch box, revealing a trio of Spam musubi, and placed one in front of me.

I accepted the peace offering. "Don't be mad," I said. "It all happened so fast. I'm not even sure how I did it."

"I believe you," she said. "I'm just . . . disappointed."

"Why?"

"I thought things would be different this time. I thought we could work together."

I gave her a strange look. "We are. When didn't we work together?"

"Near the end," she said ruefully, biting into her musubi. "You started keeping secrets from me. It's why we lost."

"I don't remember that yet," I said. "What kind of secrets?"

"Maybe it's better you don't remember and we have a fresh start." She waved her hand as if she could dismiss what she'd brought up. "The point is that we need to communicate better with each other."

"I've been trying to reach you all morning," I said, genuinely confused. "If you want to ask me something, I'm right here."

"She was trying to talk to you," Huong said. "What did she say?"

"I couldn't hear her. The wind was too loud."

She made a face. "That was weird. Did you do that?"

"No! And then I got distracted."

I told Huong about the smoke I saw behind the two of them in the hallway, and how my elements seemed to instinctively send Daphne away from the danger, but to where, I wasn't sure.

But Huong didn't care about that, and instead wanted to know more about the smoke, which she hadn't detected. "What color was it?"

"Dark. Gray? It's hard to remember. There was a lot of fog."

"Like black and red?"

We both had the same thought. We knew our brothers would find us eventually. I just hadn't thought it would be this soon.

But why not? I looked around the cafeteria, which had grown noisy with pointless chatter. What if our brothers were already here and I just wasn't strong enough to sense them yet?

From their spot near the salad bar, KT and Harsha spotted us, but when Harsha moved forward with his lunch tray, KT whispered something in his ear that stopped him.

"If it really was our brothers, they would have come after us," Huong said. "What would they want with some sophomore? No offense, I know you used to be her friend."

"I don't know. Maybe they're trying to get to me? That means we have to help her."

Huong sighed. "Okay, but we can't let it distract us entirely from regaining our powers."

"It won't."

"You don't remember yet. I do. Helping humans was what got us distracted last time, worrying over every soldier in our army. We cannot save everyone we like. We have to be more selfish this time, Jolie, and think about ourselves. Because if we don't win back our elements, our brothers will take them, and this whole world is screwed."

Before I could respond, Harsha and KT approached our table and Huong's mood brightened. As they chatted, I sat quietly, my senses heightened, pondering our last words.

For the rest of lunch, I tried to detect my brothers' spirits around us in the cafeteria, realizing I had no idea what to look or feel for. My sister and I had reincarnated into human teens. What if our brothers had done the same?

My body filled with dread, my muscles tightening with uncertainty. Learning about my past life should have felt empowering. It shouldn't have made me feel more confused about who I was or was supposed to be.

Later that evening, I filled Ông Nội in about the day's events. We sat in the dining room, where I poured him cup after cup of jasmine tea. He seemed to understand the bizarre encounter, even though he kept referring to Daphne as Daffy.

Ông tried searching for Daphne as well, since he used to consult on missing persons cases. Vietnamese or Chinese families who'd grown impatient and frustrated with the red tape of police investigations occasionally called him, asking for new leads. But the missing were usually fentanyl addicts or ex-husbands skipping out on child support payments. While Ông had known Daphne since she was little, he couldn't locate her presence, even after he held her picture and the notes she'd sent me—including the not-so-nice ones—in his hands.

I laid my head on the table. "Do you think Daphne's safe?"

"If you can feel her spirit, that is a good sign," Ông said.

"But why can't I find her? Where did I put her? Why is she even involved in all of this?"

"You should trust your intentions even if you cannot yet understand them," Ông said quietly. "She is likely somewhere safe; so safe that even you can't locate her. Or reveal to anyone else where she is."

"Like my brothers."

"Or someone closer to you."

I realized who he was talking about. "Huong is my sister," I said.

"Who you only met a few weeks ago."

"She is probably stronger than both of us." Which made me realize something. "Why hasn't she sensed your elements yet?"

"Your spirit is shielding me," Ông said. "This is how you tried to protect your warriors, but it only lasted so long against the Han."

"I can disguise my elements?"

"You do it instinctively. It's how you remained undetected to live as a human. Elements emerge when they are ready to be united. As your spirit grows, you will recognize more elements. That is how she found you. But if we are not careful, this is also how she can find me."

My phone buzzed on the table. I turned it over and looked at the screen. A selfie from Huong, sticking her tongue out at me.

Was it a coincidence? Could she sense us talking about her?

"Why can't we work together?" I asked. "She can help us against my brothers."

"There is a reason you've stayed hidden all these years," Ông Nội said. "I cannot see the full prophecy of your return. We don't know how she'll react when she learns about me. She may think you need to take back all of your elements, even the ones from me."

"But they're yours. How could I even get them back?"

"We'd have to both agree to the gift. I offer, you accept. When the elements recognize the intention, they can release to another. That is the only way elements can move from one body to another, mortal or immortal. Unless . . ."

"Unless what?"

"Unless you can trick or force them away."

That sounded frightening. I exhaled shakily. "I won't tell her," I promised. "Not yet."

"It's going to be harder than that. Your elements attract each other. You cannot help but come back together."

"Isn't that a good thing? She's my sister. We are supposed to share."

Ông didn't say anything. He leaned back, his face observant and neutral—like he did with his clients who refused to accept his readings.

"It's going to be different this time," I insisted. "That's why she came to find me. This is our second chance."

24

THE POWER OF WATER

That night, I stared at the writing prompts of my overdue history homework, but I couldn't focus. The mythology book was nestled beside me like a puppy, the butter-soft cover warm against my thigh. I pushed away my homework and rolled over to open the red leather tome.

Another chapter had appeared, the print shiny and dark against the yellowed pages, like the words had been freshly inked. I stared for a moment, debating if I should call Huong, but the text soon pulled me in.

This chapter chronicled the key battles between the Trung sisters and General Ma Yuan's army. It was a depressing read—paragraph after paragraph detailing how the Han methodically defeated us in every battle with the sheer size and relentlessness of their armies. I felt ill for these soldiers who'd sacrificed their lives and time with their families to fight for us. The Han army, on the other hand, never seemed depleted by their losses. Their forces multiplied in size with each battle.

No wonder it felt bleak. No wonder we lost.

That night, my dream travel took me back to the start of the war. My sister and I had arrived in a highland village riding two golden elephants, with a small but devoted army of soldiers following on horseback. The air felt hot and dusty in my throat.

We were recruiting volunteers from the Han-occupied villages to build our army. The soldiers—many of them women, from teenagers to grandmothers—looked determined and optimistic in their unsullied armor, their polished, bloodless weapons gleaming at their sides. They had not yet experienced battle.

In the village center, Trac and I smiled and nodded at the curious villagers below us. Some soldiers untied bags of rice, fruit, and vegetables from their horses, while others shepherded people toward the center square. When Trac was sure she had enough of a crowd, she slipped off her elephant to stand before them. I also dismounted and stood beside our soldiers.

Trac took the time to say hello and learn the name of every villager. It felt like it took hours. But Trac listened to the villagers' stories and concerns, nodding and absorbing their struggles while the Han emperor continued to take away their precious food reserves. I realized she was building their trust with her silence. She couldn't just come into the village and proclaim she knew what was best for them. That was what the Han had done. She knew to listen first.

One woman, pregnant and widowed, wept in Trac's arms and thanked her for the supplies of food, but asked how they would survive the rest of the season after it ran out. They'd already planted the rice paddies and soil with seeds, but the dirt and air felt bone-dry.

Another young woman who looked defiant and angry said she'd been orphaned because the Han soldiers had recruited her father into the army and her mother had died of grief.

The voices of both women sounded familiar, and I searched their faces, hoping they could trigger more memories. Trac then returned to the middle of the village square. She levitated up in the air, drawing astonished gasps from the villagers, and settled on top of the elephant so she could connect with every face in the crowd.

"We've lost so much because of the Han," Trac said calmly, projecting her voice. "Our loved ones. Our land. Our water. No longer. We can bring them all back if you trust me and fight beside us. We need to stop expecting to be rescued. We must achieve this ourselves. When will you step forward?"

She reached behind her for the dragon sword and raised it to the sky. Her eyes closed as the sword glowed a bright white, her face tilted toward the sun. Our soldiers and I did the same. The rest of the crowd also eventually turned their faces to the sky, their eyes closed, and a silence fell over the town square, until we could hear only the rustle of the wind through the teak and tamarind trees.

I waited for the change. When my neck began to ache, I glanced down and realized the ground was melting with the shadows. I looked up again. The sky had filled with gray clouds, hiding the sun. Shrieks of joy and laughter arrived with the sprinkles on our faces and arms, increasing as the rain grew into fat, wet drops.

The dragon sword still raised, Trac gracefully pulled more

clouds to gather above the village and commanded them to expand. The clouds multiplied and stretched until the whole village was shrouded with silvery mist.

"The power of water is now yours," Trac pronounced. "The bounty of this earth is now yours. With your loyalty, this will be our land. We will rule together with love, cooperation, and compassion. You will never be hungry again. Our descendants will never suffer again."

While the women, men, and children in the village laughed and danced, more people emerged from their homes, the suspicious, doubtful ones now converted, all of them hugging and exclaiming happiness for the rain's return. The hardened dirt softened into a rich mud. The plants and the earth exhaled in cool gratitude.

The villagers knelt to the ground, already worshipping us as their saviors. Others lined up to swear allegiance and volunteer for the new army. The two women who'd looked familiar to me stood near the front, their faces full of wonder and admiration. How did one miracle of rain convince them that we were goddesses? How were they so sure to trust us?

Trac floated off the elephant's back to the ground, the crowd gasping in delight and surprise. We rarely flew in front of other humans—that seemed to upset mortals more than any of our other powers, even fire. She landed in the arms of her followers. While Trac soaked in the attention and love, always and forever the revered hero, I suddenly felt shy, my arms folding over my chest. I glanced nervously at the growing crowd. I didn't remember feeling this way last time. Maybe I'd been tired, my spirit depleted from harnessing the divine elements of water to bring the rain. Or maybe I was tired of being cold and wet. But my eyes soon returned to Trac, like everyone else's eyes.

They wanted to be like her. And why not? I could see Huong in Trac so clearly: the sweetness, the compassion, the empathy. She made you feel worthy. She made you feel seen and safe and strong. No wonder we all loved her and followed her, even to death.

I woke to the sound of tapping on my window. It hadn't rained in San Jose in months. The news had forecasted another year of drought. I walked over to the window and opened it, breathing in the damp, fresh morning air. The drops felt plump and soothing on my fingers before evaporating, surrounding me in a faint yellow mist.

The newly returned elements surged throughout my body. I stared at the rain droplets and they dutifully grew larger and larger, obeying my will.

Welcome back to our first power, Huong said in my thoughts.

I smiled, my spirit warming, strengthening inside me. The power of water.

25

THE POWER OF FIRE

A week had passed since we'd seen Daphne's spirit and we'd regained our water power. Every morning, Principal Morris asked students to step forward with any information, for the sake of the missing girl and her family. I imagined what would happen if I actually did step forward; wondered if they'd call the police.

Lana looked catatonic whenever I saw her in class or passed her in the hallway. I didn't approach her because she glared at me whenever she could. But she no longer intimidated me, because I finally believed what Huong had been saying: humans, especially this one, held no power over us.

I did see Daphne's mom at the grocery store one afternoon, not that she noticed me or anyone else around her. Mrs. Nguyen pushed a cart full of frozen dinners and instant coffee, her face pale, her eyes vacant. When my mind uncontrollably dipped into her thoughts, I sensed pain and anguish: her last memory of Daphne, texting in her bedroom, slamming her door shut. I swiftly left the store, afraid to see any more.

In the meantime, Huong and I continued searching for our missing element fragments. This took time. After the surprising ease of regaining my water power from merely reaching outside my bedroom window, Huong warned me the others wouldn't all be as simple. Our elements could be anywhere or in any creature.

Like an injured tabby cat. We'd been driving around Atherton for hours, Huong convinced she sensed something, when she suddenly halted in the middle of an intersection. Ignoring honks and hollers, she stepped outside of her car and picked the cat up, cradling it in her arms. I got out of the car and approached cautiously, afraid it was dead. Seconds later, I watched their bodies light up, a violet aura enveloping them. The cat's green eyes blinked open; it was calm and purring. Huong looked up and urged me to come close. I touched her arm, and Huong's and the cat's memories filled my head.

If this is what immortality felt like, it was amazing. As a goddess, my mind and body had been upgraded in every way. Aside from the burning sinuses and hives, my body felt stronger than it had in months. And with all the swimming in gym and the after-school expeditions with Huong, my clothes were loose on my leaner frame, so Huong sent me home with bags of her extra, often designer-label clothes with the tags still on them. These clothes were nicer than anything I'd ever owned. They felt comforting to wear, too; even though Huong had never worn them, I felt closer to her.

In the afternoons, Huong and I played with our rediscovered water power, marveling at how easily the elements bent to our desires. We did dumb, fun tricks, like starting a lightning storm and watching people gasp and scurry inside their cars or houses. Or creating waves in the gym pool that splashed into the girls' faces.

We flirted with our other elements, too, which still felt fragile, at least for me. The slowing or speeding up of time was trickier for me, because it utilized a combination of the four elements, and it caused the worst headaches. Huong was obsessed with regaining fire next, though it was our weakest power by far. She gained great satisfaction from gliding her toes through a flame, snapping her fingers to light candles, or reheating a pizza slice in the warmth of her palms. I couldn't imagine how ecstatic she'd feel once she regained her full fire powers.

I wanted to regain air. Often overlooked and underappreciated, it was sneaky and could create great chaos. I'd gotten a taste of its potential that night when it had saved us from crashing into Daphne's car. Sometimes I just liked to watch the clouds outside of my classroom window come together in different shapes as I sculpted animals and people, wondering if anyone else was looking up and noticing. I'd light up the sky in assorted colors, preferably during sunset, when people expected unusual colors anyway. I liked to wash it over in yellow, and sometimes Huong would respond by swirling a layer of lavender through. None of it seemed too weird, with everyone so used to climate disruptions and our wildfire seasons, heat waves, and droughts. And the manipulations never lasted long. If we did anything too strenuous, we'd have to wait a few days for our strength to replenish, which annoyed an impatient Huong.

"It won't be like this when we fully reincarnate," Huong said one afternoon, when she impulsively squandered her fire power starting a bonfire at the beach before the other kids arrived. "We'll never be weak, not for a moment."

We'd stayed behind after Harsha and their other friends left so Huong could regain the energy to stand. They thought she'd just had too much to drink.

"It's not too bad," I said, wrapping another beach towel over her shivering shoulders. "Waiting allows us to appreciate our gifts."

"Queens do not wait," Huong said. "If we did, we'd never get anything done."

"I disagree," I said. "How about that? I defy you, Queen."

That brought a smile from her. "I'll accept this disobedience. Only this once."

If only it could always be like this: jumping from realm to realm, enjoying the best of these worlds and never having to deal with anything or anyone else. We hadn't experienced any further visions of Daphne or our brothers, and I felt guilty for not missing Daphne. That every second of her absence felt like a relief.

At night, we met in our dreams, where time stretched as far as we wanted and we could explore the memories of our first lives in Vietnam. We walked through our childhood village, playing with the neighboring girls who eventually grew up to fight alongside us in our army. Learned how to combine herbs and create elixirs with our mother. How to carry a sword and shoot a bow with our father. We explored our reign as queens with our army. Those were the happiest dreams, sweet memories of the sisterhood and friendship we shared with our soldiers.

Most of our dreams during these few weeks ended serenely, and I would wake up in the morning feeling refreshed and inspired. There was only one that wrenched me from sleep in the middle of the night.

Our father's murder was as gruesome as I'd feared, a chaotic midnight raid where Han warriors dragged him from his tent out to a meadow for his execution. I recognized two of the Han generals as Ma Yuan's devoted henchmen, our immortal brothers Geng Shu and Liang Song.

While our mother and I hid under the floorboards of our farmhouse, Trac searched for Father's dragon sword. She ran out to the meadow only to be tackled by Geng Shu and Liang Song. They forced her to watch Ma Yuan behead our father with the dragon sword. When I heard Trac's screams, I burst out of the floor and rushed outside.

By the time I arrived, our brothers had smuggled our father's head into a dirty leather sack, leaving his lifeless body behind in the mud. I tried to reach for Trac's hand, but she pushed me away, focusing on her rage. As the Han mounted their horses, Trac's screams grew louder, higher, escalating to a pitch so unbearable that the Han soldiers all stared at her, astonished, immobile. Then the cries transformed into flames.

Our three brothers had already escaped, but their human army could not. She burned them, spewing a sheet of fire across the wall of twenty soldiers, incinerating not only the men but their horses, too, until all that was left was ash. I watched, stunned, breathless, as Trac continued to sob pitiful little-girl tears. I stared back at the house where my mother hid, willing her not to come out.

Finally Trac collected herself, wiped her eyes, and found our father's two swords in the dark smoke. She placed the fairy in my chubby hands.

"This is yours now," she said, picking up the dragon from the scorched earth for herself.

It felt heavy and hot in my hands, like the sword could burn my skin off, but my grip remained firm. I turned back to the ashes. "Father," I said.

"He's gone," she said. "It's just us. Let's go back to Mother."

We staggered away, not looking back at the meadow—now a wasteland of embers and ash smoking in the shape of a crescent moon. The swords trailed behind us, carving through the dirt.

I awoke with a start, looking around my room in fear. I rushed down the stairs barefoot, fleeing to the backyard on instinct, realizing I needed to get as far from my grandparents and the house as I could. My mind searched for Huong, who was also awake.

Do you understand our powers now? Her tone was jarringly satisfied, even triumphant.

I felt the smoky tickle in my throat again.

This is what we are meant to do. We can burn things.

Instead of complying, I pressed my lips together.

It's going to come out; you can't stop it. I saw a burst of orange flames soar across the ink-black sky. *Where do you think the hives are from? The blisters? If you didn't suppress them, your body would be fine. Open your mouth. Accept your power.*

I shook my head, angry that she was trying to teach me something after what we'd witnessed, forcing me to relive her experience and to obey her commands once again.

This is necessary for our spirits to fully reincarnate, she said inside my head. *We need to control all four elements. Now, open your mouth.*

The smoke erupted inside of me, my throat bubbling with flames. I collapsed to my knees on the dried grass, my back arching up, my lips finally releasing the fire from my lungs into the night air. The flames continued to unfurl as I angled my rage away from the lemon and orange trees in our backyard and my eyes filled with ashy smoke.

I must have lost consciousness, because the next morning I awoke with my Bà Nội sitting on the grass next to me, hugging my sweating, shaking body. As she whispered useless comforting words, the feeling in my body returned first to my fingers and toes, then traveled through my veins back to my heart and brain.

Unlike other times, I didn't feel the euphoria of my elements activating. Instead I was distracted by Huong's energy, which I could feel humming miles away across town.

26

WINNING

Perhaps sensing that I was in no mood to go to school that morning, Huong texted that she'd pick me up.

I'm staying home, I texted back.

Don't be a baby. I'll be there in ten minutes.

I opened the passenger door to her beaming face behind a pair of large dark sunglasses. Her hair was in two long braids along her shoulders. She wore a crisp white tank top and an eggplant cardigan with black jeans. She sipped from her coffee tumbler and nodded to its steaming twin waiting in the console.

I slammed the door shut and ignored the cup of coffee.

"It's soy milk," she said. "Because I remember that this human vessel is lactose intolerant." She peered past me to the house. "How's your Ông Nội?" she asked.

I picked up the cup of coffee. "The same," I lied. "Ranting and raving about the end of the world."

"I'd like to listen to him sometime," she said as she drove away from the house.

I glared at her. "You could have warned me."

She rolled her eyes. "Is this about last night's dream? You read about our father's death in the mythology book, it's not like it was a surprise."

"I'm talking about what you made me do after."

"Stop overreacting. We have to experience these dreams to regain our powers." She waited until she was at a stoplight before leaning over to look at me. "But I shouldn't have pushed you with fire. I just knew you could do it, and I became impatient. Regaining our power of fire is important."

"We watched our father's murder," I said.

Her eyes cooled and she sat back. "It's part of our story. His death inspired our revolution."

"He was a good man," I said. "He raised us as his own daughters. Didn't you feel . . . anything watching him die again?"

"That was his destiny," she said, turning her attention back to the road. "I know it's a terrible memory, but it will make us stronger."

"It makes me hate our brothers," I said.

The morning sun filtered through a row of eucalyptus trees, casting spindly shadows across the road.

"We shouldn't call them that," she said.

"If we are sisters from the same gods," I said, "what are they? Why are they not our brothers?"

"It means something else for humans. Those dear *brothers*

have been trying to destroy us since the beginning of our existence."

"So we never got along?" I asked.

"No," Huong said impatiently, shaking her head. "Why does that matter?"

"I just wonder if there was ever a time we had peace. As a family."

She looked like I'd slapped her. "It's that kind of thinking that made us lose the first time."

"You mean compromise?" I asked. "Negotiating for peace made us lose?"

"You cannot compromise with warlords. They don't care about peace. They only want power."

"But if we reincarnate and regain our powers, they'll leave us alone."

"Don't be so naive. They're never going to stop trying."

I suddenly understood. "You want to take their elements."

Her face looked impatient, like only now was I catching up. "We have to."

I frowned at how petulant she sounded, like a stubborn toddler. "How does that make us any better than them?"

Huong reached over, picked up my hand, and squeezed it. I winced. Her long fingernails could dig and her grip could pinch when she wasn't careful.

"Because we're good," she said. "We don't have a history of thousands of years of bloodshed. If we want peace and order in this world, we need to remove the rot."

The smile on her face appeared unsettlingly calm.

"You want them to find us here," I realized.

"They're coming, sweetie, whether we want them to or not," she said. "But if we are reincarnated, we will be ready for them. It is our prophecy. This is how we win."

27

THE POWER OF EARTH

Bà Nội had mentioned that Ông Nội had an early reading. But I'd forgotten this by the time I wandered sleepily down the stairs on Saturday morning, inhaling the incense wafting through the air, still in my pajamas. At the dining room table, my grandparents sat across from Huong and KT. I blinked a few times, wondering if they were another dream.

Papers lay scattered on the table along with the usual fruit and nut trays. The curtains were open, morning sunlight streaming through the windows and casting the girls in a bright glow. KT's face looked red and puffy, like she'd been crying all night. I'd never seen her without makeup. Huong sat next to her, holding her hand.

"Your grandfather just started," Bà Nội explained. "Breakfast is in the kitchen." Her polite way of telling me to leave.

"Hey, Jolie," Huong said, raising her chin at me.

Bà Nội looked surprised, but Ông Nội didn't even glance up, instead gazing at the charts on the table, the numbers and sketches so lightly drawn in pencil.

"We know each other from school," I said to Bà Nội, my heart beating louder with each breath. "What's going on?"

"Quentin is missing," Huong said.

KT's face immediately crumpled. Her hands flew to her face as she wailed loudly into them.

"What happened?" I asked, trying not to show my relief. Huong hadn't recognized anything in Ông. So far.

"Nobody's heard from him since last Friday," Huong said, wrapping an arm around a sobbing KT.

"He was in LA visiting his cousins over the weekend," KT said through her tears. "I thought he was ghosting me after I told him to jump off a cliff. But then his mom called me yesterday. She *never* calls me." A pause for more tears and hyperventilating. "They hadn't heard from him either. His aunt and uncle said he never arrived. The police think he ran away. From what? He's always done whatever the hell he wanted. What if he *did* jump off a cliff? Oh god, he is stupid enough to do something like that."

"The principal sent an alert this morning," Huong said. "Because of Daphne, they're afraid it's a copycat runaway."

"He is not a follower! And he has everything to live for, unlike that peasant—"

"We thought your grandfather could help," Huong interrupted, shooting KT a stern look.

"We can try," Bà Nội said. "But sometimes people don't want to be found."

"He never goes off the grid," KT said sharply. "He lives on his phone."

"Where was his last location?" I asked.

"Paso Robles," KT said. "They found his car in a winery parking lot. He hates wine! They found his wallet, keys, and phone."

"You cannot reach him now," Ông Nội said, his voice startling us. "But you will."

"When?" KT asked, leaning forward.

Ông Nội's face twisted in concentration, which was unusual; he normally remained stoic during readings. I walked over to sit next to him, but he didn't react. He studied the charts. The print appeared darker now, the images clearer: two dragons flying in the air.

I glanced up, wondering if the girls could decipher the scribbling.

"He's trying to find you," Ông Nội said. "He is traveling the realm right now."

"How?" KT frantically checked her phone. "Is he alive? Is he all right?"

"He is here," he said.

"Where?" KT asked, confused.

"Which realm?" Huong asked, leaning forward.

Ông Nội gave a cryptic smile, looking at Huong. "They're coming together. Just like you knew they would. But this is a war you will never win."

My breath and body cooled. The room swirled with feelings: the calm of Ông Nội, the bewilderment of both KT and Bà Nội, and the quiet determination of Huong. What did she know? Could she feel Ông Nội's elements? I tried to reach her mind, but she was too interested in the thầy bói.

He pointed to his papers, and I followed his shaking finger. The two dragons on the papers were moving, their penciled silhouettes flying slowly across the pages, leaping around the dining table, until they landed on the page in front of me, facing me.

Protect her, they said.

I looked up into Ông Nội's ice-white eyes and understood.

My chair screeched as I jumped to my feet, reaching for Bà Nội's arm. I pulled her down to the floor, shoving her under the table. Before she could protest, the floor and walls began to shake—the furniture vibrating, the noise overwhelming our voices. Books and vases rattled off the bookshelves. The tremors grew louder, stronger. KT and Huong fell to the floor, tangling around the chair legs. Ông Nội was farthest away, still seated in his chair. His slippered feet appeared to dance along the waves of the Oriental rug.

Crack, crack, crack! The brittle sound swelled, filling our ears, until the rug softened beneath us and the tiled floor crumbled into piles of rock and dust. We scrambled to the edges of solid ground as steam and smoke burst through the exposed rift like a geyser, filling the room with a blinding white powder. I pushed Bà Nội behind me, safely away from the crumbling crevasse. The rift burst wide, slicing our dining room in half, sending Bà Nội's rosewood table tumbling into the chasm. Ông Nội's horoscope charts quickly followed, fluttering into the darkness.

With the room carved in half, Bà Nội and I lay on one side and Ông Nội and the girls on the other, all of us staring in shock at the giant hole. The dust clouds from the chasm bloomed larger, engulfing the room. KT stumbled toward the edge, almost falling in, but Huong dragged her back and pushed her against the wall.

Ông Nội's chair collapsed, and he slipped, his body sliding swiftly toward the chasm. I gasped as Ông Nội slipped farther into the crevasse, barely holding on to the floor's edge, his legs swinging above the smoky void.

As I screamed, Huong leaped forward, grabbing hold of his shoulders, trying to pull him back up. But his arms would not lock around hers. She managed to grab one of his arms and pulled, her face and body straining with effort. He dangled against the dusty cliff, looking over his shoulder, staring curiously into the abyss.

On the ground, I held Bà Nội behind me, the thick plumes of dust making our eyes water. Her fingernails dug into my waist, her body shivering against my back. My muscles strained with the pressure of holding us away from the crevasse. I couldn't risk moving and her falling in, too.

The heat from the chasm below felt suffocating, yet my body yearned to dive in. This same allure drew Ông Nội. It felt like the irresistible pull of the immortal elements reuniting. Something whispered to me inside my head. It was coming from the chasm.

This wasn't just any chasm. This was a portal. A portal that only a divine god could open.

Welcome back, sisters. Won't you join us?

Ma Yuan. His voice sounded both terrifying and familiar.

Never, I heard my sister grimly tell them.

Why so mad? another voice asked, which I immediately recognized as our other brother, Geng Shu. *You're the one who sum-moned us.* He loved warfare more than any of us and was always eager to prolong the domination and torture.

How about a trade? Do you want your little mortal friend back? She is annoying. We'd gladly exchange her for your elements, dear sister.

They were lying. I didn't sense Daphne anywhere close to them, but they knew she was missing. They must have been watching us.

They were waiting for us to jump or fall. I was more worried about them taking Ông Nội.

Through the dust, Huong looked desperately back at me. She was using all her strength to shield Ông Nội. It was up to me to stop our brothers.

I crawled toward the crevasse and peered down. Six white eyes as bright as stars gazed up at me.

There she is! It was Liang Song's gravelly voice. The cleverest of our three brothers, he'd masterminded most of the Han's attacks on our borders. *Still as tiny and precious as ever. Such a shame we have to tear you apart.*

Now, now, Ma Yuan said in a falsely soothing voice. *Can't you see she's not all put back together?*

Get away, I said. *This is your first warning.*

Aw. That's all right. The world has changed, and so have we. Don't be scared of us.

Those words, that smirk. I realized where Ma Yuan had been hiding. Where I'd heard that voice before. I looked over at Huong, horrified as she realized the same thing.

Quentin. His annoying presence these past few months,

leering, taunting, gleefully chasing after Daphne that night in the car. My impulse to burn him in that car was correct. He'd been spying on us all along.

I slammed my palms on the broken-up floor, which was littered with cracked tiles, dust, and dirt. I almost screamed in delight when I realized my brothers' attack had unlocked another element: the power of earth. Just in time.

Instead I focused, pushing out their voices. I needed to reach through the ceramic tiles, the concrete foundation, and all the other layers of sediment. The elements I detected underneath my fingers swirled chaotically.

Our brothers had quieted as I felt their spirits working together to challenge my efforts and regain control. But they were too slow. They'd weakened themselves creating the portal.

My earth elements gathered in my body. I pulled my palms together, watching as the chasm in the middle of our dining room began to mend, merging the broken soil.

Huong pulled Ông Nội up over the edge and back against the dining room wall. We watched as the chasm edges swelled and groaned toward each other, the floor reknitting itself. I sprawled back on the floor, vibrating with concentration, the powers draining from my body. My sweaty hands were red and blistered. Once the portal finally healed, I turned my head.

The room was no longer in shambles. There were clouds of dust in the air and Ông Nội's papers scattered around, but the newly repaired floor looked pristine, the elements smoothing over the earthquake's destruction. The dining table and rug had been restored, our battle effectively erased. Despite my exhaustion, my body buzzed with vitality and adrenaline. Defeating my brothers had energized me.

But the humans were not so lucky. Ông Nội lay on the floor, his head in Huong's lap, while KT crouched next to them. Bà Nội cried out, crawling across the floor to reach my grandfather.

Huong's eyes met mine through the dust. She didn't have to say it or think it. He was unconscious, barely breathing. While his body appeared unharmed, we could both feel his spirit depleting. He was dying.

Behind us I could hear KT hollering about an ambulance, Bà Nội speaking frantically into the landline in the kitchen, KT stumbling to the front door for better cell reception. I held my grandfather's chilled, limp hands, but he didn't squeeze back. I closed my eyes, trying to will whatever power I had left to him, but nothing happened. His fingers felt soft as the panic tightened around my heart. Most of my energy had gone into closing the portal. All I had left were my inadequate human senses.

I swallowed back tears of rage and frustration. How could I fail him again?

Huong pressed on my shoulder and I sat back, releasing Ông Nội's hands. She quickly moved to take my place. Lacing her fingers into his, Huong closed her eyes, her face hovering over his.

We waited, the air around us growing thick and still. A few agonizing seconds passed, and I feared the worst. Then both their eyes opened, a familiar bright white, the sign of the elements' activation. Their faces and bodies began to glow golden and purple, shining through their clothes, their skin so radiant I squinted.

Huong opened her mouth, exhaling a thin spiral of glittery

violet smoke. The elements swirled into the air for a moment before they swooped into Ông Nội's waiting mouth. The infusion of elements was immediate: his body startled awake, his eyes blinking, his skin gleaming with vitality.

"He's alive," I called out to Bà Nội, my voice hoarse with exhaustion. "He's okay!"

Bà Nội rushed back to our sides, kneeling on the floor, sniffling back her tears. She cradled my grandfather's face with her hands.

Huong and I stood looking around us, at each other, grateful, relieved. Our powers had erased most of our brothers' attack, leaving behind only the typical shambles from an earthquake: emptied bookshelves, paintings askew.

"Thank you," I whispered.

"I need to find KT and take her home," Huong said. "We all should rest."

"What if they come back?"

"It won't be for a while," Huong said. "You really knocked them out."

"Jolie," Bà Nội said.

We both looked back at her. My grandmother was frowning.

I walked back to them, kneeling on the floor, the dread returning to my chest. My grandfather continued to blink at us, his irises gray and unfocused.

"Ông Nội," I said.

"Where are you?" he asked, his eyes fluttering, his irises growing paler. "Why can't I see you?"

THE MYTH OF THE THẦY BÓI
(PART TWO)

Did you ever wonder what happened to the dragon after Lâm Xuân Hiển returned to his people?

Alone under the sea, our lonely dragon missed her new companion, who in only a few days had proven to be kinder, gentler, and more interesting than her brothers and sisters had been in centuries.

Generously giving Lâm Xuân Hiển divine elements had weakened her, and she remained in the ocean cave for years to recover. She didn't mind. She remained connected to her new friend through their shared visions, so she could see and experience the world through our ancestor.

The dragon had never witnessed human life so intimately before. Mortals always seemed so small and hysterical, screaming and running away and such, as any human would, when they encountered a dragon. But in their own communities, these humans chatted, laughed, shared stories, and helped each other. Although their mortal lives were short—or maybe because of that—they lived with more purpose, joy, and splendor than the dragon had ever known.

The dragon's older sister, however, disagreed. When Trac descended into the cave to find Nhi weak and vulnerable, she was furious at her foolish generosity. To ensure that no other human could ever possess their powers, Trac cast a spell over their divine elements.

If any human should try to eat those flowers again, they'd only taste bitter and rancid, and they would spit them out; humans could not bear to even hold them in their mouths. Nhi couldn't stop Trac's spell. She was too weak.

Trac pointed out all the mortals' deficiencies. Humans couldn't fly. Or breathe fire. They died so easily.

This debate lasted through the younger dragon's recovery, until Nhi finally convinced her older sister that they should visit the human world reincarnated as humans, live an entire human life, and then decide who had it better.

To accomplish this, they had to relinquish the guardian dragons' prime elements, which were too powerful to exist within human bodies. They hid these origin elements around the world, burying them inside mountains and volcanos and underneath oceans and rivers, dispersing these precious elements into tiny fragments so their brothers could never find them.

As for their new human home, they selected our ancestor's village. By this time, Lâm Xuân Hiển had already died, but his elements had passed down to his granddaughter, a farmer's wife with no children of her own.

We will be the daughters she wished for, *Nhi predicted.* She will show us how to live as humans.

We will protect our land this way, *Trac predicted.* No longer will we control our destiny as dragons in the sky, but as humans. We will lead our people. We will rule this world as queens.

How could they have predicted what would happen next? That their brothers, curious and mischievous, would follow? Yet it was the destiny of their making. So the world continues to suffer the consequences.

AFTERSHOCKS

At the emergency room, we told them he'd fallen and hit his head during the earthquake. But the doctors couldn't explain the blindness. Bà Nội and I waited with growing frustration as his vitals returned to normal for a man of his advanced age. Ông Nội offered no help, remaining unresponsive to any questions the nurses and doctors asked him. Upon examination, the ophthalmologist reported that his pupils had been degenerating for quite some time.

"He could see this morning," I said angrily. "It can't just happen." But even as I said that I recalled incidents of Ông Nội bumping into corners, dropping a water glass, or setting his gaze so closely to his books that his nose touched the paper. How Bà Nội seemed to guide his steps more carefully in recent weeks. He'd blame Bà Nội, accuse the furniture of moving, or laugh it off. Perhaps the doctor was right. Ông Nội hid it well or we didn't notice. We were worrying about so many other things.

I still blamed my brothers. Maybe this would have happened eventually, but they'd certainly sped it up.

Bà Nội only cried.

We returned home several hours later, exhausted and devastated. Ông Nội still hadn't said a word, only smiling and cooperating with our instructions as we moved him through his dinner and bedtime routine. When I searched his mind, his thoughts seemed completely oblivious to what had happened. He allowed Bà Nội to put him to bed without any complaints.

"I'm sorry," Huong sobbed on the phone with me after I came home. "I know how much you love him."

"This isn't your fault," I said. "You saved his life. It's the Han."

"These were never just earthquakes," Huong said. "They were hunting for us."

Our brothers had been sniffing around, patiently tracking us for who knew how long. These earthquakes, so common in California, were the perfect decoy for their attack. They'd stolen the idea from us, a trick we'd used to lure their soldiers into an open valley, where we would crack the earth open, watching as the Han soldiers fell to their deaths.

But we didn't fall into their trap. We'd shut down the portal, but there would be more. My brothers had discovered a way in, and it was only a matter of time before they returned even stronger.

"They actually helped us by opening that portal," Huong said. "We wouldn't have regained our earth power without their earthquake."

"But at what cost?" I asked.

She didn't have an answer. It was terrible, but a fact—the

stronger we grew, the easier it became for our brothers to hunt us down. And the humans around us.

Huong and I had searched Bà Nội's and KT's thoughts, and they hadn't seen our brothers. As far as any mortal understood, it was only an earthquake, a 4.2 with an epicenter in Atherton, twenty-two miles away. Only Huong and I remembered the portal breaking open in my dining room and the fight with our brothers. Even in front of catastrophic damage, humans couldn't see or remember anything from the ancient realm.

But Bà Nội rightly suspected that something else had happened, even if the details felt foggy, and studied me with suspicion that evening at dinner.

"Are you finally going to tell me?"

Instead of speaking, I held her hands, sharing my memories of the last month with her.

She didn't speak for several minutes, absorbing what I'd shared. Ông Nội's warnings haunted me. I was supposed to protect Bà Nội from these memories and I knew he'd disapprove, but after all she'd done for us, she deserved to know. I didn't want to lie anymore.

"You're immortal," Bà Nội finally said, incredulously. "And your friend is, too?"

"She's actually my sister," I said.

Bà Nội nodded, though she looked bewildered. "This does explain your mood these last few weeks. Those are her clothes you've been wearing?"

I nodded.

"And that is what you want?"

"Sure," I said, hoping she meant the clothes. "They feel nice."

"You've been . . . happier," Bà Nội observed. "Less lonely and more confident. It's been nice to see. I just don't understand why Ông Nội didn't say anything to me."

"He hadn't met Huong until today," I said. "He wasn't sure about her at first, because he'd only known about me. But Huong saved him today. And we're going to need her help."

"For what?" Bà Nội asked, looked frightened. "What is going to happen?"

I didn't answer, distracted by what she wasn't saying to me. Her thoughts had turned to my dad. The last time she saw him, he was closing the trunk of his hatchback, refusing to look any of us in the eyes. I was only seven and had no idea I'd never see him again. His eyes were swollen and red.

As soon as Bà Nội realized I was reading her thoughts, she stood from the dining table and backed away from me.

I followed her into the kitchen.

"Why are you thinking about my dad?" I asked as she put her half-eaten plate of food in the sink. "What does he have to do with this?"

"He started having visions," Bà Nội said, turning away from me like she could shield her thoughts, "that he didn't under- stand. He didn't want them."

"Am I the reason he left?" I asked, continuing to follow her. "Was he scared of me?"

She put her hands up to my chest to stop me, her face twisted in anguish. "He left to protect us. He thought . . . that by staying away, he could prevent what he was seeing in his premonitions."

"He was supposed to help Ông Nội carry the duties," I realized, my body temperature rising with my anger. "Instead he left it all on Ông. Dad's a coward."

"We cannot blame him," Bà Nội said. "He saw what it was doing to your Ông Nội. He warned us about the blindness. It runs in the family for the thầy bói, if they live long enough. Your dad thought he could find another way."

Away from me. She didn't have to say it aloud, but he was escaping me. I had placed this burden on them for centuries.

"I'm going to protect you," I said. "Both of you."

But she didn't look comforted. Only sad. Like she was finally accepting this reality. This destiny.

"Sometimes," Bà Nội said, "I would get irritated when he'd tell me the future. How I shouldn't bother with some things because he knew the outcome. Like when your dad left and I kept trying to call him, write to him, to get him to come back. Ông Nội would spoil my dreams with the truth. I would get so mad. What was wrong with hope? With trying? But now . . . I have never wanted to know the future more."

I wondered briefly if it would be a merciful act to erase today's memory from her. My powers could lift that nightmare from my grandmother's thoughts so she could sleep, and breathe, and be happy. But I quickly dismissed the idea and felt terrible for considering it.

Bà Nội's eyes had grown heavy. When she went up again to check on Ông Nội and didn't come down after a few minutes, I realized she must have fallen asleep next to him.

29

HERO

What took you so long?

My eyes opened. I was in another dream. Huong had transported us back to Vietnam.

"I'm tired," I said groggily, looking around. We stood in a stream. Above us was a shaded, misty forest, surrounded by blue-gray rocks and waterfalls. "Couldn't this have waited until tomorrow?"

Nope. Trust me, you want to know this.

I pulled at the heavy royal armor lying against my skin and squinted at the sky. *Where are we now?*

"It's an important memory," Huong said excitedly, taking my hand to lead me along the stream, catching me up as we walked. *I've been waiting.*

She shared her last few hours with me. After dropping KT off at home, Huong drove through San Jose looking for other signs of the Han. She'd found another element fragment on a walking trail near the Hayward fault line, which had unlocked new memories, bringing her back to this moment.

"Is this about Quentin?" I asked as we crossed over a bed of wet rocks. It still amazed me that he'd been lurking around us all this time. I thought he was a creep, but I didn't realize he was the original creep.

"No," she said. "But I learned why he targeted KT."

A low moaning caught my attention. Realizing what it was, I sucked in a breath. I broke into a run across the stream as it grew louder inside my ears. Huong ran swiftly behind me.

We sloshed through the stream, climbing over wet, mossy rocks until we saw her in the distance. She was crumpled between two boulders, her helmet half-off. The armor revealed her as a high-ranking general in our army. Ma Yuan stood over her, holding a spear. The warrior looked unafraid, staring at him in stunned reverence, a funnel of black and red smoke rising above her mouth.

"Get away from her!" Huong yelled, breaking the divine spell.

Ma Yuan and the soldier startled, the smoke funnel lifting above their heads. Ma Yuan stabbed the spear into the warrior's abdomen. The soldier screamed in agony.

Huong and I flew through the air. We landed next to the warrior, and the black-and-red funnel exploded, Ma Yuan's smoke surrounding and blinding us.

Instinctively, my sister and I raised our hands, expelling our own golden and purple smoke. The plumes burst through the sky, blanketing the area.

As the clouds thinned, I sank to my knees to peer into the general's face. Huong cradled the soldier in her arms, the spear still inside the warrior's stomach.

The cheeks were chubbier, her chin and forehead smeared with dirt, but her identity was undeniable. I looked over at Huong for confirmation.

KT.

This is why this general's face looked so familiar to me. KT—or Le Chan, as she was known in this realm—fighting alongside us as my sister's most reckless general, who threw herself on the front lines, always to be rescued by my sister.

I wrapped my hands around the spear and smoothly pulled it from Le Chan's stomach. Reaching into the satchel by my hip, I found our mother's herbal elixir. I gently applied the ointment over the wound, but the blood continued to seep out, down her armor and into my hands. Huong held Le Chan from behind, whispering into her ear, her white eyes unable to disguise her despair.

You should do it, Huong thought, giving me permission. I nodded, and placed my muddy, bloody hands over the wound. The energy built through my fingers, traveling into Le Chan's abdomen. The ground around us lit up, sprouting mustard flowers, the air brightening again with golden dust. I plucked one of the flowers next to me, bestowing my powers into it. I slipped the glowing flower inside Le Chan's lips. When she tried to resist, her tongue pushing the bitter flower out between her teeth, my fingers forced the healing elements back in. Within a few seconds, Le Chan's eyes opened, flashing a glittering white before returning to brown. I gently removed my fingers from her mouth. The gash on her stomach vanished, along with the blood. Her skin sparkled with vitality. Le Chan smiled up at us, still disoriented, before closing her eyes again.

Huong's eyes met mine as the world dimmed, and I knew the dream was ending. It was too soon. I wanted to stay, to speak to Le Chan and learn more.

Back in my bedroom in San Jose, I sat up, panting with excitement.

The earth power from earlier today felt like nothing compared to this discovery, which was far better than striking earthquakes, pouring down monsoons, or firing up hurricanes. While many of our powers disrupted or destroyed, this one resurrected and healed. It made sense: If we could manipulate people's thoughts and erase their memories, why couldn't we influence their bodies? We could restore life, especially to those who had sacrificed in our war with our brothers. We could help all of our soldiers.

The northern lights outside my bedroom window painted the sky a velvety purple. Hours had passed since the earthquake in San Jose.

You here? Huong asked through our thoughts.

Yes.

Call me. I'm low on power.

"This is amazing," I said after she answered her phone. "Did you know KT was a reincarnation of Le Chan?"

"No," she said. "The elements you gifted her must have gathered here, just like ours did."

"And Quentin, too? Is everyone at our school reincarnated from ancient Vietnam?"

"They must have followed us here. They sensed us. Humans can have reincarnated souls. They just can't remember their pasts like gods can."

I opened the mythology book, turning the pages until I found my brothers' faces looming among the Han, KT's face alongside us in battle. There was even an illustration of Ma Yuan ambushing Le Chan near the waterfall, right before we rescued her.

"It's all here," I said.

"Always a step behind us," Huong said, shaking her head. "Too bad it can't tell us memories before we remember them."

"How could we not recognize our brother?" I asked, frowning at the sneer of Ma Yuan's penciled face on the page.

"Quentin disguised himself pretty well," Huong admitted. "He is fully reincarnated, so at his fullest strength, he can hide from us. KT fell for him hard, the poor idiot. This is the problem with human teenagers. All those hormones."

"But why even bother hiding?" I asked. The memory of Quentin speeding down the streets of San Jose, trying to scare us, seemed juvenile and pointless compared to the destruction he and our brothers had wrought in our history. "Why not attack when he found us?"

"He realized we weren't fully reincarnated. Why attack now when he can steal all of our elements later?"

"But he can't just take our elements away. We have to gift them."

"He could torture us. Or trick us. Why do you think he was manipulating KT?"

I recalled how Huong had to restrain KT from falling into

the crevasse. But what if she was trying to keep KT from jumping in?

Le Chan's noble, kind face was so different from KT's puckered sneer, yet they were the same spirit. "Why does KT hate me? I saved her life in Vietnam."

"Oh, she doesn't hate you. She's just a bitch. Only immortals remember their past lives. She only has enough elements to remember the life she's living. Any more than that can be dangerous for a human." She shook her head. "Maybe any amount is."

This time, I was the one who fell silent, confused by what she meant. "You don't think I should have saved Le Chan's life?"

"Once we started healing our generals and soldiers, we became vulnerable," Huong said. "The more we treated, the weaker we became. It's why we lost the war."

"We lost because we were outnumbered," I said, "and too many of our soldiers died. I don't think we should regret saving our friends who pledged their loyalty to us."

"Why didn't you tell me about your grandfather?" Huong asked.

My heartbeat fluttered. "I told you he was a thầy bói."

"But you didn't tell me he was *the* thầy bói. There are phony psychics all over town, but your Ông Nội is part of us."

"I wanted to understand all of this first," I said. "I wanted to protect him."

Huong pouted. "It's happening again."

"What?"

"Your attachment to these mortals. Your thầy bói. Even our

soldiers. Giving them our elements cost us the war, our country, our spirits. You put their needs over ours."

It was an accusation, but she said the words so gently.

"Why do we have to choose?" I asked.

"Reclaiming our kingdom is our destiny. Look what has happened to this world since we left. We came back here to correct history. Our days of hiding are over."

30

SIGHT

Huong tried to lure me out the next morning, but I wanted to stay home with my grandparents.

"You cannot just sit at home with them all day," she said.

"We were attacked yesterday," I said. "Ông Nội is blind. I can't leave them alone."

"Then I'll come to you. We'll figure out a way to protect them. We're almost there, Jolie. We have three of the four elements under our control. Now, all we need is air."

"So I can fly," I said.

I could sense Huong's smile over the phone. "You want to, don't you?"

I did. To fly again, to really fly. The powers I had now only allowed me to float in the air for a few minutes. But to take a nice long flight, unencumbered, unburdened . . . Even in our last dream, when flying toward Le Chan to save her from Ma Yuan, my body surged with bliss during those brief seconds in the air.

Ông Nội sat in the backyard for fresh air while Bà Nội

prepared breakfast. I pulled up a patio chair next to him. She'd placed a pair of her oversized sunglasses over his white eyes.

"Do you remember what happened yesterday?" I asked.

He nodded slowly. "Only parts of it."

"Did the Han take away your eyesight?"

"No," he said, "Thầy bói must sacrifice their human vision in order to make room for divine sight. It was bad timing."

"I'm sorry," I said.

"I'm not," he said, tilting his face toward the sun. "There is much more to see this way. The elements are everywhere, Jolie, more than I ever imagined."

"But you can't see Bà Nội anymore," I said.

"I see her mortal spirit," he said. "It may not be as bright as yours, but I'd recognize her anywhere. I've been with her most of my life. Losing human eyesight cannot take her away from me."

"What do you see when you look at me?"

I couldn't see much of his face behind those huge sunglasses, but I could sense he was assessing me.

"Your elements are radiant and yellow like the sun, incomplete," he said. "When you reincarnate, you will shine so bright, even I will have difficulty looking at you."

I frowned at that lonely prospect.

"But you don't need to ask me," he continued. "You can use your own divine eyes to see what I see."

"I don't really like it," I admitted. When I'd first discovered the ability with Huong, it had seemed so cool. But seeing through those alarming white eyes grew overwhelming: the magnitude of colors, the vastness of the elements. The visions would stay with me long after I shifted back into human eyes. Same with the mind-reading. Aside from chatting with Huong, I'd grown reluctant to listen in on other people's thoughts, the noise feeling like it was polluting my brain.

He tilted his face toward me. "You are afraid because you still think you're human instead of a god. This frustrates your sister."

I smiled wanly. "I didn't ask for a reading."

"Free for family. You should not fear who you are. But you and your sister still have much to resolve before that happens."

"I can't if I still don't have my memories back. It's easier for Huong. She has way more elements than me."

"She seeks them out. She wants them. Your elements can sense your reluctance. They know you are not ready. Your sister is not always right, but regarding this, she is."

"It's nice to know I'm disappointing in both of my lifetimes."

"Stop feeling sorry for yourself and pay attention. Why are you here with me now? You should also be out looking for the rest of your elements. Not home babysitting us."

I looked back to see if breakfast was ready. The lecture was growing tedious. "What if my brothers come back?"

"Their attack yesterday almost worked because you were not prepared. Now you know. You have the power to protect our home without being here."

"How?"

He turned away from me to face the garden. I waited, a little annoyed at his distraction. Then my eyes turned to what he was looking at: the garden beds looked overgrown with mustard flowers, spilling across the wooden sides, popping up throughout the surrounding grass and concrete. This was odd: Bà Nội had just weeded the garden a week ago.

"Do you see them?" he asked impatiently.

I blinked several times until my pupils turned white. The mustard flowers in our backyard were glowing, glittering bright.

They were no ordinary flowers.

"You see?" he said. "You've been growing what you've needed all along."

31

FLOWERS

After the earthquake, Huong and I resolved to stay alert. We didn't want another ambush. Our brothers had possibly been watching us for weeks as we wasted our time and energy performing silly pranks. We wouldn't make that mistake again.

Our imminent reincarnation would lure out our brothers, and Huong warned that we would need to battle for our elements. But aside from our confrontation at the earthquake, I'd never been in a fight in this life.

"You'll remember," Huong said as we sat next to each other, reading more of the mythology book together in her bedroom. She smiled and then lunged for my throat with both hands.

Without thinking, I sprang back and released a rush of wind from my mouth, throwing Huong off the bed and back against the wall. She crumpled into a heap, leaving a large crack trailing up the wall.

I stared in horror as she shakily brought herself back to her feet.

"I'm so sorry," I said, putting my hand over my mouth.

"Don't be," she said, looking at me with admiration. "You just proved me right."

The mythology book confirmed Ông Nội's revelation about the flowers. A new chapter revealed how the Trung sisters harnessed their elements to guard their troops. During the war, they camped in a valley of yellow and purple blossoms infused with their powers, so at night, the flowers protected them while they slept. The enemy couldn't cross through these flowers without alerting them. When I shared the information with Huong, she suggested we recreate these protections for our houses here.

We started at Huong's house, waiting until after sunset so the neighbors wouldn't notice. The purple cherry blossoms in Huong's front yard appeared in perpetual bloom, another marvel in winter, even in northern California. The blooms never fell to the ground like other flowers. I touched a petal with my finger, but it stayed firm on the stem, glimmering in the moonlight.

Huong raised her hands, waiting for her palms to generate sparks. She gathered her air and earth elements together, swirling them toward the sky and settling them over the entire structure.

Within seconds, the dirt beneath our feet began to tremble and sputter as the elements activated the soil. The vines from the purple cherry blossoms vibrated as they grew, climbing toward the house, up the walls, spreading across the sides and roof, careful to avoid windows and doors. The black vines looked menacing, as though threatening to swallow up the house, until the buds burst open, transforming Huong's cream-colored house into a botanical oasis of lush purple and violet blooms.

Humans could pass through without seeing or feeling anything. It would only stop our brothers—temporarily—and give us enough time to return.

Despite Huong's success with her own house, Bà Nội was doubtful of my skills.

"What if you get hurt?" Bà Nội asked me over dinner. "What if you lose too much of your own power trying to protect us?"

"It will return to me," I assured her. "And Huong is here to protect us."

"Jolie knows she is making this choice," Ông Nội said.

After dinner, they waved to us from inside the house while Huong and I stood in the driveway. Everyone waited for me to begin.

"Don't overthink," Huong said, her arms crossed. "You visualize what you want, and the elements will sense your intention."

I closed my eyes, raising my hands like she had. I sought out and found my air and earth elements and gifted their release. That was the easy part.

"Ow," I muttered.

"Keep going," Huong urged. "Full intent."

The way they drained from my hands, sparking into the air, was a pain unlike anything I had felt before. Huong had barely flinched when she did it. The heat quickly burned through my body like a lit fuse. The pain grew until all I could see were white and gold specks flashing in front of my eyes.

When I blinked again, I was sprawled on the sidewalk in front of my house. Huong lay next to me on her side.

"Did it work?" I whispered.

She pushed her hands on the concrete to sit up, and I turned my head. My eyes settled on the abundant veil of yellow and violet blossoms blooming around my grandparents' house. Layers and layers of fragrant, delicate flowers.

"You passed out near the end, so I finished the flowers with my elements," she said. "How do you feel?"

"Like I just set myself on fire," I said, trying to sit up, too, and immediately feeling dizzy. "Why didn't you pass out?"

"It's going to take time," she said, her hands smoothing my disheveled hair. "But you're getting stronger."

"You keep saying that," I said.

"Because it's true. Once we reincarnate, we can finally go home."

I looked back at my house: the only home I'd known for sixteen years, up until a few weeks ago. Bà Nội was probably expecting us to come in soon. I sensed my grandparents inside, safe and cozy, waiting for me.

"What if this is our home?" I asked. "What if we were meant to stay here?"

Huong pursed her lips, like my questions were distasteful. "That isn't the prophecy."

She was always saying that, like she knew what it actually was. She sounded so confident. But beyond overthrowing our brothers and reclaiming our thrones, she lacked crucial details. Because she didn't know either.

"How are you sure?" I asked. "There's a reason we lived among humans as the Trung sisters. We've found good things in this life."

"But they're temporary," Huong said. "They cannot stay with us."

"What is your favorite thing?" I persisted. "What will you remember?"

She looked at me for a moment, then rolled her eyes and considered. "Besides you?"

"Yes, besides finding me."

Her face looked thoughtful, relaxed, for the first time in a while. "I don't think I've ever seen another a creature, human or immortal, like Harsha. He's the closest this world has come to perfection. His face, his entire being, is beyond comparison."

She sounded so unlike herself. Earnestness looked oddly attractive on her. I could have said something funny or snarky, but I didn't. Instead I watched her face, the contentment and sweetness that felt so rare these days, and I wished for it to last.

32

PRESENT

Over the next few weeks, we continued searching for air. I tried to project more confidence and queenliness, and while this made school easier (my grades had never been better; my classmates no longer hassled me; in fact, they seemed overly friendly, even afraid of me), it didn't convince any more air elements to emerge.

As we ventured around San Jose, Huong taught me how to drive, which was much easier to master than my powers. I surprised myself with how quickly I picked it up. Within a few days, I could merge smoothly onto the freeways at rush hour, weaving between lanes to pass the slower cars. Huong was happy to hand over driving to me. The sky smoldered a myriad of rusty colors during our sunset drives. Sometimes when I glanced in the rearview mirror, I thought I spotted a trail of black smoke behind us, but when Huong looked out her window to check, she never saw anything.

Huong spent more time at my house, having dinners with me and my grandparents and occasionally spending the night on the weekends. We'd either read from the mythology book or do homework together. My grandparents gladly welcomed Huong. She was always a gracious guest, offering to help with cleaning up and guiding Ông Nội around the house.

The anticipation of our reincarnation felt like finals week, but much, much worse. It was hard to concentrate on anything else. Every morning, I awoke with a start, imagining, hoping, but also fearing feeling something new. At school, Huong acted uninterested in almost everyone else, only paying attention and responding to things I said. Harsha and KT didn't seem to notice, still distracted by Quentin's unexplained absence. Students had gone missing from our school before, but never two at the same time. Quentin's disappearance overshadowed Daphne's in conversations, mostly because his oblivious mortal parents had posted a $20,000 cash reward for any information that could lead to finding him. If only we could tell them that he didn't want to be found.

It's better people forget Quentin altogether, Huong shared in our thoughts one day at lunch, after we'd heard another announcement reminding us to report any clues on Daphne's and Quentin's whereabouts. At the other side of the table, KT and Harsha were judging Milo and Basil in a belching contest.

KT loves him, I reminded her, *and he's Harsha's best friend.*

They'll get over it, Huong thought. *Humans always do. That's one of their few advantages.*

Resilience?

No. That they can forget things. Her words sounded bitter inside my head. *Their lives are free of burden.*

Not for my grandfather.

"You should have thought about that before you created him." Huong chose to say that out loud.

I looked at her face to see if she was serious. She was.

"I didn't create him," I whispered, discreetly checking to see if anyone at our table had heard us. They hadn't, still engrossed in their own discussion.

"Yes, you did," she hissed back. "You changed him and his descendants, and now it's something we'll always have to deal with."

"I gave him a gift," I said. "We are meant to share our powers."

"Who said? Our parents? Great advice. And where are they now?"

I glared at her. "Why are you in such a bad mood today?"

"Because I'm the only one taking this seriously. This world went to shit while we were gone."

"You said we didn't have a choice but to leave."

"All of our choices, right and wrong, led us here. You messed up, and I'm tired of pretending you didn't. Nothing we give humans will change their mortality. Have you ever considered that humans aren't capable of handling our power?"

Huong stood and stomped out of the cafeteria. KT hesitated for a moment, then followed her, calling out for her to slow down. Milo and Basil had wandered away from the table, too, leaving only me and Harsha.

Harsha put down his burrito and turned in my direction. "Is Huong mad at me?"

"What did you do?" I asked, half-serious, half-avoiding.

"Nothing," he said. "When she wants space, I give it to her. When she wants me around, I'm there. Lately, she barely notices me. Unless it's to tell me to shut up or to get her something."

"I wouldn't take it personally," I said, slowly unwrapping my bánh bao.

"It's hard not to," he said, fiddling unhappily with his water bottle. "Maybe we need a break."

I looked up at him in alarm. "Are you serious?"

He nodded without meeting my gaze.

I peered around to check if anyone heard him, if this was a prank. Did he think I wasn't going to tell her what he said? "Why are you telling me?" I asked.

"I don't know," he said, pausing, like he was reflecting at that moment. "You're her favorite, at least right now, until she gets bored with you, too."

I sighed. He wasn't wrong. Huong was a notoriously inconsistent love-bomber; nothing felt better than when she lavished all her attention on you. Like all of your problems and concerns mattered, and she wanted to solve them with you. But when she pulled away and moved on, the loss felt disorienting. Maybe this was Huong's way of preparing for our reincarnation, when we'd have to leave this realm. How she could deal with hard goodbyes.

I didn't want to have deal with them either.

"You should talk to her," I suggested.

"I'm not even sure she cares," he said. "So why should I?" He looked more irritated than sad, and I wondered if maybe that was better.

Someone from another table called out to me. Isabelle Gomez from my chemistry class asked me about a lab that was due next period. Then she asked where I got my skirt. I continued the chat, grateful for the distraction. It was happening more often—kids who normally never spoke to me reaching out, smiling, wanting to talk to me, texting me to hang out, wanting to be my friend. Classmates smiled at my jokes, complimented my clothes (mostly Huong's), asked and listened for my opinion.

Huong's popularity had rubbed off on me. If she found me worthy, so did the rest of the school. Despite knowing this, it still felt good, like a warm blanket after months of feeling cold. I'd catch my reflection in a window or mirror and startle at what I saw: my better posture, my smoother and sleeker hair, my smile. This was what happiness looked like on me.

A few minutes later, Huong and KT returned to the table, their faces pinched with annoyance. KT gestured not-so-discreetly to the back corner. "Your ex-friend keeps staring over here," she declared.

I turned. Lana sat by herself, absorbed in her phone. A few months ago, that was me.

"She's not anymore," I said.

"I can feel her thinking about us," Huong said, glaring in her direction.

At that moment, a breeze wafted in from the open cafeteria doors, a funnel of wind and leaves hurtling from the courtyard. Student conversations quieted as more kids watched the wind twirl down the aisle, growing in speed, straight to Lana's table.

As Lana glanced up, the wind lifted her tray and swiftly over-turned her vitamin water and applesauce into her lap.

A stunned pause, then snickers, until more students gave each other permission to laugh. At our table, KT howled, pulling out her phone to document the moment, along with a bunch of other kids. Harsha's friends Milo and Basil were also leering, while Harsha stared at Huong uncertainly.

Had he realized what happened? Or was he just disappointed in her reaction?

Lana pulled the soggy food and napkin off her lap and set them back on the tray. As the laughter continued, she gathered her backpack and fled the cafeteria. Her long hair hid most of her face during her frantic exit, but her thoughts lingered behind. *I wish I could disappear. I wish I could disappear, too.*

I looked over at Huong, who snuggled shoulder to shoulder with KT as they grinned into her phone, looking at the shots she'd just captured.

Why did you do that? I asked Huong.

She didn't even look my way as she and KT snickered and swiped the screen together. But Huong's response spoke clearly in my head.

Why did you let me?

33

SANTA CRUZ

Over the next few weeks, our dreams moved away from memories and into premonitions of an impending disaster. One night, wildfires burned up the mountains. The next night, an earthquake decimated the Bay Area.

On the third night, a tornado spun and spun our houses in the air before dropping them by the sea cliff in Santa Cruz—the same place where we reunited as sisters. When I stepped out of the house, I saw Daphne standing at the edge of the cliff, the ocean waves roaring behind her. She was dressed in our troop's armor and looked terrified. Her skin glowed as bright as the sun. As I walked toward her, she began mouthing words to me.

Where are you? I asked. *How can I find you?*

She mouthed her words even faster, her face stretching with panic.

Daphne! I tried again. *Where are you?*

Her eyes glazed over white as the sky around us darkened. Another set of white eyes appeared behind her, then another, then three more sets, multiplying throughout the air, as plentiful as constellations in the night sky. Flames erupted from Daphne's body. Her hands and feet disintegrated, turning into violet and yellow ash, the fire consuming the rest of her body, until the last thing I saw were her ice-white eyes.

I woke up shaking and looked over at my phone. Four missed calls from Huong. When I called her back, Huong confirmed she'd had the same dream, too. I checked the mythology book for anything new. There were additional blank pages at the end but nothing printed. Our reincarnation, and the battle it would bring, felt imminent. Huong was convinced the final element fragments were reuniting and we had to be there to meet them before our brothers found them first.

"We need to go to Santa Cruz," Huong said. "Like, now." She had it all figured out: Harsha and his friends were already planning to ditch school that morning to hang out at his family's beach house. They'd keep him occupied while she and I snuck off to finish our reincarnation.

"I have a chemistry quiz," I said.

"Who cares?" Huong asked. "That quiz doesn't matter. This *life* doesn't matter. Only our prophecy."

"I studied hard for it," I said. "Let me have one last day."

"What about Daphne?" Huong reminded me. "You saw her in the dream."

"She's safe," I said. "I can feel it." It was true. My elements, whenever they sought her out, assured me of her distance and safety.

"We can wait a few more hours," Huong said. "But you're delaying the inevitable."

It wasn't about the quiz. I needed time and space to think,

especially away from her. Huong's attention, while often flattering, could also feel suffocating. So much was happening. So much would change, and soon. Maybe I was clinging to petty human worries. They still felt real and manageable, unlike our dreams.

At school, Lana looked miserable. She was wearing the same Vaquero hoodie and sweatpants I suspected she'd worn the day before. Several nights that week, my phone had buzzed with calls from an anonymous number, but they left no voicemails. The one time I picked up, I sensed Lana's panicked thoughts in the silence. She wanted to talk to me about Daphne's disappearance but was too afraid.

I was tempted to say something, to assure her that Daphne was alive, but there wasn't anything I could say that wouldn't create more problems.

At the end of World History, I approached her desk.

"How are you?" I asked.

She glanced at me uncertainly. "Okay," Lana said. "Not okay."

"It makes sense," I said. "She's your best friend."

"She was yours, too," Lana reminded me. "You should care, too."

"I do," I said.

"You haven't been at any of the search parties or vigils Daphne's family has organized."

I had heard about them. The local news programs and newspapers were covering them, too. "I didn't think I'd be welcome," I said.

"This is about Daphne's life, not your hurt feelings." She looked disgusted—an expression that had become painfully familiar to me. "You've changed. New clothes, new friends, even the way you talk. I don't even recognize you anymore."

A wave of self-consciousness washed over me. "If I try to talk to you, I'm desperate. If I ignore you, I'm selfish. If you don't recognize me, it's because you haven't talked to me for over a year."

The classroom had emptied out. It was just us. She lingered. I fought the urge to read her thoughts, too frightened to know the truth she couldn't speak.

"It wasn't supposed to last this long," Lana said. "Things just got so weird with you after the swim meet. Every time we thought about trying to talk to you again, something strange would happen. Like the night before Daphne disappeared. After you texted us."

The powers inside me stirred curiously. "What happened?" I asked.

"Remember that earthquake in Berkeley the night she disappeared? Daphne and I started feeling it hours before anyone else. But my parents didn't feel anything, even when I stood right next to them. Daphne's, too. We checked the news and the seismic monitors online. We thought we were imagining it, even as we went to bed. But no one talked about the earthquake until the next day. By then, Daphne was gone."

Memories of that night crept through my thoughts, the dread gathering inside me. "Did you . . . did you dream about anything that night?" I asked hesitantly.

Her eyes brightened instantly. "Why?"

"I don't know," I said, suddenly regretting it, picking up my backpack and moving toward the door. "It's nothing—"

"Wait—" she said, trying to follow me. "Jolie!"

I rushed off, turning a corner and slipping into a group of students in the hallway.

Huong had arranged for Harsha to drive me out to Santa Cruz after school, since he had to stay for an econ test. She'd ridden ahead with KT that morning.

While Harsha drove me home so I could change clothes, I caught my reflection in the side-view mirror and blinked at myself. The shiny, sleek hair, the eyeliner and lip gloss, Huong's clothes. I had changed. I looked like my sister.

Lana was right. Not just about my appearance. How much had I really tried with Daphne? Wasn't I really only worried about myself and Huong and our reincarnations? I could have easily talked to Lana or Daphne's family to put together the clues.

My brothers had been circling Lana and Daphne for weeks, possibly even months. Was it to threaten me? I tried to recall the dream again: the egg, the girls laughing at me, my fiery response. I didn't remember seeing or sensing Ma Yuan or the others anywhere. Ông Nội said I'd hidden Daphne for her own protection, but where?

I had to get to Santa Cruz. Once I fully reincarnated and we completed the prophecy, the gaps in my memory would close. And this nightmare and uncertainty could finally end.

34

TRUST

Harsha waited in the car while I ran into my house to drop off my backpack and change outfits. I tried my best to keep up a casual, cheerful face, but Bà Nội didn't need any elements to see right through me. I wasn't sure why I felt the need to change clothes. How does one dress for a divine reincarnation?

"When will I see you again?" she asked.

"I'm not sure," I said, pulling on jeans and my dad's old Berkeley hoodie. I hadn't worn my own clothes in weeks, and they felt soft and comforting. "I'll try to let you know."

"Do you promise?" she asked.

I couldn't lie to her.

"I can't," I said, "I'm sorry." I turned around. She looked tiny and frail sitting on the bed. "The house is safe. You and Ông Nội should stay inside for as long as you can, okay?"

"You're coming back," she said.

"Yes," I said, zipping up my backpack and slinging it over my shoulder. "I won't stop trying."

When I ran downstairs, I found Ông Nội standing in the living room.

"You don't have to worry about us," he said. "It's time to fulfill your prophecy."

"I don't feel ready," I admitted. "Can you see what will happen?"

"Some," he said, after a long pause.

"But you won't tell me," I said.

"You know what to do," he said. "The guardian dragons chose you above the rest of them for a reason."

"But I don't have all my memories back."

Ông Nội shook his head. "And you may never get them back. That is a risk you took when you left this world the first time. Memories shouldn't tell you what to do. Sometimes they prevent you from doing what you need. You should only trust yourself."

"I will. I'll be back."

"Yes, I know," he said, his eyes full of sadness. "This isn't the last time we will be together."

35

THE PARTY

By the time we arrived at Harsha's beach house, the driveway was already full, and a line of cars was parked alongside the road. I frowned at the random kids wandering up to the house, the music we could already hear from the car.

"Did you know you were hosting a party?" I asked.

Harsha didn't reply as he handed me two grocery bags from the trunk. He'd been silent for most of the car ride, radio music filling the hour-long drive while I tried to memorize the trees and landscapes around me, wondering if this was the last time I'd see them in this life.

"Well, I'm glad the two of you worked it out," I said.

"What are you talking about?"

"You said you wanted to take a break," I reminded him.

"No, I didn't," he said, holding a bag of ice in one hand, a confused frown on his face. "Did Huong say something?"

I searched the thoughts behind his increasingly suspicious face. He genuinely did not know what I was talking about, like our lunchtime conversation from a few weeks ago had never happened.

"My bad, I got confused," I said, disguising my concern with a dopey smile. "Sorry."

We carried the extra snacks and ice bags to the house. After dropping off the groceries in the crowded kitchen, I navigated through the throngs of people, looking for Huong. Every room spilled over with kids. I finally found her and KT playing a video game with Milo and Basil.

At the sight of me, Huong dropped her game controller, walked over, and dragged me upstairs to the second-floor balcony outside of Harsha's bedroom. Beyond the pool and the wrought-iron fence surrounding Harsha's family's property, the coastal preserve jutted into the ocean. It felt like years, not just a few weeks, since Huong and I had discovered we were sisters. But maybe time had always done that, shrinking, expanding, until you could no longer tell the difference.

"Why did you invite all these people?" I asked as soon as Huong slid the balcony door closed.

"I didn't." She explained that when she and KT arrived that morning, Milo and Basil were already here. One of them sent out a group text about the party that was forwarded to most of the junior class.

"It's not a big deal," she said. "They're not going to get in our way."

We watched from the balcony as two girls puked into the pool while another one live-streamed it on her phone.

"I'm not sure Harsha appreciated it," I said, then looked carefully at her. I told her about our weird conversation outside the car. "What did you do to him?"

"Oh, it's not a big deal," she said, waving her hand. "He got huffy and insecure that I was ignoring him, so I fixed it. Now he's happy again. We're leaving soon anyway. This way, he only has good memories of us."

"Who else have you done that to?" I asked warily.

Huong shrugged, seeming annoyed that I wouldn't let it go. "Nobody. And they're my elements, okay?"

Of course if I'd ever suggested doing anything like that, she would have scolded me for wasting my powers.

"Anyway, we needed his house," she said, looking up at the colorful sky.

"But not all these people. I don't understand why you're friends with them." But even as I said that, I realized I did. Of course Huong surrounded herself with the most powerful, influential kids. She admired their meanness, which she mistook for strength, and had promoted the most ruthless soldiers to command positions in our army. Like KT.

Huong shot me a look of annoyance. "I guess we're both bad at picking allies. But it won't matter soon."

The marine layer was growing wider and thicker across the horizon. The sunset looked even more vibrant tonight, shining through the pastel ribbons of rolling fog.

The balcony trembled, and I put a hand on the railing to steady myself. No one else at the party seemed to notice except for me and Huong. Maybe they assumed it was just the bass from the music. My sister and I knew better.

"They're becoming more frequent," Huong said with satisfaction. "It's like the earth is cracking open for us."

I looked up at the cloudy sky. "Maybe our elements are returning to us in the rain."

She smiled and nodded toward the ocean. "Or a tsunami."

I frowned, imagining our classmates washing away—if our brothers didn't wipe them out first. "That would put everyone here in danger."

"We'll be here to protect them." She watched me step back from the balcony, my arms crossing over my stomach. "What is it?"

"I feel ill," I said.

"No, you don't." She set her cup on the balcony. "You feel great. I know because I do."

She leaned backward over the balcony rail, tilting her face to the moon, like she was going to backflip over, while I leaned my shoulders against the glass door. Her hips swung to the bass of the music.

"This is what we've been waiting for," she said. "All this time waiting around in these pitiful human bodies. Our patience finally rewarded. Tonight, our spirits will complete, and all of our powers will return. We will fulfill our destiny."

"And we'll find Daphne," I reminded her.

Huong shrugged her shoulders. "That, too."

"I'm serious. Her family is suffering. She is suffering. They don't deserve this."

"Fine. If we can reincarnate our immortal spirits and defeat our brothers, then, yes, finding that little mortal should be easy."

"And we're supposed to do this in front of a hundred teenagers?" I asked.

"They probably won't even notice."

"You think they're that stupid?"

"Teenagers are the most ideal humans to manipulate," she said, leaning back to drape her arm over the handrail. "Their bodies are growing fast and strong—the best they'll probably ever be—but their minds, oh, their minds are still so soft. You can pour anything into them. They are the perfect soldiers."

"That also makes them impulsive and dangerous," I said.

"Not if you control them," Huong said. "They're not going to remember any of this anyway. They just need to stay out of our way."

She swung her legs over the balcony, placing one bare foot, then the other, against the side of the house. I looked around nervously as her hands released the railing. Slowly, she levitated. Once she landed atop the roof, her hands drifted to her sides for balance, a smug expression on her face.

"Stop showing off," I hissed, my body tensing as each step along the tiles crackled under her feet.

"This is the best view of these humans: us up high, them down low," she said, peering over to give me a reassuring smile. "They can't hide from us here."

I flinched, and she noticed it.

"You still think they're our equals," Huong observed. "Even after all that has happened. Why? We created this world. These humans you worry about are insignificant. We are divine."

"Just come down," I said, my eyes flickering down to my sneakers, both securely planted on the balcony behind the handrail, then looking back up to make sure she was still there.

The ocean breeze swept through, lifting our hair, tickling goose bumps along my arms. "Someone will see you."

"Tell me that we're more important," she said as she traveled farther away from me, striding across the rooftop tiles like they were solid ground, her hands now on her hips, her eyes still surveying the crowd.

"What if I don't?"

She looked up suddenly, her eyes flashing white for a moment, her face dark with rage. The recognition startled me. Trac's face.

"Why do you always take their side?" she barked.

My heart pounded and my mind whirred, trying to come up with the right words to calm her. This wasn't the time or place to fight. "I'm not. I just don't think they're the enemy."

Huong smiled, almost in relief, dampening that brief spark of temper. "But you're always protecting them, when they took this world away from us."

"They didn't."

"Yes, they did. After we gave them everything. Mortals use up this world, and then they die. But not us. Never us."

An ocean breeze filtered by. Fog gathered along the navy-blue sky, the band of stars growing clearer. It no longer looked white but iridescent, revealing a new shade of the rainbow with every blink. She was still so bitter about our final battle, blaming humans instead of ourselves. They had nothing to do with our power struggle. Yet she chose to blame them. And me.

"It belongs to all of us," I said. "We're supposed to protect this world, including everyone and everything in it."

"And what if they get in the way?"

Huong was so good at sweet-talking people into believing her: her boyfriend, her best friend, the students at our school. But on this, I'd never change my mind.

"I'm not going to fight them, Huong," I said.

Something in her posture shifted. I could feel her pulling away, leaving a cool emptiness between us.

"That's your choice, Nhi," she said, sighing. "It's always been your choice. We'll have to see what happens."

It was high tide, but we couldn't hear it over the music. I held my breath at the memory of standing over that cliff, our toes scraping along the crumbly edge.

When Harsha came into the bedroom, calling out for Huong, she tiptoed back to the balcony. I left them, my stomach feeling queasy. Something was wrong. I slowly tracked a loop through the kitchen, dining room, and multiple living rooms.

In the family room, Milo and Basil continued to massacre each other's avatars on the television screen, and they now had an audience of girls cooing at every explosion. They hollered at me to come watch, but I ignored them. Outside by the pool, kids hovered in tight circles.

When I walked through the living room, I recognized the source of my nausea. I sensed her the second she snuck inside the house. After setting my empty drink on a windowsill, I made my way through the party, my breathing measured, and darted upstairs to one of the open bedrooms. I didn't even have to look back to know Lana had followed me.

"What are you doing here?" I asked after closing the door behind us.

"Why did you ask me about my dream?" Lana asked. She wore a marigold-colored puffy vest, her face flush from the heat in the house.

"Did anyone see you?"

"I remembered," she said, her eyes wild and alert. "What you did to us."

My thoughts flashed back to the dream: the egg, the girls laughing at me, my fiery response. The bedside light flickered for a few seconds, but Lana's eyes remained focused on me.

"You should go," I said.

"You had the same dream, didn't you?" Lana asked. "Is this like what happened at the swim meet? You said something was inside me. I never forgot that. Jolie, what is it?"

"I was having a psychotic episode," I said. "I wanted to cut you open, remember?"

"Daphne has been missing for almost a month," she said. "What did you see? Why were you watching her locker that day?"

"I wasn't," I lied. "Sophomores shouldn't be here. You weren't invited."

"Jolie, please," she said, stepping closer to me. "I'm here and I want to listen to you. I will believe you."

I retreated toward the room's balcony and opened the sliding glass doors. This one was smaller than the balcony in Harsha's room and had a low stone ledge around it, so a person could easily pitch over and fall two floors onto the concrete below. I turned to face Lana and sat on the ledge.

I knew she wouldn't follow me. Lana was afraid of heights—

couldn't even hike up a trail with any significant elevation. She had to sit with one of the chaperones at the trailhead during our sixth-grade hike on Mount Tam.

But she did. With one hand clinging to the patio door, she stepped out on the balcony, her other hand reaching out to me. I responded by swinging one leg over the ledge.

"You don't have to be scared," she said. "Even . . . if you had something to do with it, just tell me where she is. I promise I won't tell anyone."

I couldn't believe it. "You think . . . I took her?"

The music pounded into our ears and veins. Hadn't we heard this song a few minutes ago? Or were they all blending together now, an unending loop of noise? I swallowed the saliva in the back of my throat. The sky spun around us. My grip slipped and I started to fall back.

"Jolie!" Lana cried, catching my hands.

Our touch felt electric; my body grew warm and calm all at once. I looked into Lana's face, her hands still on me, noticing the faint golden glitter behind her skin. My body relaxed in recognition.

Our eyes shifted white as my spirit stirred, the memories returning, our elements reaching for each other.

The pool. The swim meet. What I had done, what she had done beneath the water was finally clear. Lana had been wrong. So had I. Now I knew what really happened.

36

THE SWIM MEET

It was the second day of the county semifinals, and we were competing in the third heat of the morning. We'd posed for selfies in a corner of the warm-up area and finished our morning stretches. While the other girls chatted, I tried to maintain focus on the race, following my teammates to the edge of the pool, preparing for my part in the relay.

When it was my turn, I dove in. As I dolphin-kicked through the water, I saw her: Trac racing toward me—eyes grim and clear—intending for us to collide.

Our first meeting in thousands of years.

In that instant, I remembered. Our past lives. Our previous realm. What she did.

We were not happy to see each other.

I crossed into another lane, not caring if I tangled with the other competitors, but she swiftly followed. We both swam down, skirting the edges of the pool, until it suddenly gave way to the South China Sea, our first chosen home in this world.

Instinctively, our bodies reverted into our original forms, our human flesh ripping open to reveal the enormous muscular length, the rigid plates and scales of our dragon bodies. We needed to engage each other in the vessels we knew best. Trac immediately turned her sharp fangs to clamp her jaw onto my tail. Her spiky arms reached for my body to flip me under her, but I wriggled out of her grip, hissing my own fire to throw her off. She somersaulted away, then circled around to face me.

We panted at each other, little bursts of steam between us.

It's been a long time, sister, she said, her white eyes full of pride. *I've missed you. Care to introduce me to your new friends?*

We watched as the girls swam above us. I pulled up to her, face-to-face, our flames flicking at each other. *Leave them alone.*

Her long purple tongue darted a few times. *Nhi. You know better than to attach yourself to mere mortals. It always breaks your heart. What happens when they find out who you truly are?*

This is who I am now.

You think you can deny who you are, little sister? We are not meant to cower. We are dragons. We are meant to rule this world together.

I don't want to be like you.

Even in dragon form, with fangs and fire, I could read the hurt on her face. It hid behind the eyes, in the way their light dimmed. *Then renounce your elements if you have no use for them. If you don't, these humans you've grown so fond of, I'll burn them to ashes right here.*

You don't have the power.

Are you sure? I'm not the one who's been asleep for two thousand years.

Without further words, we charged at each other.

The water flashed violet and yellow with our struggle. Our battle, as vicious as it was—tearing into each other's skin, smoke and fire clouding our eyes and our lungs—also felt like a reunion. We hadn't fought in centuries. My sister, who'd seen, experienced, lost, and achieved everything by my side—I clung to her, even as she tried to destroy me.

I pinned her head between my arms, my tail wrapped around her torso. I could feel her heartbeat slow and squeezed tighter, despite the gnashing of her fangs into my skin. This was it. I could end it here, demand her surrender, and she'd be no more. I'd be free of her. I'd be alone.

My arms relented, just a little, perhaps from mercy or from cowardice. No matter. It was enough that her tail thrashed back to wrap around my throat. I choked and gagged as she roared fire into my face, and then she threw me across the ocean floor.

We retreated, staring at each other, snarling with uncertainty.

She was the only one to speak afterward: *I'll be back, little sister. I promise. Run back to your human life. See what's left. I'll return for you soon.*

Meanwhile, above us in the water, the humans continued their race—they couldn't detect the spaces between realms, couldn't witness our battle. From their viewpoint, they could only see my human body floundering at the bottom of the pool.

When I didn't come back to the surface, Lana dove in after me. As her hands wrapped around me, my divine elements transferred to her, and when Daphne helped pull me out, some transferred to her, too. Now that my sister had rediscovered me in this world, I knew my friends would need protection. So I gave them the most precious protection I could.

Lying on the concrete poolside, I could not see my teammates or my coaches' faces. I could not see my weeping Bà Nội. When Lana knelt beside me, trying to hold my hand, I pushed her away roughly, only seeing my sister's dragon face.

"Get away from me! She's going to destroy me! She's going to burn you all! We need to hide now! Why don't you see it? It's inside of her!"

The screams echoed throughout my head. I lunged and clawed at Lana as two assistant coaches held me down. I'd seen myself in that viral video, but now, experiencing it through this memory fragment, I finally understood. Once again, I had thought that giving away the strongest part of my spirit would protect the people around me. I hadn't realized how it could harm me.

37

THE POWER OF AIR

After experiencing the memory, Lana's entire body began shaking, her eyes filling with tears. We sat on the floor of the balcony, the party below us, but that didn't matter anymore.

"You felt that?" she asked. "That was real, right?"

I couldn't answer right away. My sister. She was not my ally. She was not my queen. She was my traitor, my enemy.

I could finally recognize Huong's manipulations this past year. The ambush at the meet was only the beginning. Huong was also responsible for kicking off my confusion, grief, and forgetfulness that destroyed my friendships and reputation.

When we started our freshman year, Lana and Daphne had already begun pulling away from me. Huong had enrolled at West as a transfer student from Vietnam, establishing her influence and popularity while keeping a close watch over all of us. She was the one who planted the Loser Lam posts and videos about me on Schoolbook. She haunted Ông Nội's dreams, unable to leech his divine elements, but successful in confusing and disorienting him so we'd all think he was crazy.

She was the dragon flying over our house who stalked us at the Vietnamese seafood restaurant, forcing both of my grandparents into solitude at home.

When Huong had determined I was sufficiently isolated and vulnerable, she'd arranged to enroll in the same gym class as us and conveniently crash into Lana in the pool so I could save her. When she revived the bullying posts shortly after and offered to help me delete them, she had identified the IP address as belonging to Lana. She'd rescued me from the social hell she'd put me in so I would be grateful for her kindness and never notice she'd been responsible for all of it.

She was patient, methodical, and thorough in her battle plan. It would be impressive if it wasn't so revolting.

"That bitch," I said, shaking with fury. "That monster."

"You were telling the truth," Lana said, her eyes wide and clear with understanding. "I didn't believe you."

But I'd already moved on to another, more disturbing realization. When Huong had said the reincarnation was arriving tonight, I'd assumed she was speaking of the unaccounted element fragments we'd been randomly finding these past few months.

But none of them had been random.

A chill coiled down my spine. "This is a trap," I whispered.

Right as I said that, the bedroom door slammed shut. Our heads turned. Huong walked toward us, KT behind her, and stopped between the balcony doors. The sky was a dark, heavy velvet, except for the half-moon. A misty haze rose from the heated swimming pool.

"Jolie?" Huong asked.

"I'm fine," I said, fighting to swallow back my anger, pretending to still be dumb and clueless. "Lana was just leaving."

They hovered in the doorway, like predators cornering their prey. My hand reached for something behind me and found only the ledge.

Huong smiled faintly, serenely, deceptive as ever. The same face that masterfully navigated through negotiations, threats, and ultimatums of war. But now I could see her malevolent glow, her sinister eyes that I mistook for cleverness. I had been so stupid.

"So soon?" Huong exclaimed, stepping onto the tiny balcony. My eyes scanned for an escape route. "It's just starting to get fun."

Someone had cranked up the music, straining the surround-sound speakers wired throughout the house and the backyard. I grasped for the powers within me, calculating if they were enough to allow us to escape.

"I just came to ask about Daphne," Lana said, her voice shaking.

Huong and KT stepped forward again, forcing Lana to fumble back and bump against the balcony ledge.

"Let her leave, Huong," I said.

"Why would I do that?" Huong said. "You're the one who insisted she be involved. So now she is."

The noise and music around us drained away. Lana frowned while KT smirked behind Huong's shoulder. I inhaled quickly, trying to control my rage. Between Huong and KT, I had no chance. They'd easily overwhelm me.

"I had this big speech planned," Huong said, "in case you weren't smart enough to figure it out. Your memory has been missing for . . . for . . . ever."

"No need," I said, moving quickly to shield Lana. "I'm done listening to you."

KT tackled me, shoving me to the balcony floor. My head cracked against the stone ledge. When I turned and looked up, Huong had already grabbed Lana by the throat, sweeping her up. They lifted off the balcony, hovering in the air.

I stared after them. Huong continued to choke Lana with one hand, their skin twinkling bright against the night sky. Lana's eyes glowed white as she struggled in the air, her arms and legs flailing.

"Give up now," KT whispered fiercely in my ear, her grip around my shoulders tightening. "You won't win here." Her eyes had also turned white, revealing the spirit of Le Chan, the loyal general to my sister, Trac.

I looked at her, stunned, suddenly feeling very stupid. KT remembered me. She always had. Huong had lied about mortals not remembering their past lives. The divine elements that brought KT to this realm must have also carried these memories across lifetimes.

Screams and hollers rose from below. The kids at the party looked up at Huong and Lana, their faces stunned and smartphones raised, recording. Harsha, Milo, and Basil had rushed into the bedroom and stared at us in shock.

I smiled into KT/Le Chan's grim face. She was wrong. Her words felt sad and weak and futile, a fog of distraction. We both knew I could win. That was why she'd been such a bitch, spent so much time trying to make me feel bad about myself.

The more I remembered, the more powerful I became, and this frightened both her and my sister. In touching me, Lana had restored my power of air.

My final power.

I closed my eyes, stretching time so everything quieted and calmed beneath us. Only Huong and I continued at our godly speed. KT still held me down, but her grasp softened, her body succumbing to the slowing of time. Her miniscule amount of elements were no match, and I cast her off smoothly and jumped to my feet.

Huong looked down at me, smiling gleefully, her grip on Lana tightening.

I couldn't believe it at first, she told me. *You chose to hide your remaining elements in these . . . teenagers? The cockroaches who rejected you? Maybe secretly brilliant. How could you defile your own elements in these creatures?*

I sent a gust of wind around Huong and Lana, trying to pull them both back to the balcony, but Huong easily deflected with her own air. My feet lifted from the balcony, the air pulling me up.

I shot up, the wind flowing through my hair, soaring along my body. Huong responded swiftly, elevating higher into the sky but remaining close enough to taunt me. Lana clung to her side. The violet dust glimmered as Huong climbed higher into the clouds.

Those elements are mine, I told her as I chased them through a cluster of clouds.

They're Lana's to gift now, not yours. Anyway, I just wanted you to see me take them from you. How does it feel to watch a part of you get stolen away?

My elements will never be yours.

We'll see, little sister.

Lana had gone limp in her arms, possibly from the elevation of our flight, but it was frightening to see how lifeless she looked in my sister's grip, her skin engulfed in Huong's violet dust. Huong continued to gleefully race through the sky.

You've proven your point, I said, struggling to sound calm. *Let her go.*

Sister, I'm the stronger one, so you listen to me. A true queen does not wait. She takes. She determines her own prophecy. Watch me.

The sky burst into purple-tinged flames. The heat pushed me away and I somersaulted back several times in the air. I strained to regain control, still spinning, unsure what was up or down in the thick haze.

When I finally righted myself, I was alone, choking on smoke, our mental connection severed. Huong had vanished. I flew desperately around the sky, following a violet trail of smoke, only to find myself circling in chaotic loops. I flew and flew, searching. But it was dark and all I could see were the stars around me, the wind roaring in my ears.

My body felt raw and cold in the ocean air, but I didn't give up. After a few more circles between Harsha's house and the sea cliff, I spotted it: Huong's portal, a silvery, dusty oval emitting a dull, steady glow on the horizon. With my remaining strength, I soared toward the portal, trying to rush through before it closed. As I entered, I felt my body warm, then grow raging hot, sparks flashing in front of my eyes, around my limbs, burning as I passed between realms.

38

PRIME ELEMENTS

That little liar. That backstabbing, treacherous, lying liar.

The poems, songs, and stories about our deaths were wrong. What my sister had told me was wrong. It wasn't a sacrifice or suicide. It was a betrayal.

I knew the truth about the final battle with the Han. And what really happened in my first and only battle with my sister.

THE TRUTH OF THE PRIME ELEMENTS

The war with our brothers had ravaged our land. Our desire to win had driven us all to amass more power than we ever had before, sucking every element from the world in order to fight each other. The world suffered from our greed. Humans and animals starved. Our soldiers died. Our land, once plentiful with natural resources, burned with the scars of our battles and neglect.

I begged my sister to surrender, but she refused. I knew our brothers wouldn't either. So I secretly began to infuse elements into our people, into the land and creatures, in the hope that they could survive and fight back for themselves.

But my elements were not enough. I needed to weaken my siblings.

In the valley between the mountains and the ocean, our armies met again for the final time. Our soldiers were outnumbered and demoralized. Han reinforcements poured in from the mountainside, but Trac gave specific orders to not retreat for any reason.

I had other ideas. During the battle, I jumped on my horse and pretended to chase after several Han soldiers. At a juncture around a mountain bend, I led my horse uphill through the forest and climbed toward the sea. We slogged through mud and grass, slowly at times, but I was determined to stay ahead of my sister.

Trac followed me to the sea cliff. I pointed the fairy sword at her face and warned her to go back to our soldiers. Unafraid, she dismounted from her horse and turned to me, her face flushed with fury.

"You are a traitor!" she screamed as she stomped toward me. "A coward!"

She pulled me from my horse and tackled me to the ground, throwing our weapons aside, our fairy and dragon blades clattering in the dirt. She wanted to hurt me but with her bare hands, without weapons getting in the way of her satisfaction. We wrestled and rolled close to the edge of the cliff, leaving streaks of our blood across the earth, trails of our struggle that would stain and crack the world.

In the past I'd give in to her, my love for my sister, my only partner in this world, reasserting itself. Not this time. With every punch she threw at me, I struck back harder. Using my remaining strength, I hurled us over the cliff, our bodies tearing at one another, until the wind intervened and wrenched us apart.

This was our legendary death, the jump that had never been a jump. It was a push. From me.

The fall into the water felt as shocking as crashing into hard earth. Our growls and screams submerged. We sank our nails into each other's skin, extracting blood, roaring fire, which quickly turned into steam. The water was a bright, cloudy scarlet as we descended deeper into the ocean. I blinked through the water and found Trac's scarlet-rimmed eyes staring up at me.

We should be dying, I thought with a surprising calm. We were still fighting each other, struggling for dominance. But we couldn't die. We would do this forever.

Sometime during our battle, the ocean waves threw us back onto a beach, and we wrestled on the rough sand, the ash thick on our faces and bodies. "Let go of me," *I gasped as her hands wrapped around my throat. I twisted my neck, but all I could see around me was fire and smoke.*

I don't want to fight anymore, *I said through our thoughts.*

You were going to betray me, *she replied with her mind, her hands tightening around my neck, the frown on her face deepening.* Betray our soldiers and abandon me. What kind of queen are you?

I struggled to speak. "I'm trying to save us."

"How? By surrendering and giving our enemies all the power?"

We can end all of this. *My hands settled over hers, trying to calm her, as I shared my discovery through our thoughts.*

One day during a battle, after getting tossed into a ravine by my horse, I noticed the tiniest, faintest glimmers lingering in the air, stirring my feet so I could stand. These glimmers felt familiar, and I soon realized why. They were the prime elements, the original elements our guardian parents gifted us, that we hid and protected for thousands of years.

When we surrendered the prime elements, we assumed we'd never find them again. But here they were when I needed them most.

They surrounded me, swirling around my body in joyful reunion. It was like our parents had never left—they'd only transformed. Their spirits infused our world, in particles so miniscule that no creature, not even their divine children, would notice. This was their legacy: sacrificing their vessels to become part of the world.

It was also our prophecy to do the same, but we'd chosen not to listen. We'd grown scared and selfish. Our powers had become too familiar, too seductive. How could we be expected to give them up? Who else on earth deserved these elements more than us?

What probably frightened us even more than the loss of powers was the loss of our existence as we knew it. What would it mean to not live as a dragon or human or any other creature? To truly return to the origins of this world? Could we think anymore? Would we remember any of this? Why did we have to sacrifice ourselves? Why did the humans get to stay?

The greatest trick the gods ever pulled off was convincing the humans that they were ordinary. That they were not deserving. But our parents had known better.

To be true queens of this world, to protect and preserve its future, we had to sacrifice ourselves for it.

My spirit absorbed the prime elements, our parents' memories returning to me slowly but surely, offering me their wisdom, their experience, and their responsibility. The power to release ourselves to this world was our destiny. Any god could do it. We were supposed to. We could return to the divine dust we began as, what our parents became. We would liberate ourselves from these vessels, explode and scatter our elements across the world. It would take centuries to find our way back to each other, if we ever did.

Instead of being filled with wonder at this revelation, my sister glared at me.

"You rat. When did you find them? Why didn't you tell me sooner? And why didn't they return to me?"

Why didn't they? These were good questions. "It only recently happened. I wasn't sure what the prime elements meant until now."

It wasn't a total lie. But it wasn't the total truth. Perhaps my sister could sense this because she still regarded me suspiciously. "The prime elements cannot remain within human bodies. That's why we gave them up to become human."

"I don't know why I can hold them. Maybe because the prime elements know it's only temporary and I'll release them."

"Then give some to me. Half of those are mine."

"They're not for us. I'm going to give them back to the world."

"Are you crazy? You receive the greatest elements, more powerful than anything our brothers and I have, and you want to give them up?"

"We were never meant to keep them."

"You want to sacrifice yourself like our parents did," she seethed. "Abandon the world. That is your brilliant plan?"

I was determined not to let her sway me. "You know we can't win this war."

The look on her exhausted face told me she agreed, but her fingers remained locked around my throat.

"We reinfuse the land," I said. "The prime elements together with our divine elements will protect our people."

"We could do that anyway, if we possessed the prime elements," she said. "We can return to our dragon forms—"

"No," I said. "This world cannot survive us as gods. Not as dragons or as queens. This is the only way."

Her grip loosened slightly.

"I saw it, Trac. This is our parents' prophecy. We do it together."

Her grip relaxed, our arms softening around each other as she read my thoughts, tried to understand how sacrificing ourselves could bring peace. We rolled onto our backs to stare at the sky.

We hadn't lain next to each other so peacefully like that for a long time.

"Aren't you scared?" she asked.

I reached over for her hand. "Not with you here." I turned my attention to the clouds, still red and black from our brothers' destruction.

"I gift my elements to this world," I said.

After a few moments, I heard her voice—faint, soft.

"I gift my elements to this world."

Once our intentions to dissolve became clear, our gifts declared, our powers stirred, the transformation commenced. It started with our shoulders and backs melting, the elements oozing into the soil. Our thighs and arms collapsed through the earth, our skin and hair growing transparent. It was working. My mind calmed.

During a slow blink, I spotted a twinkle in the sky. Through the smoke, a bright scarlet V formation appeared in the corner of my vision.

Our brothers. They'd found us. Timing was crucial, but if we stayed still, our elements could scatter before the Han touched ground. There'd be nothing left for them to take.

"Don't move. They're coming."

Those words. My eyes lit up in shock. The dream I'd shared with Huong back in her room in San Jose. She hadn't said them. I had. But my sister was squirming, refusing to lie still.

"Please don't move," I said again.

She'd already jumped up, turning to me, her body taking shape and color again, her human vessel rebuilding itself, eyes dark with guilt.

She rescinded her gift, reversing her intentions.

As my vessel continued to deteriorate, the elements flew away from my dissolving body, searching for their intended home. But before the earth could absorb them, my siblings surrounded me, trapping the elements for themselves. I watched helplessly as my orphaned yellow dust surged into my brothers' greedy mouths and seeped into their skin. My brothers stood over me, pushing and shoving at each other, trying to angle for the most exposure, growing stronger and larger as the dust swirled frantically around them.

But that wasn't what broke my heart. No, that privilege belonged to my sister, my dear queen, who stood among them, fighting and shoving her way to the front to devour the most from me. Even as she flourished with my stolen elements, she paused long enough to look at me with pity.

"I'm sorry," she said as I slowly lost consciousness. "I'm sorry. But I can't let you do this to us."

Sensing danger, some of my elements attempted to flee. They soared as far as they could across the earth, the preservation instinct strong. It would take centuries for them to come out of hiding, to rebuild our spirit. To reincarnate me.

I hadn't betrayed her. She had betrayed me. In that moment, when she should have chosen sacrifice, she instead joined our brothers against me. My vision dimmed, my sister kneeling over what was left of my face. Was she experiencing regret? It was too late to stop it now as shards of my spirit continued to disintegrate.

With the precious remains of our mental connection, I shared with her one final parting thought.

I will return.

She and my siblings wouldn't know how, but this was far from over. They called me little sister, smallest goddess, lost queen. But they underestimated me.

39

VIETNAM

I awoke, blinking through a metallic fog. I struggled to sit up, alarmed that I was off my feet. The back of my head throbbed, pressure pounded in my ears. My arms and legs felt heavy. I drew in a breath, my heart quickening. The clouds must have parted to allow sun, because the fog thinned. I recognized the muddy water, mossy rocks, waist-high elephant grass, and soft, tanned earth.

I was in Vietnam. It was the day of our last battle. Trac had created a portal back to our final day together. Everything Ông Nội had said about regaining my memories now made sense. I couldn't truly understand until my memories returned. There was no way his words or the mythology book could ever explain all this to me, and all I would have to do.

With Lana's element fragments, my spirit was approaching complete reincarnation. I only needed a few missing pieces— and I could feel them out in the realms, aware of me, wanting to return. Memories of my life as Nhi had been restored, but I still felt fuzzy, my spirit settling back into this realm.

I wore heavy armor with the engraving of our army's crest, a fairy and a dragon. Behind my back, the weight of my sword, the fairy, lay along my spine. At my right shoulder was my bow and a quiver full of arrows.

I stood in a meadow of glowing mustard flowers—the same ones from my home, the same ones I'd eaten in Bà Nội's garden. With every step, flowers bloomed in my path and the grass and soil around my feet lit up with gold dust. As did the mountains, the trees, the animals, the insects, even the dew on the smallest branches and leaves. My elements were infused in the land, every piece of it illuminated with the golden dust I'd only seen glimpses of before. It was like walking through a cloud of wondrous, glittering light.

A horse neighed through the mist. The twinkling dust vanished in a cloud of fog. My body filled with anticipation. And rage.

"Huong!" I screamed, relieved to hear my hoarse yet familiar voice. My cold breath plumed in the air. "Trac!"

She'd been pretending the whole time, acting like she was waiting to reincarnate alongside me, when she'd had her powers all along and was spying on me, manipulating me. I'd given up, just as she'd done centuries ago.

I had to focus. New time, new location. Above me, between two mist-covered limestone mountains, a slate-gray sky growled with thunder. Somewhere in the distance a waterfall roared, hidden behind a blanket of fog.

Horse hooves clomped toward me, closer, louder, closer.

The collision was sudden, but not painful. Oddly, the contact felt reassuring, solid and sharp, the crunching of metal against my face and chest. My body bounced back into the soft grass. I heard a low, deep whinny and blinked my eyes, focusing on the muddy, restless forelegs of a horse. Above the horse, a dark shadow hovered over me.

"Bubbles," Ma Yuan sighed. "Welcome back."

My spirit recoiled in disgust at his stupid nickname. The shadow shifted as it came closer, revealing a Han warrior in full bronze armor and mandarin red garments. His coat of arms boasted an ornate engraved dragon. Behind the scarred cheeks and scruffy beard, his eyes glittered with Quentin's mischief.

"How did you find me?" I asked.

He smiled, his thoughts providing me his answer. Those two idiot boys playing their video games were no simple mortals. They were my immortal idiot brothers Liang Song and Geng Shu.

"Milo and Basil?" I cried in disbelief. Their sleepy eyes, their slack-jawed expressions. I realized they were around, always around. How easy it was for them to pose as a couple of teenage dirtbags. "Did they need to be so obnoxious?"

"I think you mean popular. It doesn't matter the era. Kids are drawn to power. That will never change."

I reached back for my fairy sword and pointed it at his face. He looked unimpressed.

"I'm not here to fight you," he said. "And you should be happy I found you before our dear sister did."

I stood to face him. "She can't surprise me anymore."

"Always thinking about her," Ma Yuan said. "Your biggest flaw of many, little sister. It's what slows you down. Now, if you were a little more selfish, focused on your own needs, maybe you'd find success."

"So I should just attack you now?" I asked, stepping toward him, thrusting the fairy in his face.

"Oh, no need to do that yet," Ma Yuan said, slowly dismounting, holding his hands up, and walking away from his horse and weapons. "You may have your memories back, but you've been out of action for two thousand years. Except for what that Jolie experienced, and that is, what, barely sixteen years? Don't you want to learn what you've missed?"

"I'm supposed to believe anything you say?" I asked.

"How did trusting Trac work out for you?" he asked.

"More reason not to listen to you," I said.

He slowly circled me, leaving plenty of space as he rustled through the grass, touching the boulders and trees around us as if checking for stray elements. But they remained loyal to me, silently humming around Ma Yuan like a warning. I realized he couldn't hurt me. In our territory, the elements infusing our land wouldn't let him. All he could do was talk.

"I will admit," he said, "I've missed you. Sure, we've had fun running around this world, causing all sorts of trouble, but you provided a balance. A little bit of mercy and restraint. The yin to our yang. But it was your choice to destroy yourself. Do you realize now how stupid that was? You gave up your powers and memories for centuries. And for what?"

"You can't understand," I said. "It requires traits you lack."

"Oh, you can have your virtue and compassion. Your great plan to destroy the gods and put us out of work failed. You wanted to make the world boring. You destroyed yourself and wasted your powers."

It was hard to remember if Ma Yuan had always been this immature, or if too much of Quentin had rubbed off on him.

"They don't belong to us," I said.

"Then why do we do so well with them?" he asked. "You've studied world history. You've seen what we've done."

"What, cause chaos?" I asked. "And war, destruction, starvation, suffering?"

"I know," he said, unable to hide the smug glee. "We exceeded my expectations."

I felt a nudge at my mind and looked up at the sly smile on his face. Begrudgingly, I allowed his thoughts into mine, so he could share his memories.

After my destruction, our sister had disappeared. Ma Yuan didn't care—as long as Trac stayed out of their way. Along with our brothers Geng Shu and Liang Song, Ma Yuan continued to play in Asia. Happy to realize that humans would pillage and murder with only the slightest prodding, our brothers eagerly exploited the human frailties, nurtured jealousies and resentments, and ripped apart truces and alliances, kickstarting the period of Five Dynasties and Ten Kingdoms. They whispered into feuding warlords' ears, feeding their egos and stoking their bloodthirst as imperial states struggled for dominance.

"It was some of our finest work," Ma Yuan said fondly, looking almost sentimental. "The land was so clean and pure, a blank canvas for bloodshed and annihilation."

The land and sea wars in Asia entertained them for centuries, and they heard news of our other siblings wreaking havoc in Europe, Africa, and the Americas. They reveled in the world wars, in how easily they could manipulate humans into giving up their peace. The Vietnam War eventually led to their reunion with Trac.

"She was still trying to keep invaders out of that tiny little sliver of land you both loved so much," Ma Yuan said. "She even convinced us to help get the Americans out. So it is crazy that, of all places, you turn up in her former enemy's territory."

"Why did you come to America?"

"For you, of course! When word got out that your spirit was reincarnating, of course we wanted to welcome you back. You, little sister, contain some of the best elements a god could ever want. We got a little taste, and we'd love some more."

He meant it. Ma Yuan gazed at me hungrily, like even being near my powers stoked his appetite. At the same time, I could detect my former elements in him, how they yearned to return to me but couldn't. This was why it was so easy for my siblings to find me. They all had a little of me in them.

"America is not such a bad destination, I suppose," he said. "That land is also drenched in genocide and hostile takeovers."

"So you all were just waiting around until I reincarnated," I said. "What makes you think you can just take my elements?"

"You didn't want them before," Ma Yuan said. "I bet you wouldn't even know what to do with them. It would be a waste."

"I think you underestimate me."

"Do I? Let's look at your history. How easy it was for dear sister to fool you into thinking you were worthless. Jolie went from being an elite swimmer with friends and a life to a loser nobody. Now, tell me: Do all teenagers succumb so easily to shame? She knocked you down, rebuilt you, and regained your loyalty. Like it or not, little sister, she beat you. Again."

"Not yet," I said.

"She will. So far, you've done terribly in this human lifetime, just like your first one. And as you can see, in this world, we've been doing fine without you."

I stared at him in disbelief. "This world is a mess."

"You think you could do better?"

So that was his offer. My eyes narrowed in disgust.

"You want to double-cross her," I said. "Didn't you just call me a loser?"

"Trac has grown too ambitious for her own good," Ma Yuan said. "She's decided that this world needs a queen, and with your powers she thinks she can be it. Can you imagine that? A woman warrior?"

I couldn't resist my own grim smile. "I can, actually."

"But you," he continued. "There must be a reason our parents chose you. Why they decided to cut our sister out so their elements would only return to you. So why don't we see? We'll help you defeat our sister and save your little community back in California. In gratitude, you can share some of the elements our parents gave you."

His eyes glittered, unable to hide his ravenous envy of my powers, the very ones protecting me from his attack. "Sharing is caring, you know. Can you imagine what I could do with such power? You present so many possibilities."

"But I don't have them all," I said.

"They're coming," he said. "They're trying to find you."

He said it with such reverence. He was scared of me. Once they returned, I'd be more powerful than the rest of them.

My siblings, for all their macho arrogance, had weakened. After centuries of fighting and exploiting their powers, their struggles had settled into a disappointing stalemate, none of them strong enough to overtake the others.

My arrival had provided an enticing disruption. They feared what would happen once I fully reincarnated, but they couldn't resist their curiosity.

"What makes you think I'll side with you?" I asked.

"Because you're not stupid," Ma Yuan said. "You can make a smarter choice this time. Not nice, not kind, but smart. You detest war. So what? What is your alternative, besides abandoning the world?"

"Humans have come up with other options."

"But have any of them been nearly as effective? We didn't teach these mortals to fight, sister. They just needed direction. And they like it! I know because I watched it all happen. You really think you can achieve world order without fighting for it? At least we're here. At least we're doing something."

"You're saying you cared enough to stay and kill."

"These humans will never stop fighting. But if you want the wars to end, you carry the solution inside of you. I can help you. And if you want our sister out, let's take care of her together."

During his lecture, I finally oriented to being in Vietnam, my

powers of earth and air acclimating to my first realm. I remembered the location of my army's camp. I put away my sword,
and reached behind my shoulder for my bow. I loaded an arrow
and pointed it at his face.

"You're talking about world domination, not order," I said.
"No thank you."

Ma Yuan laughed. "Still so stubborn. Why don't we just let
that offer sink in? Go back to your sad army and your deranged
sister. See if you can do better. We'll talk again."

I followed him with my bow and arrow as he mounted his
horse, turned, and galloped away. But his memories and words
lingered as I walked toward my army's camp, back to my sister.

THE BIGGEST LIES ABOUT ELEMENTS

Here are the lies I believed about my elements. About me.

1. They're all the same.

The guardian dragons are made of the prime elements. Their children are made up of lesser, though still formidable, divine elements. No matter how hard they try, the divine dragons will never be as powerful as the guardian dragons.

2. Only gods have them.

This may have been true in the beginning, but not any longer. We thought they couldn't be gifted to mortals, given their delicate bodies. But the thầy bói broke this rule, and others after them.

3. Elements can be gifted to another spirit, which requires the consent of both the giver and receiver.

Not every spirit can give consent to receiving elements. The world cannot give consent, a dangerous loophole that immortals and mortals have exploited. Past catastrophes in the world demonstrate ample evidence of how consequential this vulnerability can be.

4. The guardian dragons selected two heirs to inherit the prime elements.

   No one ever said there were two.

5. We cannot control our dreams.

   Yes, we can.

6. We cannot change the past.

   Yes, we can.

40

CAMP

Eventually I found the camp—a cluster of tents, horses, and fire pits surrounded by a bamboo grove. Without stopping or addressing any of the curious soldiers who began to recognize me, I walked into the largest tent.

Our eyes met as soon as I entered her headquarters, and I felt the anger rush through my body, warming me head to toe. Trac looked like herself and not herself all at once. As Huong, she exuded sweetness—generous with her smiles and laughter— but with our true origins revealed, our pasts exposed, she reverted to her genuine scornful demeanor: her locked, defiant jaw, her imperious glare.

Two familiar people flanked her: her faithful generals, dressed in metal-plated armor and violet and gold. Their uniforms couldn't disguise their spirits. Le Chan's natural black hair was tied in a messy knot atop her head—much less severe than KT's peroxide blond hair in the other realm. Her proud chin was streaked with dirt, a thin gash of dried blood along her cheek. The other general was Phung Thi Chinh, who had disguised herself as Huong's housekeeper back in San Jose. She looked noble and calm, a chief strategist in our army.

Huong had brought back her biggest allies, taunting me by hiding them in plain sight.

"Finally," Trac said, her voice deep and sharp. "Did you get lost?" Her hair was longer, a single braid swinging down her back, and her face looked older, with creases in the forehead and around her eyes. A violet turban was wrapped around her head.

I took a step closer. "Where is she?" I could feel Lana's spirit close by.

A cruel smile bloomed on her face. "Our soldiers are dying every day in our name, and you are more concerned with some spoiled teenage American."

"She doesn't belong to you."

"Why? Because you hid your powers in her? You found the stupidest creatures in the realm to carry the world's most precious matter. You certainly fooled me."

"You fooled me, too, about everything. You said you were going to help fulfill the prophecy."

"Yes, my own. I'm still going to do that."

"Not if I stop you."

She shook her head. "I tried listening to you. I left your family alone. I helped you find your runaway elements, and you still screwed everything up."

"How? Because I didn't just hand over my elements to you? I'm glad I didn't."

"You do not deserve them."

"And neither do you," I said. "And stop taking credit for things you didn't do. My elements would have returned to me anyway. You were simply spying and leeching, just like our brothers."

She eyed me uncertainly.

"That's right," I said. "I bet you're wondering what memories I've got back."

"I don't care if you have all of them," she sneered. "Do you know where we are now? It's a pretty important chapter in our story."

I did. It was our final battle. All that talk about sisterhood and ruling as queens together—the Trung Sisters was a myth.

"This isn't what our parents wanted. This isn't why they gifted us these powers."

"They're not here to tell us what to do. I decide."

"Do you really think siding with our brothers is better?"

"It's a temporary alliance. We take care of you, then I'll take care of them."

"That didn't work out for you the first time."

I looked past her to Le Chan and Phung Thi Chinh. "What do you think Ma Yuan will do when he finally has what he wants?" I asked. "What will he need with the rest of you?"

"You never deserved to be a god," Le Chan said, taking a step toward me. "But we've proven our loyalty."

"Oh," I said, finally realizing, my gaze going between these two foolish generals. "You think my brothers and sister are going to make you immortal? Make you gods? Did they promise you some of my powers? Is that the lie they told you?"

"You don't get to talk to them that way," Trac said. "They've done more to save our country than you ever have."

"And what about the rest of our soldiers out there? You still intend for them to go out and fight for you."

"That's their destiny. Their sacrifice will unite our country."

"Because you know they would never side with Ma Yuan. You are lying to all of them."

"Do you really think they'd believe you over me?" Trac asked. She smiled insincerely. "They would all die for me. They want to do it."

She dismissed her generals with a lift of her head. They nodded obediently and departed the tent, Le Chan turning back one last time to shoot me a look of triumph.

Trac really didn't care. She had no qualms about repeating history, leading our army to guaranteed destruction for her own pride. As long as she had soldiers to sacrifice, her foolish mission could continue.

I stared at her hatefully. *What would our army think if they knew you were plotting with their enemy? That all their sacrifices and deaths were for nothing?*

She had the gall to look offended. *I am doing this for them. You're the one who abandoned them. But you can change that, right now, if you want to. Join me, and we can overpower our brothers. This is your last chance.*

I'm not joining you. Once I find Lana, I'm leaving.

Her smile faded. *Go look on the battlefield. See if you can get to her before our brothers.*

You know I'll get to her first.

We'll see. We are meant to rule this world. If you will not take the throne with me, I'll stand on it by myself.

She left, walking the long way around the tent in order not to cross me. I sat down on a stool, peeling off the weapons from my back, which had grown heavy, making sure they stayed near me in case my sister returned. When the tent flap re-opened, I assumed it was Trac again, returning to lob another snide insult. But after recognizing the person's face as she stepped toward the light, my anger melted away.

"Mother," I whispered, exhaling.

"My Nhi," she said, walking quickly toward me, pressing her damp cheek against mine. She seemed smaller and thinner than I remembered.

As we held each other, she absorbed the memories and experiences of my life as Jolie. She understood. She knew. There were many things she'd taught me. But at that moment, all I could think of was her being right there in front of me again, her face, her eyes, her arms around me. My eyes filled with tears.

"You have to leave," she said.

"I can stop her," I said. "I'm almost fully reincarnated."

"That is why I am here. You hid your elements well, Nhi, so well that even you couldn't find them."

She was right. My mother and I had prepared for this potential outcome, casting protection spells and hiding as many of my elements as possible in case my brothers won. As a farmer and healer, she had taught us how to combine the materials of this world with our immortal elements.

From under her garment, she pulled out a worn, yellowed journal of bamboo strips. Although it didn't have a red leather cover, I immediately knew what those pages contained.

"How do you have the mythology book?" I asked.

"Why do you think only one exists?"

When I placed my hand over it, the book lit up and I remembered. We'd made two of them. One for each of us.

During the final weeks of the war, my mother and I created an escape plan. At night, while Trac and her generals choreographed battle strategies against the Han, my mother and I hid in the medical tent. Everyone assumed we were grinding and mixing herbs, not realizing we were recording our histories and memories on bamboo strips, anticipating a day when my spirit could return to this world.

We imbued the bamboo strips with elements of water and fire, plus a combination of my mother's herbs to disguise their contents. If one of my siblings found them, the words would transform to what they'd like to read and believe. Afterward, my mother sent the strips with a loyal foot soldier back to our village to hide them with her relatives. The writing was then passed on through the thầy bói as a secret record, eventually bound and disguised in these books.

So the mythology book had been written by me. They were my memories and thoughts, collected and protected by the thầy bói all these years. As I turned the battered pages, I realized that those previously appearing blank when I was with Huong had materialized here, filled with texts and illustrations.

My fingers hovered above the words, trying to read quickly and deeply. Once I got into a rhythm, the words came faster, my fingers trying to keep up with the page turns. As I read, the words grew darker, the letters plumping into bold, then bleeding darker until the ink, wet and black and shiny, stuck to my finger pads, dripping down my fingers. Now that I was here to finally reabsorb them, they no longer needed to remain in the book. My body began to hum as I drank in these words, sucking in the ink through my fingers. The elements inside the ink made my blood swell and sing.

Another creation myth of Vietnam is that the land emerged from a battle between two dragons. Their intertwined bodies crashed into the South China Sea, creating Vietnam's curving, porous, mountainous S shape. The illustration of the dragon battle was nothing special: a sketch of two scaly reptilian monsters clawing and snarling at each other, a large, foreboding wave of rippling ocean water behind them. It looked very similar to Ông Nội's scribblings.

I closed my eyes as the illustration lit up inside my head, the outlines of our dragon forms animating themselves, their vibrant colors filling in, deep mauves and sharp purples and sunkissed yellows. The snarls and roars thundered in my ears, their struggle playing across my brain, their fire scorching down my muscles.

These words contained not only the strategies on how I could beat my siblings, but how I could locate the rest of my prime elements.

When the sensations passed, I opened my eyes, bright white, and turned to my mother.

"This isn't all of it," I said, sounding ravenous, incomplete.

"No," she said. "You know where the other half is."

I closed my eyes, searching for the book in the other realm. I located it next to my grandparents' bed. It was safe under Ông's protection, for now.

"You need to go back," my mother said. "You need to find the other book before she does."

"Come with me," I said. "I can take you with me and Lana."

She shook her head. "My place is here. You cannot save me. You need to stop trying to save everyone."

"I can!" I said. "Once I reincarnate, I can protect all of you."

"You don't understand. Your spirit was broken. The cracks will always remain. You will never have all your memories and powers back, not like before. It is a miracle you can reincarnate now. But you cannot risk doing that to yourself again."

The ground beneath us shook. The rumbles, the shaking of the tent, the chilling, familiar dread. The earth was cracking, crumbling. My brothers. Right on time.

Trac had brought me back to this moment to choose differently. To choose her. Our brothers had done the same thing. If I chose neither, they'd destroy me anyway.

They were all waiting for me to decide.

To leave would put all of our soldiers in danger. I remembered what I had to do here in this moment, not only for my soldiers, but for everyone. Even if my first mother was right, that I was forever broken, I still had to do something.

"I can't change the prophecy," I said.

My mother's hand tightened around my wrist. "Who says?"

"If I stay and fully reincarnate, we will only grow stronger," I said "We cannot help it. We'll overwhelm this world."

"How do you know?" she said. "You sacrificed yourself once,

and we are back here again. You thought the world couldn't survive you and your siblings. But what if it cannot survive without you?"

I didn't know. But my mother's words held possibility and hope. I wouldn't run away, but I wouldn't surrender either.

"I'll find another way," I promised.

Another tremor rolled beneath us, and we both stumbled, nearly falling to the ground. I assembled my bow and arrow and put on my sword, the long, thin fairy. The weight of the sword grounded the nervous energy in my body.

I stepped out of the tent. The ground felt soft and damp from an earlier storm, but now the sun shone brightly against a calm blue sky. Peaceful, but not for long. One of the captains had already begun drumming—awakening and alerting soldiers to prepare for battle. In the mountains, I could see the Han torches, a trail of light marching toward us.

Across the field, our troops gathered, replenishing their weapons and preparing the horses. The generals helped Trac mount her golden elephant as soldiers surrounded her, waiting for instructions. Trac addressed our troops before every battle in our royal circle. I was supposed to sit quietly by her side: supportive, silent. But instead of listening to my sister—to those words she'd said so many times that no longer inspired, that only revealed her hypocrisy and deception, her contempt for humans and everything else I loved in this world—I heard our mother. And I heard Ông Nội.

How could I find another way?

Trac preferred to stand on top of her elephant's back for her speeches as she outlined battle strategy. While she lacked the flirty sweetness of Huong, her charisma and strength commanded everyone's attention. She appeared like a good leader because she pretended so well to care.

She could have levitated, flown, or done many other things, but we tried not to overwhelm our troops with immortal actions. I walked across the field, the drumbeats vibrating through my body. My elephant recognized me, hearing my call through our thoughts, kneeling forward on his front legs, allowing me to step up. He felt soft and stable under me, prepared to follow my instructions.

He stood carefully, so I didn't falter as we rose from the ground. We walked slowly through the grass toward the royal circle. Phung Thi Chinh saw me first; her mouth dropped open, but she remained silent. Le Chan narrowed her eyes in suspicion. The troops eventually parted to allow me to enter the royal circle. I was supposed to sit, nod, listen, follow, like I had the first time.

This time, I realized, I wasn't going to do any of that.

I climbed atop my elephant, planting one foot, then the other on his stable back. I wavered only a little before finding my balance and turning to face my sister.

THE CHOICE

Standing above our soldiers, eye to eye, my sister glared at me.

What are you doing?

She couldn't say it aloud with our troops on the ground, waiting. In the distance, we heard the drumbeats and galloping horses of the Han army steadily approaching. A funnel of gray and red smoke hovered between the mountains and red tendrils of fire curled along the horizon, warning of our brothers' impending arrival. The earth rumbled with thunder, the sky brightening every few seconds with a streak of lightning.

We only had a few minutes. What could I say quickly that would convince these women to listen to me after Trac had led them for nearly three years?

"I want to thank you all for your service and loyalty," I said after clearing my throat. "You are released from your obligation. You do not owe your lives to us. You do not owe us anything."

Confused murmurs and grumbles filled the air as the troops and horses grew unsettled.

Trac's eyes narrowed. "I agree, Queen Nhi," she said loudly, turning to gaze out at the soldiers and generals. "She speaks truth. We have no obligation to each other. We choose to be here. We choose to fight together."

Soldiers cheered, raising fists and weapons into the air, while others bowed in prayer. I waited a few seconds, gathering my breath, and tried again.

"No," I said, louder this time. "That isn't what I mean. You've fought this war for far too long. It's time to return home to your families."

I'd been practicing, thinking, and believing these words for years, but I'd never had the courage to speak. They flowed easily, like a long-held exhale.

"So you want to surrender?" Le Chan asked angrily. "What about the Han? What is going to keep them from attacking our land?"

"We will protect our land," I said. "But we're not sacrificing any more of your lives to do it."

"You've saved us before," a soldier spoke up. "You can do it again."

"We can't. Not any longer. There are too many of them and too few of us."

She looked at me in disbelief. I didn't blame her or any of them. For so long, I had only served as Trac's echo, amplifying her voice, her commands. Always in agreement, I was a leader only on the battlefield. It must have been confusing to hear me speak up now.

I wanted to say more. I wanted to explain that they were

marching toward inevitable doom, that Trac, their queen, had no plans to save them or their families. But that would only cause more confusion and heartbreak. What they needed to do was run away and save themselves while they still could.

"Queen Nhi is right." A voice spoke up that usually never did. Our mother stepped forward from the crowd, looking around at the other soldiers. "I've treated your wounds. I've watched many of you die. I've witnessed our queens heal and bring you back to life. These are nothing short of miracles. But these miracles have also weakened your queens and made our army vulnerable."

"It is not your place to speak for your queens," Trac interrupted harshly.

"She is our mother," I said.

"Gods do not have mothers," Trac said, her eyes turning white.

The soldiers murmured in confusion, looking at each other.

"So the solution is to surrender?" Le Chan asked, the mockery dripping from her words. "We are minutes away from a crucial battle. If we do nothing, we will be slaughtered. As our queens, you swore to protect us."

"And we will," Trac said. "Queen Nhi may have given up, but I haven't."

Her eyes flashed white again. She wanted to strike me, do worse than that, but she couldn't, not in front of our troops.

"You cannot win this battle," I said, trying to sound strong and not desperate. But I could feel our soldiers' thoughts swaying toward Trac. "I wish you could. I wish we could fulfill every promise we have made to you. But it is time your queens finished this war without you."

We were all shouting now, out of frustration and anger but also in an attempt to make ourselves heard. The earth continued to shudder under the thunder and lightning strikes.

"We don't need to win to have peace," I said.

"She doesn't believe in us. She doesn't believe in you," Trac said, reaching for her dragon sword and raising it to the sky, her signature move before battle. "But I do. I will fight alongside you. So take up your weapons. Those of you who wish to prove your courage, come with me. It is your choice. It always has been."

Our soldiers' eyes glittered in the glow of the bright white dragon.

"Loyalists to Queen Trac, prepare for attack," Le Chan bellowed, pulling her helmet on.

Don't even try to stop us, Trac warned as our troops brushed past me and our mother to assemble at the valley. Some of the captains and soldiers shot me terrified, uncertain looks, but continued to march behind their queen.

The sky brightened with silver smoke, making it hard to see. I brought in a gust of cool wind from the ocean, trying to clear the haze for our troops, but the smoke returned once again. I did this several times, watching anxiously as my sister led our army to meet the Han.

I felt a hand on my foot and looked down at my mother.

"Leave," she said urgently, her eyes large and determined. "This is your chance."

But I couldn't help myself. My eyes returned to our troops as they marched forward into the valley to confront Ma Yuan, our other brothers, and their army. The war cries rang through the air followed by the familiar clatter of metal against metal, the whistles of launching arrows. My heart began to race as I foresaw the bodies crumpling, collapsing around the valley. Our brothers would be merciless. Without me to help, this battle would be over in minutes.

"Do not worry," my mother said. "We will find another way."

Then I saw her: Lana, trapped in the body of one of our lowest-ranking soldiers, a quiet, young officer who had never experienced battle before. She stood on the front line of our troops—bewildered, confused, pushed forward by the soldiers surrounding her.

She was going to die.

I looked around frantically for an available horse. I summoned one to gallop toward me and jumped from my elephant onto the horse as it raced into the valley.

As we hurtled through the black and red dust, I freed my fairy sword, swinging it over my head.

The bodies already littering the muddy grass slowed my horse. The valley radiated crimson flames from the arrows cast by both sides. I blinked away the tears and dust, still pushing forward to where I sensed Lana. Whenever a Han warrior came close for an attack, I easily deflected them, sending them tumbling across the smoking grass.

Suddenly my horse collapsed, struggling to settle his hind hooves. I looked down and realized the earth was crumbling beneath us, wrenching our army in half. Above us, on the fiery horizon, I spotted our three brothers, Ma Yuan, Liang Song, and Geng Shu, perched high in their war chariots, their hands raised and swaying as they orchestrated their magnificent assault.

Face-to-face, I could finally recognize my other brothers: Liang Song's clever smirk in Milo, and Geng Shu's brutality in Basil. They'd always managed to sit near me in World History, no matter what seat I chose. And I had believed they only wanted to copy my worksheet answers.

My horse neighed in agony before finally falling through the cracked earth. A thick geyser of smoke and fire erupted from the crevasse. I floated to higher ground and raised my hands, bringing down water from the clouds, smothering the fires and filling the sky with hissing steam.

Violet, yellow, orange, black, and red sparks burst in the air, exploding into billowing clouds of smoke. Ma Yuan stretched out his arms and brought down a lightning storm, demolishing trees and igniting fires in the wild grass, while Liang Song hacked away at the ground with shuddering thunderbolts.

Trac held her dragon sword to the sky and harnessed a windstorm, gathering our brothers' fire to force Ma Yuan and Liang Song back toward the crevasse.

I struggled to stand on wobbly dirt that kept crumbling, finally bringing up a wind that wiped Geng Shu off his feet. While I could hear Trac battling Ma Yuan and Liang Song, I pulled out my bow and arrow, prepared for Geng Shu to fly up and meet me again.

"I should have known," I called out. "You've always been a

shitty fighter, whether you're holding a sword or a game controller."

And you're still a scared little loser, he replied in our thoughts, *whether or not you think we're around to show you up.*

As soon as I saw his face peek out from a boulder, I lit the arrow with my fingers and sent it flying toward him.

Geng Shu responded quickly, catching the burning arrow with one hand and throwing it to the ground. I used that opportunity to unleash a gust of wind, knocking him to the ashen, smoky ground. As he fell, he threw back his own air, sending me clattering to the earth.

It was amazing to see how Ma Yuan and Trac batted you around like a toy. Just like old times. Amazing and also embarrassing.

You're still mad that our parents loved me more.

The sky had grown thick with smoke as we battled for control: I couldn't see, breathe, or hear much that wasn't right in front of me. But as the shadow of Geng Shu's sword fell across my face, I struck back with the fairy. Every time our blades clashed, they crackled and sparked, the air smoldering in yellow and red. Every collision seemed to aggravate him further, his frustrated screams growing louder, his face more incensed. I was overwhelming him, the air slowly but steadily glowing more yellow.

Look at you keeping up with me now, Geng Shu taunted. *How much longer can you really last, little one?*

For centuries, my siblings had pillaged this earth for their own selfish reasons. They didn't care about any of the creatures suffering from their carnage. They only craved power. I had destroyed my spirit trying to stop them, but that hadn't fixed anything. The world continued to rage. Did I really want to reincarnate in another two thousand years to a realm that was even worse?

It is not that bad, Ma Yuan interrupted, revealing his invasion of my thoughts. *At least we have a vision for this world. Unlike our deadbeat parents, we acted. What is it you do, little sister, besides revolt against us?*

Ma Yuan released a shower of lightning strikes. The fairy sword lit up and deflected the lightning back to him, sending him spinning and smoking through the air. He landed on the ground right next to Lana.

Trac's thoughts followed me through the field of wounded and dying soldiers from both sides. As I neared Lana, Trac announced herself not far from us, the violet air around her shielding her from the fiery arrows and lightning strikes. She raised her hands, creating a swirling wind, and Lana immediately hurtled into my sister's arms. They ascended to the clouds, Lana's legs kicking frantically.

I sprang after them, soaring through the clouds. Trac and Lana rose together, struggling in a frantic embrace. As I neared them, Trac turned toward me, breathless.

"You don't need her," I said, panting.

Trac smiled, tightening her arms around Lana's throat and chest. "And neither do you, little sister."

Although we were thousands of feet above our soldiers, my senses could feel their retreat, our mother leading them to safety. She'd done it, just like she promised. But Trac, in her selfish fury, hadn't noticed. This was my opportunity to distract. If our mother could find another way, so could I.

"If humans don't matter, then let go of this one," I said. "You're giving them all the power, when what you really want is me."

"I know they don't matter," Trac said. "She will die and turn to useless stardust, like the rest of the mortals in this world. But you are my sister. You are supposed to choose me first. Not some pathetic mortal."

Lana screamed as Trac's grip loosened, her arms and legs flailing like a rattled puppet.

"We'll trade," I proposed, trying to not to sound or feel desperate. "Lana and our mother for my elements. You will be stronger than me, Ma Yuan, or any of us. You can finally be queen."

Trac considered this for a moment, then smiled. "Interesting offer," she said, "but I want what you don't yet have."

The prime elements. In my exhaustion, she'd slipped into my thoughts as the realization arrived.

The mythology book.

The book she'd derided for weeks as inconsequential and useless.

"Oh," Trac said in understanding. "I should have known. Clever, but I guess not foolproof, right?"

Her hands flew up, releasing Lana to freefall to the earth. I immediately dove after her, but Trac's voice flooded my mind.

That is your biggest weakness, Nhi. Your need to protect your human pets scattered all over the realms. You need to choose. You have to pick favorites.

Once I caught an unconscious Lana in my arms, I quickly flipped, soaring back to the clouds, returning to my sister.

Trac, I said in my mind, still holding on to our divine connection. *Trac!*

I could feel her listening but saying nothing.

Then I sensed someone else. Two voices. Ông Nội, Bà Nội. They were screaming. Huong had traveled back to California, to my grandparents. I tried to listen and make out their words.

Then, silence.

Trac had been looking for the mythology book but found them instead.

I activated my powers, creating my own portal, carving a fiery circle in the clouds. Golden sparks surged through the air like fireworks, growing hotter and brighter as we burst through.

42

THE BEACH

When I opened my eyes, I was no longer weightless. The ground beneath me felt granular, damp. The scents of salt and cypress glided across my senses. I reached out to my sides, my fingers picking up gritty, wet sand.

I was back in Santa Cruz. Alone.

My eyes gazed into the sun, at the undulating colors of red, black, and violet. The laughter of my siblings rang in my ears.

Trac. I sought out my sister's spirit but found no response. I tried to locate my grandparents and the mythology book, and again felt nothing. She was hiding them.

And Lana. The last thing I remembered before diving through the portal was carrying her. My eyes strained to look all around me. Where was Lana?

My mind and body felt so weak. I needed more elements to return so I could recover and find them.

A shadow stepped into the bright white halo of the sun, revealing a familiar shape: big hair, thick eyebrows, that frown.

Their face came into focus. Harsha.

I sat up on both elbows, blinking, then pulled myself forward to sit upright. Harsha wore a black wetsuit, ocean waves rolling behind him. He side-eyed me like a disapproving parent.

"Have you been here all night?" he asked.

"What?" My voice felt dry and parched. Next to us, the white ocean surf rolled toward us. My hand stretched out and scraped against cool metal. I looked over. The fairy sword lay next to my hip, speckled with sand.

He knelt next to me, his eyes thin and suspicious. His thick black hair was still dry. He hadn't been in the water yet. "I thought you left with her."

"Who?" I asked, digging the sword further into the sand.

"Huong," he said impatiently. "You guys just bailed without saying goodbye. And I haven't been able to reach her for hours. Is she pissed again?"

"Probably," I said, trying to sense for her but feeling nothing.

"This is weird," Harsha said. "I had a few beers, but not that many. I don't even remember going to sleep. But I woke up this morning and the house is cleared."

I hardly cared about his problems. What I was more interested in was the glittery halo around him, which I'd never noticed before. Huong's violet elements flickered enticingly around him. So I hadn't been the only one who cared to share.

I felt bone-tired, nearly depleted of elements. But maybe I had just enough to connect with him. I reached over for his hand, which he at first resisted until our elements engaged. His body relaxed, allowing our palms to touch, our fingers to interlock.

Our spirits connected, exchanging memories. I allowed him into my experiences of the last few months and watched as a wide range of emotions spread across his usually placid face: shock, disbelief, anger, and finally understanding.

I learned about how he and Huong had first met. He'd spotted her in the hallway and followed her to English class. I saw their first date at Huong's favorite Cambodian restaurant. Their late-night texts. The first time they kissed. Witnessing these events didn't reveal why she'd chosen him, so I kept searching for a reason, because Huong rarely did anything without a purpose. The people she paid any attention to during both of our human incarnations had to prove worthy of her time.

The elements she gave him changed his life. His swim times improved and he broke the school butterfly record. He earned a starting position on the water polo team. His grades shot up and he made the principal's honor roll for the first time. He stopped arguing with his parents. Despite all these positive events, he and Huong eventually grew tired of each other, or at least reached the end of their relationship, which had already been impressively long for high school. Harsha thought Huong was always distracted, which she was. Huong seemed annoyed by most of Harsha's concerns and barely listened to him. Yet she wasn't willing to break up, always conveniently manipulating his thoughts to believe they were fine. While Huong had managed to delete most of their arguments from his memory, I could sense the lingering unhappiness. He was ready for them to be over and move on. But she was too proud to let him go.

While I could access his memories, I couldn't take his elements.

He'd need to gift their release, and if he did that, he could lose his memories of Huong. I pulled my hand away. He sat there, still savoring the last of those memories. His face looked over- whelmed after finally learning what was behind all of Huong's frustrations and silences.

"She's your sister," he finally said.

"Yes."

"And . . . you're immortal," he said. "Q, Milo. Basil? What the hell. All of you?"

I nodded.

"Why are you sharing this?" he asked.

"Because they're coming here," I said. "They're coming to re- trieve all of the elements, including the ones in you."

"They can have them! I don't want them. I don't even know what to do with them."

I suddenly remembered that back in this realm it was Thurs- day. "Why are you here? Why aren't you at school?"

"Didn't you hear about the wildfires?"

"In San Jose?"

"Not yet, but it won't be long. They're already evacuating Marin and the East Bay."

Once again, my elements reached out for my sister and my grandparents. Still nothing.

"I thought I'd take an hour and surf before the air got too smoky," Harsha said. "And I find you and these weird giant eggs on this beach—"

"What eggs?" I asked, my face whipping around, searching.

I climbed to my feet, which felt weak and shaky on the wet

sand, and squinted to look around the beach. Harsha led me, but I already knew where they were. A vision grew brighter, clearer, like connecting two puzzle pieces—my dreams and my reality—to finally create a clear image. We stopped in a rocky cove and found two cream-colored eggs the size of boulders nestled in the sand.

"I thought they were rocks at first, but then I saw the crack in that one," Harsha said.

One of the eggs wobbled. A muffled sound came from the right side.

"Shit, it definitely didn't do that before," Harsha said.

I stepped toward it, the egg nearly as large as me, and pressed my ear against the hard shell. At first it sounded like laughing, from both eggs, like in my dreams, but then I realized it wasn't laughter at all. It was screaming.

"Get back," I said, gesturing him away from not only the eggs, but me. Once the space was clear, my mouth opened and unleashed a torrent of fire through the air, burning across the surface of the eggs.

Harsha said something, but I couldn't hear him over the roar inside my ears. I aimed the fire to sweep across every surface of the eggs, until I began to see the cracks and fissures spreading along the shells. I strode toward the smoking eggs and punched my hand into the shell of the nearest one, pulling a piece of it away. My hand throbbed, but the sensation soon turned cool and soothing. I continued punching and pulling until the hole was large enough that I could wrench Lana out of the egg.

She was covered in a sticky, iridescent, buttery goo, eyes shut.

"Hold her," I instructed an astonished Harsha, and once he held her dripping, exhausted body, I walked over and did the same with the second egg, ignoring the growing cuts along my hands and forearms from scraping away the jagged shells, until I found Daphne's hands and yanked her out.

We dragged their sticky bodies to the shore, allowing the waves to wash away the glutinous yellow slime from their skin. The water around them glowed momentarily before returning to its normal blue. Lana and Daphne panted heavily, their chests bobbing up and down, their eyes still closed from the egg goo.

Harsha's eyes stretched wide, his chin quivering like he wanted to cry, but he was too stunned to ask for more details.

Lana eyes blinked open after a wave splashed her in the face. She sat up, sputtering, coughing out more goo from her lungs. Daphne followed soon after, and they squinted into the sun for several minutes, recovering.

Harsha ran back to his house to look for blankets, looking relieved to have an errand and be helpful, while I sat with the girls. They were still disoriented, like they'd stepped off the longest roller-coaster ride of their lives, not yet aware that they were sitting naked on a beach.

At least they were calm. We huddled shoulder to shoulder, leaning against each other. I buried my feet under the sand, feeling the waves lap over them, trying to determine what to do next. Daphne and Lana extended their legs into the water, too, our feet touching each other. I activated the elements between the three of us, power surging, replenishing our bodies.

As they bathed in the ocean water, rinsing off the egg goo, we shared our experiences over the last few weeks. I dug up the fairy sword from the sand and they stared at it in awe. They learned about my life as Nhi, while I absorbed details about Daphne's and Lana's abductions.

Daphne's memories confirmed my suspicions. That night during the car chase, Ma Yuan had detected the elements I'd hidden in her. He went hunting for her in her dreams, hoping to trick her into gifting her elements to him. Instead my embedded elements protected her, transporting her to the egg, hiding her from my siblings and me. The apparition I'd seen with the principal and her parents had been her spirit; she was mouthing to me warnings about Huong.

Lana's missing time, while shorter, felt more chaotic. After kidnapping her from the party, Huong had stashed Lana's spirit in the body of a low-ranking soldier in our army. She'd witnessed the battles my sister and I fought against the Han. What had been just hours in this realm was weeks in the Vietnam realm.

Daphne still looked dazed. She swallowed, her eyes closing as if burning, then looked back at us. "How long was I in there?" she asked.

"For a few weeks," I said.

"It doesn't feel like that," Daphne admitted. "It feels like time stopped in there."

"Were you scared?" I don't know why I asked. I knew the answer.

"No." She exhaled. "I felt safe. I was happy."

I understood. It was the closest a human could ever feel to returning to the womb.

"How did you know where to find us?" Lana asked, her voice cracked and dry.

"Harsha saw the eggs," I said. "And then I remembered the dream."

"So did I," Lana said, looking overwhelmed. I could feel her thoughts processing my memories: the excitement, the fear, the guilt.

"You were right to be scared of me," I admitted. "I didn't mean to pull you into all of this."

Lana reached over to touch my shoulder. "You were protecting us," she said.

"We didn't know," Daphne said.

I couldn't remember the last time they'd looked at me without disgust. And now, their faces were full of wonder. I dug my heels into the wet sand, enjoying the refreshing waves of cool water rolling along my overheated skin.

"It makes sense now," Daphne said. "The strange things that would happen when we were with you."

Lana nodded. "Remember that day we were walking back from getting ice cream? And those yellow flowers started sprouting from the cracks in the sidewalk. They were everywhere. We called it our yellow brick road. But when I tried to take my mom back later to show her, they were gone."

They recalled the strange moments from our childhood, details they noticed that I didn't. How I could sit underwater in a pool or hot tub longer than anyone else, only emerging when they dragged me up. How I never felt too hot or too cold, barely breaking a sweat on hundred-degree days in summer or running into the ice-cold waves while they shivered in hoodies on the dry sand. How I never fell or stumbled or broke a bone, no matter what I was doing. I'd climb trees and balance on fences and rooftops while they screamed for me to come down and to stop showing off.

"And I remember the fish in the pool when we were little," Lana admitted, looking ashamed. "I pretended I didn't because I was scared."

"You changed after the swim meet," Daphne said. "We didn't know how to act around you anymore."

She reached over and placed a hand on my shoulder, understanding how this connection worked. Daphne shared how I looked to them through their eyes. I used to laugh, smile, make jokes. I was assertive and determined. My sister's attack and my release of elements had transformed Jolie into a nervous, insecure ghost.

"You'd try to talk to us about it, but you just sounded crazy," Lana recalled. "So we avoided you. And when you wouldn't leave us alone, we got mean."

"Should we call you Nhi?" Lana asked. "Is that your real name?"

"I'm still Jolie," I said. "And Nhi, too, I guess. I'm both."

Daphne stared down at her hands and legs, still glistening in the sun. "How much of your elements did you give us?"

"Enough to protect you and my family," I said. "At least that was my hope. I didn't realize it would make you bait for my brothers."

We were silent for a moment, breathing all of this in, trying to make sense of it. The waves grew larger, noisier, icy white crests tumbling toward us, yet we didn't move.

"You should take them back." Lana said. "All of them, before you meet them again."

"She's right," Daphne said. "If you're ever going to have a chance against them, you need every element you can get."

"My siblings know that," I said. "They're expecting that."

My siblings were so foolish. They didn't care about world order—only power. They were willing to repeat history, destroy their legacies for my elements, even if it was temporary, even if the elements were destined to always leave them. Their greed for power overwhelmed any common sense. They'd fight anyone for it. I had to be different if I was going to defeat them. I couldn't do the same thing.

I looked at Daphne. "What happened to Ma Yuan? How did they say he died?"

"If I remember it right," Daphne said, "he died of a plague, along with most of his army. But before that, his deputies had accused him of war crimes. The emperor stripped Ma Yuan of all his titles and land. People think Ma Yuan faked his death to escape the charges."

"The deputies," I said. "Were they Geng Shu and Liang Song?"

"I think so," Daphne said.

"So they turned on each other," I said. "They're only uniting to try to get to me."

If their truce relied upon taking me out, then my siblings

would only need a sharp nudge for that union to fall apart. And I understood my siblings' vulnerability all too well.

Harsha returned with some beach towels and draped them over the girls' shoulders.

"We've got to go," he said. "They're evacuating Santa Cruz."

Our heads tilted up. The smoke from the wildfires had poured in from the east, staining the sky orange and red. A column of ash and smoke rose from the horizon. The sand rumbled beneath our feet.

They were coming.

"Jeez," Lana said. "Is this another earthquake?"

"No," I said. "That is my brothers."

There was no point in hiding. The element fragments were gathering strength and speed in their journey back to me. They would find me, as we were destined to reunite.

My siblings had timed their attack perfectly with my full reincarnation. And they expected me to give up my elements. Again. By force this time. I needed another strategy.

My eyes lingered over my former friends. Their bodies were still recovering from breaking out of the eggs, their skin twinkling with energy. Ông Nội had told me that every living creature in this world could be imbued with elements, from people to animals to plants, and even the earth and water themselves. My elements were everywhere, in everything that I cared about.

A queen is supposed to lead. A queen is supposed to protect her people. A queen is supposed to know what to do. What can a lost queen do?

The answer revealed itself simply, quickly. Words whisked softly and urgently across my mind. The idea, wild and preposterous, became clear.

It could blow up in my face again. But it could be our only chance.

"What's your plan?" Daphne asked. "How can we escape?"

"We're not going to escape them," I said. "We're going to find them first."

"Where?" Harsha asked.

I looked at all three of them, their eyes wide and naive, their skin sparkling.

"We're going back to school."

43

SCHOOL

We drove through plumes of smoke, the freeway surrounded by hills burning against a pink-streaked sky. The signs were barely legible through the haze, but Harsha followed my directions through the gloomy air.

Our drive was fast and smooth. Most of the traffic was going the opposite direction, with people fleeing the wildfires. Cars were packed with families, pets, and essentials. My fingers continued to clench and unclench around the fairy sword, which my friends eyed with wary wonder. We observed the somber, frightened faces of drivers and passengers surrounding us. Despite sealing the windows and running the air conditioning, Harsha and the girls coughed on the smoke leaking through the cracks of the SUV. I could have tried to clear our path, cleanse our air, but I knew we needed to preserve elements for the confrontation ahead.

While the radio reported evacuations in Santa Cruz County, the wildfires seemed to be cropping in every city but San Jose. It didn't make any sense until Daphne pulled up a map of the wildfires on Harsha's phone. Indeed, only San Jose remained clear of the fire threat, the calm center in a chaotic swirl. My sister and brothers had surrounded us.

We'd found some old gym clothes in Harsha's trunk. Lana and Daphne pulled on some tattered shirts and sweatpants without complaining of their smell. After parking the car, I made them put on another layer of hoodies, despite the heat.

"You need to cover up as much as possible," I said, helping to put the hood over Lana's head. She put her hands on my shoulders to stop my fussing.

"How are you feeling?" she asked nervously.

"Better," I assured her, though there were brief spells during the drive that I felt myself fading. "Imagine our relay team. You're going in first."

"And you'll finish it, right?" Daphne asked.

"Yes," I said. "I'll be right behind you."

"Let's just stay close together," Harsha said.

"Keep our connection and follow the plan," Lana said, nodding.

It was what I kept repeating on our drive, drilling it into their heads, and my own as well. I put on Harsha's swim parka, the thickest jacket I could find. With a bungee cord from the trunk, I tied the fairy sword across my back.

The faculty and student parking lots were empty as we walked onto the desolate campus. There was a faint rumble in the distance. Harsha, Lana, and Daphne gazed around the quad in both wonder and terror, taking in all the colors they could now see in the courtyard. The quad's meandering brick pathways, sprawling lawns, and camphor trees must have appeared especially vibrant and dazzling. The glass windows of the surrounding buildings sparkled in the sunlight. My friends would never look at this world the same way again.

I tripped over a loose brick on the pathway, the sword heavy against my back, and I winced. Daphne caught my arm, looking at me with concern.

"I'm okay," I promised, straightening my posture. "We're ready."

Once we stepped into the middle of the quad, we had nowhere to hide. The campus-wide intercom crackled through the air, followed by static and then the familiar bell signaling the start of announcements.

The jumbo outdoor screen flickered on, illuminated in a purple halo of my sister's elements. Huong and KT appeared, sitting behind the *Vaquero Vision* desk like it was a normal school day. We halted our steps, startled by their supersized images glowing and glaring down at us.

I scowled at my sister's enormous, scornful face. She'd transformed the giant screen into her personal portal, where she and KT could watch our impending demise like a gladiator event.

"Greetings, Vaqueros!" KT declared loudly, her voice echoing through the campus. "We're happy you could join us at school today. Even under the threat of climate change, you all want to continue pursuing your goals."

I searched Huong's face, her mind, for any regret or hesitation. It wasn't there.

"We appreciate your courage and resiliency," Huong said. "And while your goals will now burn to ash along with your feeble minds and bodies and everything else in this shit school, please know you are being kindled for a greater purpose."

"So true!" KT said. "Not every human can witness a coronation."

Your coronation includes burning down the state? I asked Huong in our minds.

She smiled down at me. They could see us through the screen. I sensed her eyes, not just two but many, as plentiful as stars, surrounding, watching us.

"Our brothers' idea," Huong said. "You know they like a show. They'll have their fun here, torturing some of your favorite humans. I'll take your elements. We all win."

You already have the mythology book, I said. *Release my grandparents.*

Huong shook her head. "The thầy bói stays with me. And your grandma, too, just because I want her. They're my insurance."

I smiled in understanding. *You're scared of me.*

Huong frowned. "You're too weak. I can barely sense your elements now."

She didn't suspect or detect because she was so absorbed in her own power. I needed to keep it that way. Huong's gaze shifted coolly past the girls to Harsha, possibly realizing only now that he was here. I held my breath, wondering if anyone else could see the hurt behind Huong's scorn.

"Why are you even here?" she asked him. "Don't you have any preservation instinct?"

"I think I trust your sister about my safety more than you," he said. "She hasn't lied to me our entire relationship."

KT smirked scornfully. "So now you two have a relationship?" Her eyes shifted darkly to me. "I knew you always wanted him for yourself."

"That's not why Harsha's here," I said.

KT laughed. "So he's going to fight? Seriously? These are the broken queen's chosen soldiers? Do you plan to hide behind them?"

"This is why you will lose again," Huong said, sighing. "How do you think this will end?"

Before I could answer, the ground rumbled, vibrating and cracking. As we stumbled backward, the earth in front of us groaned, splitting open across the courtyard, spitting bricks and dirt into the air. Clouds of dust and fire exploded from the crumbling crevasse, the blast sending us to the grass.

My shoulders throbbed from the impact, but I scrambled back to my feet, looking for my friends. Their bodies had landed safely, but their sooty faces looked stunned, disbelieving at the sight in front of us.

From the chasm, my brothers levitated to the surface, black, orange, and red smoke swirling around them. While they wore their full Han armor, their bodies were from this realm: Ma Yuan in Quentin, Liang Song in Milo, and Geng Shu in Basil. Behind them, Huong and KT watched from the TV screen, their eyes glittering with anticipation.

Go, I told the others while my eyes stayed fixed on Huong and KT. Lana, Harsha, and Daphne scattered obligingly to their designated corners of the campus. I took off, running toward the humanities wing, ignoring my brothers' laughter. They easily followed me, enjoying the leisurely speed of a human chase, their fire nipping at my sneakers. I threw open the wing's doors and hurtled down the hall, heading to where I would usually be at this time.

Ah, taking us to history class? Geng Shu asked.

The classroom doors slammed shut, and the hallway filled slowly with billowing smoke. I turned a corner to the staircase and ran up several flights until I reached the highest floor, then traveled down another maze of corridors, trying to stay ahead of the smoke my brothers blew into my path.

I stopped abruptly in front of my World History classroom, where I could see through the glass to Mr. Sheridan's maps of ancient China and Vietnam on the wall. I sensed for evidence my friends had completed their mission and were ready.

A piercing pain invaded my head, tearing down my spine, and I nearly blacked out from it. My feet slipped out from under me, my neck snapping back. I crumpled to the linoleum floor. I blinked a few times. When my vision returned, I saw my brothers floating above me. Ma Yuan had stolen my sword, and twirled the fairy in the air like a baton. My brothers' elements crawled under my skin, searing into my bones and bloodstream, sending my body into convulsions.

They scanned my body like an already conquered carcass, searching for elements to seize. My head lolled to the side, bright white sparks crowding my vision. I'd grown so used to the power the elements had afforded me that I'd forgotten, temporarily, what human pain felt like.

Aw, man. Are we too late? She's barely got anything!

Their shadows peered down at me, sniffing, their eyes white and probing, truly confused when they realized I had only a fraction of the elements they were expecting. I only had enough to keep my telepathic connection open with my friends. Nothing worth seizing at all.

Geng Shu knelt next to my head, his fingers wrapping around my throat.

Why are you so obsessed with me? I asked.

You have something we want.

But they don't want you. Why not move on?

Ma Yuan tossed the fairy against a locker, and it clattered down the hallway. *You even drained your precious sword? It's as useless as its name implies now.*

You fool, Liang Song said. *You knew we were coming and you chose to ditch your elements, leaving you defenseless. Again.*

Then why are you chasing me when you know Trac has them? I gasped as his grip tightened, pleased that the distraction was working. *Or do you take orders from her now without asking questions?*

Geng Shu pulled me up by the neck. My feet dangled above the floor for a moment before he threw me against a wall of lockers. His mouth opened, releasing wind into the hallway. I fell backward to the floor, my shoulder blades cracking against the tiles, the air dragging me up to the ceiling and throwing me down again. My body writhed and throbbed with pain, yet the memory of these sensations also felt familiar. Predictable. Even comforting. No matter how many times we beat on each other, we could never die. They tried their best to destroy me, and I would always return.

Maybe they knew this, too. Ma Yuan waited until my body stirred to speak again.

We could have taught you so much, he said, *if only you cared to understand. We made this world. We know it. But you never wanted to listen to us.*

Didn't you learn anything from last time? Liang Song asked as his heavy boot crunched into my kneecap.

I sure did, I said, even offering a smile to my long-lost brothers. *Did you?*

In response, Liang stomped harder onto my leg so I gasped, but soon I was overcome with the giggles, then outright laughter. The mustard flowers growing in the earth under the building had gathered strength, preparing to break through the floor. Geng Shu's brutality had helped them along, allowing the flowers to burst through the cracks, their petals tickling my skin. The blooms caressed my wounds, lifting me to my feet as they continued spreading throughout the building.

The blossoms, created by my friends outside, flowed down the hallway, covering the floors, lockers, and walls. I climbed to my feet as the mustard roots traveled up my brothers' legs and torsos, dragging them to the floor, twisting around their arms, entwining around their faces and necks.

I held out my hand and the fairy flew from the floor into my palm. Stepping over my brothers, I stood above Ma Yuan, his eyes barely visible underneath the bed of flowers.

"Who's lost now?" I asked.

44

HAN VS. TRUNG

These damn flowers again, Liang Song muttered as I scraped the edge of the fairy under his chin.

If you had some of your own, I said, *maybe you'd know when they were coming.*

We don't need protection. We're not afraid of destruction, Geng Shu said from beneath his veil of yellow flowers.

You're not strong enough to do this alone, Ma Yuan whispered sulkily, sounding so much like Quentin. *Who is helping you?*

The three of them dipped into my thoughts to find the answer: the sight of three lowly human teenagers, newly empowered with my divine elements, patrolling the grounds of the school, casting a circle of protection flowers around the perimeter.

An interesting strategy, Geng Shu admitted. *But limited. So you surprised us. But how long do you think you can hold us here?*

The ground began rippling again, hard enough that I held both hands out to maintain my balance.

Can you see them now? Geng Shu said. *They'll be here any minute.*

I walked toward the window. The campus shimmered with the yellow mustard flowers covering the lawns, walkways, and buildings. The sky had turned from orange to a dark blood-red. From an unusually large silver cloud, a spinning flock of black birds appeared to be falling.

Liang Song laughed at the concern he saw flicker across my face when I turned back to them. *You didn't think we'd come by ourselves, did you?*

I stared out at the glow of the fires, recognizing the dread I used to feel every time the Han army approached for battle. Through the rip in the cloud, they descended on horseback and on foot, their swords glinting in the red sky.

It has been so long since they've experienced the ecstasy of carnage, Geng Shu said, his smug face thankfully muffled by the flowers. *Release us now and we'll make sure your suffering isn't as long as you truly deserve.*

Hide, I urgently whispered in my friends' minds. *Hide.*

I abandoned my brothers and ran down the staircase, out of the building, and back to the courtyard. Huong and KT were still watching from the portal, observing the Han soldiers circling in the sky. I stood in the center of the courtyard and tilted my chin up, blowing the stray hairs off my face. A gash was bleeding on my cheek.

"You look wrecked," KT said, shaking her head in disgust.

"You look scared," I said, resting the fairy in front of me, trying not to look like I was leaning against it for support. "It's okay to feel regret for your very bad choices."

"You can be so conceited," Huong said. "And no fair using

our own flowers against us. I'm impressed those pathetic humans could even do it after you needed my help."

"You're underestimating me," I reminded her, discreetly surveying the area, satisfied that my friends were still safely in hiding.

Huong smiled. "My math skills are fantastic, actually. You can still do math, right?"

A lightning bolt crackled in the sky, illuminating the space around me, followed by ground-shaking thunder. Within seconds the wind began to whistle, then it grew to a howl. From the hills, the funneling air picked up leaves and debris, building into a cyclone. It quickly dove into the courtyard, shredding through the flower fields.

"My calculations say . . . you won't last long at all."

I dropped to the ground as Huong's cyclone continued to pick up speed. It devoured the flowers and untangled the mustard roots from the building, yellow petals and green leaves bursting through the air like confetti. From their hiding positions, my friends struggled to resist the wind and regrow the flowers, but they couldn't see anything through the vortex. They couldn't keep up with Huong. They could barely hang on to the ground, which they clung to as the cyclone ripped through the school. Everything they tried to plant the vortex ripped up and tossed into the air. When Huong's whirlwind attempted to sweep me off my feet, I crouched low and deflected with my sword.

"You saved so little for yourself," my sister marveled, "you can barely hold up the fairy. You don't deserve Father's sword."

An explosion from the humanities wing turned our heads.

Dark smoke burst from the ceiling, rolling down the building walls. The remaining blossoms began to scorch and wither away.

"You see?" Huong said, smirking. "Basic math. You're out-numbered."

The cyclone swirled off, Huong satisfied with the resulting destruction. Within seconds, the remaining mustard flowers around the school shriveled up, the once-brilliant yellow fields now a carpet of ash. Our brothers, untangled from the flowers in the building, had returned outside. They swooped into the sky, circling the school, hunting for Lana, Daphne, and Harsha.

There wasn't enough time. They'd find them soon, and I could sense my brothers' bloodthirst. My mind raced quickly to search for another delay.

Liang Song returned first, dangling Harsha by his ankles. Harsha's scared eyes met mine, but I whispered in his mind to stay calm.

I looked up at Huong, who was also observing him.

It's not too late. I told her privately through our thoughts. *You could have Harsha, this life. I experienced the memories. I know you care about him.*

And what will we do? Get married? I'll take care of his home and have his mortal babies? I don't want this small, pathetic life. I want my throne back. My world.

They don't deserve any of this, I said.

What did these humans ever do except reject you? They always leave you. Your mother died. Your father abandoned you. Your sup-

posed friends dumped you. But you're still as determined as ever to save them.

Geng Shu returned holding a struggling Daphne over his head, while Ma Yuan dragged back a weeping Lana. Our brothers tossed the three of them together onto the ashen ground, the dust billowing around them. My brothers' eyes glittered at the look of fresh meat.

"Enough," Liang Song said, glaring at me and Huong. "You talk and talk when we all know we're going to fight anyway. Let's get to the good part."

"As a welcome-back-to-the-world present, we're granting you the honors, little queen—how would you like to see these creatures perish?" Ma Yuan asked. "It can be quick, if you relinquish their elements to us, or slow and tortuous if you refuse."

"The elements are theirs to give," I said.

"Come on," Geng Shu whined. "They're yours and will always be yours. You know once your friends perish, they will go right back to you. So why delay it?"

"Take them, Jolie," Lana urged me. "Take ours and fight back!"

Harsha and Daphne nodded solemnly in agreement, their bodies trembling with panic. They'd risked everything to come with me here to fight my siblings. Now, they were willing to die to allow me to escape. On the drive from Santa Cruz, I'd given them nearly all of my elements, taught them how to control the powers I remembered, but how could I have prepared them for a moment like this?

"I've already given them away," I said. "They don't belong to me anymore."

Liang Song shook his head in mock dismay. "You never thought to give such a present to your brothers."

"Or sister," Huong hissed.

I jumped at the opening. "Why would I give them to a bunch of proven losers?"

That seemed to startle my siblings, and I could feel them collectively pause to ponder my question.

"Losers?" Geng Shu repeated, confused. "We *win* our wars."

"You may win wars, but you can't manage peace. After I died, you bullied Trac into hiding. Then the three of you betrayed each other. You killed your own army with a plague. Your legacy was in shambles over your childishness and greed."

"She's trying to distract you," Huong said, disgusted.

"By pointing out your phony alliance?" I said. "You are all as immature as the teenage bodies you're posing in. You squandered your opportunity the first time you stole my elements. And you'll do it again. You can't help failing."

"It was Geng Shu's idea!" Liang Song cried. "He thought spreading germs would be a more effective murder weapon, not realizing it could infect our human vessels!"

"Liar!" Geng Shu screamed.

"And that we should tell the empress Ma Yuan was to blame and is unfit to lead!" Liang Song continued.

"Aah," I said, nodding emphatically. "That explains why Ma Yuan was so eager to make a secret alliance with me."

Liang Song and Geng Shu whipped their gazes to a stunned Ma Yuan.

"That's right," I said. "Both he and big sister made me separate offers to join them. I guess they realized who would make the stronger ally. Don't worry, I turned them both down."

"That is enough!" Ma Yuan roared, but Geng Shu and Liang Song continued to exchange worried looks.

"These humans are more deserving than we ever will be," I said. "They have everything to lose, and they still choose to fight."

"It is not our fault they're not immortal," Geng Shu said. "That's how they were created."

"They can barely survive the short lifetimes they already have," Liang Song sneered. "Why are you trying to complicate things? Once they've outlived their usefulness, they die."

"Our parents didn't think so," I said, looking up to the sky where the Han soldiers continued to buzz, slaves to our brothers for eternity.

"They were cowards, just like you," Ma Yuan said. "They weren't brave enough to rule, but we are. We have. At least this way their deaths have meaning because they served their gods."

The Han soldiers had started to touch ground, their horses and chariots lining up around the courtyard and school building. I tried not to turn my head as I assessed everyone, counting the seconds we had left. As they landed, the archers shot flaming arrows into the dirt, reigniting fires in the grass and trees, the air around us darkening once again. But it was okay. I'd stalled them long enough. I stayed patient, watching, waiting for the sky to change.

Eventually my siblings caught on to what I was staring at, and their gazes followed mine to the clouds. The portal, which had been swathed in our brothers' black, orange, and red dust, was now undeniably glowing yellow.

"Anything you'd like to tell us?" Ma Yuan said, glaring over at Huong on the screen.

The Trung army—generals, captains, soldiers, and horses—galloped out of the portal, fanning across the sky, staining it deeper with our divine colors. As they floated closer to us, I recognized each one of them, their eyes bright and determined, until the last horse flew down, carrying our first human mother.

Our brothers floated in front of their soldiers, brandishing their swords, waiting. The air felt heavy and suffocating, simmering with energy and anticipation. The Trung soldiers parted to allow our mother, flanked by two generals, to stand in front of our brothers.

"I like this game!" Liang Song said, breaking the tense silence. "Same players, unusual location, new challenges. And some last-minute surprises."

"This is a surprise," Huong said, her insincere smile betraying her. "Welcome. I am grateful for your loyalty and devotion, risking such danger to stand with your queen."

"We're not here to help you," our mother said. "We know you've been deceiving us. We're here for the true leader of our people."

If Huong hadn't seen it before, she could now: our soldiers' faces and skin sparkling with yellow dust. Not a trace of purple on them. While I'd been preparing my friends here for this final battle, our mother had organized our soldiers in the other realm.

"You never loved me," Huong hissed.

"I do," our mother said, raising her chin, her voice unwavering. "That is why I'm here."

Now, I whispered to my three friends.

Harsha, Lana, and Daphne had silently crept back to their feet. During the armies' arrival and my siblings' distraction, my friends' elements had been restoring themselves. They soared through the air above the rest of us, summoning the clouds to cast shadows vast and looming across the courtyard. They raised their hands to the sky, spreading out the mist, watching it undulate across the courtyard.

My brothers and sister looked over, startled, as my friends pulled more and more dense clouds toward the ground until they blanketed the courtyard in a thick, billowing silver fog.

"Stop them!" Ma Yuan screamed, and Geng Shu and Liang Song flew up to the sky, their swords raised, cutting through the mist.

The fog can hide so much. Anything can sneak up on you. Without sight, you have to depend on your other senses to help you. My brothers and sister would be fine. And my army, along with my friends, would be fine, too, equipped with the elements my mother and I shared.

But the Han army, brought from the other realm without any preparation or protection, would not. This was what I'd been counting on: my brothers' selfishness leaving their soldiers unprotected.

My brothers tried to rise above the fog, barking orders at their soldiers. The shouting and clashing, the horses neighing around us, added to the confusion. The shadows around me jerked and stretched, trying to adapt to the smothering, suffocating fog.

Harsha continued to pull in more clouds from the sky to press into the school, while Daphne and Lana wrapped and tightened the fog around the soldiers, choking out their vision, muffling their voices. In the meantime, my army had time to react, working quickly to take down and disarm as many Han soldiers as they could.

The fog grew denser, exploding in clashes of red, black, orange, purple, and yellow. The clouds squeezed around us as our armies continued to battle, my brothers desperate to maintain dominance. They'd risen farther up in the sky, hurling lightning and thunderbolts to the ground. The soil trembled, Han and Trung soldiers rolling across the burnt grass, horses falling into the cracks of the earth.

On the glowing TV portal, KT stood, her face coming closer and closer until she broke through. Her face, her shoulder, her arms, the rest of her body pushed beyond the portal; one enormous stiletto heel, then the other, stepped onto the ravaged courtyard.

The warriors continued to battle, undisturbed that a giant KT loomed over them, jostling the already wobbly ground. She slowly shrank back to human scale, but looked no less frightening, a deranged smile on her face as she threw herself into the chaos, betraying her former soldiers.

But I was more interested in what was left behind in the portal. Huong had disappeared.

The lightning strikes ignited fires in the grass and bushes around the school, the thick black plumes combining with the rising fog and elements swirling in the air. Harsha, Lana, and Daphne orchestrated a rainstorm to contain the flames.

KT, armed with a crossbow, pointed an arrow at Lana in the sky. Before I could warn Lana, a gust of wind lifted KT into the air, throwing her across the lawn. I looked back at a satisfied Daphne. By this time, my brothers had retreated to their own portal in the sky, hurling thunderbolts at my army. But every successive bolt appeared smaller, dimmer. They were weakening.

My mother rushed at me, lifting the fairy sword from my hand so it lay between us as she hugged me. "Time to go," she said.

I hesitated and she pushed at me again.

"You've helped us enough. Trust us. You have to find them."

Huong's portal had vanished. Harsha, Daphne, and Lana patrolled the sky, controlling the rainstorm as yellow mist slowly but surely overwhelmed the black, orange, and red smoke from my brothers. She was right.

I didn't need any elements to tell me where Huong had escaped with my grandparents. I could sense their location and fear.

I ran toward the swimming pool.

45

THE CAVE

It took several minutes to reach the other side of campus, climb over the gate, and find the pool. It looked calm and pristine, the eye of the storm, where the raging winds, rains, and fire couldn't touch. I toed off my shoes and peeled off my hoodie, and leaned over the smooth, glassy water. My face was covered in soot; gashes bled on my forehead and neck. I took a few steps back, inhaled a lungful of air, and dove in.

Once underwater, I swam down, down, down, until I found the portal that Huong had left open for me. I glided through the swimming pool into the next realm. The clear, bright water darkened. My fingers and toes brushed along craggy limestone walls and stalagmites.

I recognized the cave and felt my throat and heart constrict. The colors around me flickered with each blink, blue and green and brown, the water muddled with the sediment and dirt I recalled from my dreams. My nostrils flared, blowing out tiny bubbles. Unable to hold my breath in any longer, I released. Despite the water filling my mouth, flowing down my throat, it didn't affect my lungs. I could breathe.

I exhaled, inhaled, the bubbles fizzing along my airway. I followed the moss and stalactites decorating the cavern's walls and ceiling until my knees bumped up against rock. I searched with my hands and toes for grooves or dents in the rock to climb up the cavern. When I spied the water's surface, my energy surged. My head broke through; my mouth opened to swallow a lungful of air. My arms reached through the water, searching for something to grab hold of. A pair of hands folded over mine and lifted me out.

After rolling across the mossy limestone floor, I looked up to the enormous ceiling and walls around me. My grandfather's shadow hovered over me. He was still wearing his pajamas.

"Are you okay?" Ông Nội asked softly, his words echoing off the cavernous walls, his eyes shining like two tiny flashlights in the dark.

The shadow sharpened, the outline of his tired face becoming clear. Behind him, the stalactites hanging from the chamber ceiling glowed in the darkness. The air felt frigid and prickly to breathe.

I nodded and couldn't help but smile as his eyes gazed around. "You can see here."

"This is your home," Ông Nội said. "Where we first met. We are surrounded by your elements."

"Where is Bà Nội?" I asked, struggling to sit up.

Ông Nội reached inside his bathrobe and pulled out the

mythology book. It looked battered and thin, pages clinging to the broken spine, but once he passed it to me, the book awakened. The spine knitted itself back together, the pages smoothing over, the words inside growing darker, the illustrations brighter, radiant in the cave's darkness.

I turned the pages until I found the new illustration: my grandmother, safely encased in an egg on the same beach in Santa Cruz. No one could harm her there. The illustration warmed under my fingers. I could hear the soft waves of the ocean and feel Bà Nội's steady heartbeat.

My eyes closed in relief, my breaths growing long and slow. When they reopened with my divine sight, I could truly see the cave. Humans had only recently been exploring underwater caves in Vietnam. Located far below sea level, they were the largest subterranean caverns in the world, so big that they had their own microclimates, rainforests, and wildlife. But this cave, my home, was far deeper than any human would ever find.

My sister and I had lived here after our parents left us. A refuge that no human or even our brothers could find, until the first thầy bói. He was the only human to ever discover it, and the world had not been the same since.

I stretched my aching, throbbing back. "Where is she?" I asked. "Did she hurt you?"

"That is not important," Ông Nội said. "I saw what you did, Jolie. How you helped your friends and led your army to save us. You didn't use brute power or force, like your sister or brothers. You were clever and compassionate and shared your gifts. I am proud of you."

A howl sailed through the cavern, the echo whistling in our ears.

"She'll be here soon," Ông Nội warned.

"I can protect you," I said.

He shook his head. "We both know what will happen. You cannot stop it."

I turned from his doubtful face, spying the shadow climbing along the cavern walls. I cautiously stood. The shadow traveled in wide, lazy circles, up and over, around the stalactites and stalagmites. The chill tightened its grip around my throat as she moved closer, revealing more of her enormous form. The colors of Trac's dragon's body alternated between blue, green, purple, and black. She glided elegantly, almost languidly, in our direction, our attraction already feeling natural and inevitable.

When she finally landed in front of us, the ground and walls shook, stalactites falling from the cave ceiling. She roared into the air, the flames threateningly close to us, the glow illuminating her horns, snout, and fangs. Ông Nội and I hugged each other tightly, burying our faces in each other's shoulders.

When the flames drifted away, her white eyes twinkled. She lowered her head to confront us face-to-face.

It took you long enough, Trac said. *Shouldn't you have known we'd return to your first place of treachery?*

"Will you stop?" I asked, stepping forward, between her and

my grandfather. "Your lies are getting old. You're just mad that I beat you."

I opened the book to show her an illustration of my friends and our army—that those tiny, insignificant humans were successfully defeating the Han army back at the high school. Many of the Han soldiers had already retreated through the portal, while our brothers had fallen back into the cracks of the earth, trapped by Harsha, Lana, and Daphne's unrelenting torrent of rain and wind.

"This is what happens," I said, "when you trust humans with our gift."

"Yes, they can destroy us," she said. "Thanks."

"You're such a hypocrite," I seethed. "Our brothers attacked us, tortured us for years to take our land. They betrayed you. They murdered our soldiers. I make one decision without you and I'm the enemy?"

"I didn't expect their loyalty," Trac said. "I raised and protected you after our parents left."

"Can't you see what they did? They knew the best way to beat us was to turn us against each other, so we'd do all the work. And you fell for it, again."

"But they're gone now. It's just us. Wasn't it always about us? Our brothers don't matter. No one else matters."

There was no point in arguing with her. Ever. She'd only ever see her own pain. In a way she was right: it always came down to us.

"Then release my grandfather," I said.

A cold, long silence.

Trac cocked her head, exhaling another ring of violet smoke. "As soon as he gives them to me."

"I gave him those elements thousands of years ago. They're his."

"I'm not talking about yours. I want what our parents gave you. What they should have given me. I tried to do it without troubling you, but apparently you both have to gift them, since the two of you are so connected."

"You want the prime elements from the book?"

"Why are you being so stupid about this? Yes."

Trac's eyes glittered at the mythology book in my arms, her pointed tongue flicking around her lips with delight. I tried to control the trembling in my mind and spirit.

"Release him first," I said.

She bowed forward on her front legs, lowering her head, waiting for her crown of power. "We'll do it at the same time."

She was lying, but Ông Nội already knew to prepare to run.

I lifted my shaking hands, holding the book between us, gazing into my sister's joyful eyes, and then back at Ông Nội's.

"We gift these elements from our book," Ông Nội said, nodding.

"We gift these elements from our book," I repeated.

The book twitched and sparked for several seconds, the elements sputtering to life. We watched the golden dust rise from the pages into the air, collecting in a glittery funnel, twirling and soaring as it settled over Trac's entire vessel. She closed her eyes as she accepted the gift, allowing the elements to infuse and strengthen her spirit, while Ông Nội backed away.

I stood there, surprised at how long someone could fool themselves into believing a deception, as if sheer will and desire could force this lie into reality. So convinced humans were beneath us.

Now she'd know. She'd underestimated them—and me—all along.

Trac's eyes opened, flashing white in understanding.

"These are divine elements," she accused.

"Are you sure?" I asked, my heart pounding.

"Prime elements are supposed to be too powerful for human bodies," she said, looking past me at Ông Nội, her rage rising with realization.

We had been so quick to believe in the guardian dragons' rules about ourselves and what we could do, when all along, we'd always determined our destiny. Who said we couldn't gift the prime elements to whomever we wanted? Who was going to stop me?

"I guess we were wrong," I said, turning away.

I ran as my sister released a spray of fire, and I quickly caught up with my grandfather, grabbing his hand to help us move faster. The flames stung our heels as we scrambled swiftly through the boulders, descending deeper into the cave. If we continued on this path, we could stay ahead of her. She wouldn't be able to reach us quickly without abandoning her dragon vessel.

Though she couldn't follow us, her elements could. While she didn't have our parents' elements, she had some of mine, and she was certainly more powerful than me. The air had grown colder and thick, her wind hurtling through the caverns, knocking us down several times.

She was trying to collapse the cave.

She was going to destroy our home, and us in it.

We had to find a path out. The cave was composed of countless winding passages and chambers. As we climbed through the rubble, blinking away the dust and crumbling rock, the ground beneath us softened like sand, giving way to my sister's scorching fury. When the dirt finally broke free, the ground crumbling away, my hands grabbed for the closest boulder, hanging on as tightly as I could. I looked over to see Ông Nội, his arms wrapped around a nearby rock, his body swinging above the void Trac had created. Never-ending darkness hung below us.

Our bodies clung to the cliff and my mind spun for a solution. My grandfather began trembling, but before he could fall, I reached over to grab his hand. Slowly, his shaking arms embraced my waist, so that we both hung from the cliff on my strength.

My boulder began to soften. My fingers pressed into the rapidly deteriorating limestone, searching for something hard to dig into. I willed whatever remaining power I had to bring air to support us, but there wasn't enough. I tried to motivate my grandfather's elements to rescue us, but he was too weak to respond. His arms hung around my waist, but I could feel his grip slipping.

Jolie.

Don't let go of me, I said as I searched below for an escape route, one I knew did not exist. *I have you. Just don't let go.*

I've held on to these elements for you, Ông Nội said, *and it has been my deepest honor. I'm grateful to return them to you.*

That's not part of our plan, I reminded him. *Stay with me.*

Your gift is now my gift.

With absolute reluctance, I consented. The elements soaked through my body as Ông Nội's arms were released from my grasp. When I reached for the cuff of his bathrobe, he firmly pushed off from my hand, falling back into the darkness, his eyes closing, his calm face growing smaller, fading.

I dove after him into the void, searching for him. My eyes lit up bright white, shining into the darkness.

"Ông Nội!" I screamed. "Ông Nội!"

In that instant, I realized his body had disintegrated into the air. In its place, his elements gifted me his memories and the history of his ancestors. Their voices and experiences swarmed my mind. They understood this moment was coming. This was part of the prophecy.

The first thầy bói. My first human mother. Every thầy bói up until my beloved Ông Nội and my father, who rejected his legacy. The many, many times they protected my spiritual essence over the years, from a nascent cluster of elements on a page in the mythology book to the book growing with each generation to my final human rebirth as Jolie. They nurtured and raised me, realizing one day they'd have to give these powers back to me.

Despite knowing this truth, I continued to search for him, my heart aching, my body racing faster and faster. As I descended, the black of the void turned scarlet, until all I could see was red surrounding me, deeper and darker shades growing so vivid and thick that it soon seeped into my flesh.

I flew through the void, my empowered senses experiencing everything around me. The overwhelming memories, the insects, the birds, the ferns and foliage along the walls. Everything, except Ông Nội.

46

REINCARNATION

As I continued to fall and weep, the temperature around me rose, not only outside, but inside of me. The newly gifted prime elements bubbled in my veins, stretching through me, suffocating my human body. They felt familiar, comforting, but also overwhelming.

They needed more room or else I'd erupt. I consented to transform.

The prime elements spun and swirled, reconstructing my dragon's vessel, enveloping me in our parents' words and memories, replenishing my strength.

My spirit began to acclimate to this vast body, my blood pumped throughout my elongated veins, bones and muscles stretching my torso, tail, and feet.

My head craned up toward the cliff from where we'd fallen, where my sister still lurked, and I exhaled a column of fire into the air. My scales perked up, my whiskers and horns twitching, the prime elements humming, energy coursing through my body. I soared up toward the dim light of the cliff.

In these vessels, our spirits were at their apex. In these enormous, flexible bodies, we could see, hear, taste, touch, and experience everything. We effortlessly ran, swam, and flew faster than any other creature in this world. Nothing escaped our senses. This also meant we were at our most dangerous. As dragons, we could do anything. Destroy anything.

My sister sat calmly at the edge of the cliff, waiting for me to land in front of her.

We stood across from each other in our original bodies for the first time in centuries.

"I'm going to kill you," I said between puffs of smoke.

Instead of looking scared or even offended, she gazed at me with wonder. "It's remarkable. You are as bright as the sun."

I looked down at myself. My skin glowed in alternating colors of the rainbow, my scales radiant with our parents' prime elements.

"How does it feel to hold all that power?" she asked. "Power you don't even want? Should I bother suggesting the obvious?"

My eyes returned to hers. "Never."

"Oh, come on. What happened to girl power?" *Imagine a realm where we can rule instead of our brothers.*

The same words she'd used in our first battle. My sister hadn't learned anything.

"We tried that," I said, "and I was miserable. The world was miserable. Shouldn't it tell you something that I chose to give up my life rather than spend any more time with you?"

"But I changed! I was good to you!" She looked away, her snout curling petulantly. "It was supposed to be different. We were going to learn from our mistakes. Evolve. Didn't you like us getting along?"

I thought of the last few months, since pulling her out of the swimming pool. Our friendship had felt immediate and intense, a joyful, soothing balm.

"It was a lie," I reminded her. "That's the only way we could ever get along."

"We are gods. We do what is necessary. Why can't you just own that? Our power is glorious. It is not meant to be suppressed or hidden away or destroyed."

I shook my head. "The world can't survive us."

"This world is only here because of us."

"That doesn't excuse the deaths," I said. "Ông Nội didn't have to die. You didn't have to hurt everyone you did."

"You weren't here," Trac said. "I've seen how vicious humans can be to each other. You think they are so innocent and helpless. Maybe our brothers encouraged them, but they are capable of more cruelty than you can imagine. Didn't your little girlfriends give you a taste of that? And you want to give them the tools to be even more destructive?"

She unleashed memories into my mind to support her argument, making me witness from her perspective the many sufferings and atrocities that humans had unleashed on each other. I couldn't deny her point. They could be vicious and ruthless.

She also showed me her suffering. Her loneliness. Constantly running away from our brothers' annihilation. Never at peace anywhere in this world. Trying her best to protect our country.

"I do regret it, Nhi," she said quietly. "I never wanted you gone. I didn't know it would be like this—how awful it would be living in this world without you."

I exhaled tiredly. "Then why are we fighting now?"

"Because you're still wrong. What do you think your little friends will do now?" Trac asked. "You've unleashed three hormonal teenagers with divine elements. You really think the world will be at peace?"

"I trust them," I said. "It's not our world. It never was. They get to decide. *That's* the prophecy." I knew she was stalling, her mind whirling for an exit strategy. She was panicking. It was time.

"Your trust in them will be your downfall, Nhi," she said sadly. "But not mine."

I lunged at her, knocking her on her back, my claws wrapping around her throat, talons piercing into her skin. She howled, spraying a fireball into my face.

The earth trembled and cracked as we crashed against the limestone walls, sending another cascade of stalactites tumbling to the floor. Trac twisted on her side, struggling against me, exhaling another fireball and filling the space between us with white smoke.

As I blinked away the dust, Trac seized the opportunity, wrenching away from my grasp. She sprung to her hind legs, and dove past me and into the void. I plunged after her, swerving to avoid the fireballs she released on her circular, swirling path through the blackness.

She looked back occasionally, her scaly chest heaving while flying through the darkness. I trailed after her, targeting the perimeter of violet sparks she left behind, the cold air spitting against my seething, burning body.

We continued our descent until the air shifted from black to orange, farther from the cave's surface, deeper than we'd explored before. She was leading me somewhere, but I wasn't afraid. Trac scuttled past another limestone canyon, turned up alongside a crimson grotto, then dropped out of sight.

I paused for a moment before gliding forward. The wind snatched me up, tossing me backward through the air. My body spun and spun, so quickly I was afraid I'd pass out, until I crashed with a thud on my back, my scales scraping against a crumbly, jagged surface.

Flipping quickly onto my hands and feet, I sniffed around, peering into the dark, until my eyes found warm swirls of soot floating through the air, irritating my eyes. I was standing on a crumbly rock island, surrounded by boiling magma.

My nostrils recoiled from the stench of boiling sulfur. Once my eyes blinked away the ashy dust, I could see bursts of black and bubbly geysers sprouting from craters and mingling with dark water. The rocky floor groaned and cracked beneath me, throwing me forward as it shook and slid, the heat rising, the water pushing and pulling around me: an earthquake.

It wasn't just any cavern. She'd lured me inside the chamber of an active subterranean volcano. The ground below me was softening, melting into magma, and I scrambled to stay on the highest perch of the crumbling rock island. Even as young dragons, we knew to avoid these volcanos, the magma containing the potential to overwhelm and cripple even our armored bodies.

There inside the heart of the volcano, the magma glowed brightly even from above, dripping in clumps from the craggy basalt walls, turning more of the rock into an orange sea around me. I turned slowly, my tail scraping across limestone dotted with pillow lava and steaming ponds of molten sulfur.

I could sense Trac's heartbeat and breathing close by, so I crawled slowly, gingerly across the bubbling rocks, leery of the hundreds of hydrothermal vents that could erupt at any time, especially if I triggered one with an unfortunate move.

Did you know this was here? my sister asked inside our heads. *This volcano underneath the caves kept us warm. This is where we were born, where our parents created us. They never showed it to us. Another secret.*

The heat seeped deep into my skin. My eyes traveled around the volcano chamber, the gurgling seafloor, the crumbling walls already closing in on us. The long-buried memories bloomed inside our thoughts, how our shared egg cracked in the magma, how our parents lifted us from the ashes, molding our first vessels. Their love had been different from our human parents'— not as gentle, even frightening at times—but it was still love.

Don't you want to know why? she asked. *I did. They didn't give me their memories like they did with you. I don't get gifts like you.*

The pressure around us rose. Another shudder beneath our feet, and I gripped the crusty molten floor with my talons, my muscles straining with the effort. My eyes warily watched the bubbling magma rising and sloshing around the rocks as more of our parents' memories descended into our minds.

This wasn't just our birthplace. This was where they died. It was the hardest thing they ever did, abandoning their children to the world, crawling down into the volcano and remaining here when every element in their bodies urged them to escape. They sacrificed their vessels as the volcano erupted, their spirits disintegrating into the lava, until eventually their prime elements found their way to the earth's surface—and to me.

Our parents waited here a long time for the right time to die, Trac said. *Can you feel what they were thinking? How convinced they were that they were doing the right thing? Sounds like you, doesn't it?*

A hydrothermal vent burst on the seafloor, releasing a thick plume of mineral smoke around me. After the clouds faded, I saw my sister perched on a large boulder, peering down at me. A river of bright red magma separated us.

You have to watch for the signs to know when this volcano will explode, or else you can miss it. But when it happens? It makes your death two thousand years ago seem like a paper cut in comparison. It's why we'll never see them again. They couldn't gather back together, even if they'd wanted to.

Magmatic bubbles erupted between us; white puffs of smoke mingled with swirls of orange and black. The crackle of magma gurgled above the ground, hardening into a fresh crust of smooth pillow lava. The boulder beneath my hands and feet grumbled with the pulsing gas as a blanket of ash dimmed my vision. I whirled around to follow the flicker of light along the cavern walls. In the darkness of the volcano, only the faintest silhouette of my sister's horns and scales appeared visible.

Her face glittered from the sparks of lava. The steam filled my snout, clouded my eyes. My grip on the rocky floor began to slip, my talons wobbly.

It's a waste of time denying who you are, Trac said. *We are a part of each other. Same egg. Maybe we were never supposed to be split apart. If we reunite, we can make things better. We can improve the world.*

Several seconds passed, the air and heat smothering our senses.

No, I said again, feeling more honest, more brave than I had before. It hurt, pushing the words out of my mouth, but it was necessary. *Never. Do you want to know why I chose people over you? Because they believed in me. They trusted me. You never did. You are no different from our brothers.*

With a roar, Trac leaped across the magma river and onto me, her talons sinking easily into my shoulders, pinning me down against the crumbly bedrock. My tail swung up and wrapped around one of her limbs, trying to pull her off, but she easily slapped it back with her tail. I pushed my hind legs up underneath, dragging us across the rocky seafloor. I felt a sudden coolness beneath me and realized it was the blood from my freshly shorn scales mingling with the heated rocks underneath us.

My sister's face lingered inches from mine, steam emitting from her snout and curling into mine. Soon our faces touched: the same almond-shaped eyes, upturned horns, and noble spikes along our heads. The only difference had always been our coloring, but now that didn't matter. Our skin tinted in the sooty water. We had never looked more identical than in this moment.

I realized we'd dance like this forever—attraction, revulsion, escape. It was our curse: stronger together, better apart.

This world, these humans, they deserve better than us, I whispered as we both panted from exhaustion.

You mean me. She sounded quiet. Stunned. *That's what you mean.*

Her talons retracted from my shoulders, and I managed to twist away from her grip. Or maybe she was letting me go. The blood flowed out of the gashes where her talons had broken my skin. Swirls of bright white punctured my vision, yet I managed to swing my tail up to wrap around her neck, throwing her off of me.

We stared at each other on our rock islands, a pool of bubbling magma between us. In the lava's fiery glow, her face looked weary and broken, sadder than I could ever remember. Her head swung away from me, her shadow stretching across the cavern walls.

That's it, then, she said. *This is what you want.* She rolled to her hind legs, backing up as she spoke, her eyes reflecting the magma around us.

My heart began to race in realization.

No, I said, panicking, reaching for her. *Stop!*

This is for you, my queen, she said as the lava engulfed her.

47

ALWAYS

The crater full of bubbling magma eagerly swallowed my sister's body, absorbing her legs, tail, and head. The magma responded with larger bubbles, multiplying, rumbling, until the chamber became engulfed with smoke. The volcano began to erupt, pulling me into its heat, and I could feel myself passing out.

When I opened my eyes again, squinting at the now pale-yellow light, I realized my sister and I were back on land, in the meadow near the cliff.

I pulled up from the grass, returned to my human form, not as Jolie, but as Nhi. I crawled on my hands and knees, blinking around me at the shadows in the tall grass, until I could see the largest shadow in front of me—Trac, naked and bloodied.

I reached over to gently push her to her side, so she lay on her back. In the middle of her exposed abdomen was a glowing swirl of blue and purple dust. I recognized this from my first experience. It was the core of our elements. Her spirit was dimming.

"You need to take them," she whispered, "before our brothers come for me."

"I don't need your elements," I said.

"Don't do it for the power, then. Do it for me. I want you to understand me."

"I do." I wept into her soft, bloodied hands, which were feeling lighter with every second. "I'm listening."

Her eyes were dimming to a soft gray. "Tell me. How does it feel to be left?"

"Awful."

An unexpected smile sprouted on her pale lips. "That makes me happy."

I breathed in sharply, my eyes filling with tears. "None of this makes me happy."

"Not right now, but you will be. You've gone on fine without me. I was the one with the problem being alone. Not you."

I sat next to her, crossing my legs and gently pulling her limp body toward mine, settling her head and shoulders into my lap. When I tried to push her long black braid to the side, some of the hair strands crumbled between my fingers, turning to dust. For a few minutes, we listened to her breaths grow short and shallow. Her limbs began to soften in my arms.

Trac cleared her throat and I looked down at her, still lying in my lap. Her face looked as soft and gray as the clouds surrounding us, the sparkles from her skin drifting away from her.

"You have to take them now," she said.

"We still have time," I said, not caring if my words weren't true, holding her closer to me.

"We don't," she said.

She was right. But when the other half of your spirit is leaving you, you will say anything to keep her. Did Trac realize this?

"Do you remember when Mother first realized who we were?" Trac said. "She asked Father to take me out to the fields and teach me how to shoot with a bow and arrow. And then she carried you into the garden, sat you underneath your favorite banyan tree, and cried. She never did that with me."

"I was the crybaby. She probably saw me doing it so many times."

"She saw me as the warrior and you as her child, even though I found her first. Even though she pulled me from the water first."

Trac's eyes lowered, avoiding my direct gaze, and I realized this wasn't a trick—the tears, the self-hate she radiated were real. She was right: I had always assumed she followed our father out to the fields, begged him to learn. But our mother had pushed Trac there, while she kept me with her in the garden.

"So I am that warrior. That is what I will always be."

"No," I said, swallowing the tears in my throat. "You're my sister first. Always."

She exhaled slowly, watching our fingers thread into each other's, mine already looking larger and darker than hers. Her eyes met mine, then looked past me, above me, straining with the effort. I followed her gaze.

Our swords, the dragon and the fairy, sat in the weeds, glittering with mist. "You will take the dragon," she said.

"Okay," I said.

"Don't let them have it."

"I won't."

Her eyes glazed over, and she blinked several times. "You think I'll be better the next time, if we ever meet again? More like you?"

"We'll both be better," I said, wondering if that could be true, but only smiling reassuringly at her.

She smiled. "You always have more hope than me . . . Nhi?"

"Yes?"

"I want to stay in this body when it happens. Can you help me? Don't let me change."

"Okay."

"I gift them to you, Nhi. Only you."

My memories of Trac had always come from my perspective. But as I held her body and slowly drained her elements, transferring her energy to me as her limbs relaxed, her bones and flesh disintegrated, her memories had nowhere to go but inside me. Perhaps this had always been her wish: for me to finally see her side.

As Trac led me through her memories, from our too-brief childhoods with our dragon parents to our lives under the sea, to our human childhoods and reign in Vietnam, I could see now how our human mother's eyes had always shone upon me with happiness and love instead of the fear and trepidation that she gave to Trac. How our father's only kind words to her were of encouragement to win and conquer at all costs. How she took on the responsibility and duty of a queen far more seriously than I ever had, because she felt she had to. Worst of all,

I saw how I appeared through her eyes: the petulant younger sister who she had to prod along, who always needed to be watched over, even when she had a country full of people to care for. How my departure had indeed left a hole in Trac, taking away her desire for pretty much everything until she could have me back.

For so long I had blamed her, but never myself, for our past betrayals and mistakes. We always thought our losses and pains were someone else's fault.

"I didn't know," I said, choking back the tears as the onslaught of memories continued to flow.

I wasn't sure if she heard those last words. Her eyes had closed, her face as still as glass. So I eventually quieted and held her, as I'd promised, pretending she didn't feel lighter with each passing minute as she left this realm, and me.

Trac's eyes fixated on something in the air, and I turned behind me to look: a rainbow. The biggest, brightest, most dazzling rainbow I'd ever seen stretched over our heads, as wide as the horizon. Every shade across the spectrum, all of our siblings' colors, glowed vividly, like they were all here with us. The violet shade, my sister's shade, seemed the most luminous of all.

I wasn't sure how long it took—it felt both interminable and mercilessly short at the same time. But her body softened, her spirit melted through my arms, lifting and filtering through the air, so eventually I was only clutching my own gleaming, vibrant arms, crossed over my own intact stomach, grief quickly filling up the space in my lap and in my heart.

In the haze of the sunlight, I watched the particles of her

human remains float away in every direction, almost merrily, with thousands of years of relief. These were her human particles, what the gods called mortal dust because they lacked divine powers. The dust that made up every creature on this earth, what remained through the life cycles. But they were no less precious to me. Indeed, as I watched them lift into the air, I realized they were the most important part of my sister. They were what had changed her mind.

Goodbye. She seemed to sing as these particles drifted away from me. *Goodbye. Will I see you again?*

Goodbye! I promise, you will see me again.

Goodbye, sister. Goodbye.

Her voice faded with every goodbye, but I sat. Sat for a long time and listened.

ACKNOWLEDGMENTS

This book owes everything to my village of friends, family, and allies.

For reading the very first chapter and encouraging me to keep going: Nova Ren Suma and the brilliant writers at the Djerassi Young Adult Novel Writing workshop. For my early readers who provided critical feedback: Terry Shears, Anh Thang Dao, Stephanie Brown, Mika Tanner, Amelinda Berube, and Rachel Sarah.

For providing the gift of time to write: the Djerassi Artists Colony, the Headlands Center for the Arts, the Rockefeller Foundation's Bellagio Center, the Writing Between the Vines writing residency, and Hedgebrook. For my thoughtful and supportive writing group: Valerie Miner, Camille Dungy, Tess Taylor, Toni Mirosevich, Vanessa Hua, Beth Nguyen, Angie Chuang, and Patricia Powell.

For offering me countless opportunities and community over the last decade: the Diasporic Vietnamese Artists Network, led by the fearless Isabelle Thuy Pelaud, Viet Thanh Nguyen, and Kathy Nguyen. For providing inspiration and creativity in a writing collective of badass Vietnamese women: She Who Has No Master(s), guided by visionary founder Dao Strom.

For my fierce colleagues at the California College of the Arts: Jasmin Darznik, Faith Adiele, Eric Olson, Anne Shea, Juvenal Acosta, TT Takemoto, and Jackie Francis. For my students at CCA who remind me over and over that creativity can survive the darkness.

For the endless patience and support of my super agents and readers at WME: Janine Kamouh, Oma Naraine, Dorian Karchmar, and Anna Dixon. For the editing prowess and divine vision of my editor, Tiara Kittrell, and everyone at Putnam Young Readers.

For their friendship over the years: Beth Nguyen, Kirstin Chen, R.O. Kwon, Angie Chau, Vu Tran, Julia Fierro, Christine Lee, and Mika Tanner. For the Five Families, led by some of the strongest warriors I know: Ellen Lee, Anu Gomez, Vanessa Hua, and Eveline Chang.

For the Phan and Shears families, whose love, resilience, and dreams are all over this book.

For my children, Amelie and ZZ. There is so much in this world that can make us feel helpless, but the right words can make you strong again.

And for Matt, who has sacrificed more for me and our family than I can ever say or ever pay back. He should already know this, but now you all do too.